# FORTUNE'S SON

# FORTUNE'S SON

Hannah Louise Shearer

MUTINY INK, LLC.

Published by Mutiny Ink, LLC.





PUBLISHED IN THE UNITED STATES OF AMERICA

ISBN 978-1-7379397-0-2  paperback
ISBN 978-1-7379397-1-9  ebook

COVER PHOTO © Linda Schwarz / www.LindaSchwarzPhotography.com
AUTHOR PHOTO © Linda Campanelli
DESIGNED BY Barbara Tada / www.pixelgardendesign.com

www.hannahshearer.com

Phillip Herbert Shearer: Pip, I miss you every day.

# PROLOGUE

## Friday, September 28, 2018

THE LITTLE BOY curled up as tightly as he could in the stern of the motorboat. A frenzied wind was lashing the waves and he needed shelter from the bitter cold spray. They were in a good-sized craft, going fast; it was a wet, dark night with no stars, and nine-year-old Garth Fortune had little protection. The Evinrude E-Tech G2 motor was very loud as the Man steered the boat into the San Juan de Fuca Straits. Garth shivered, miserable, terrified and more agitated by the moment. He longed to move, but it was hard with his hands tied in front of him, and his feet bound.

Garth struggled and looked ahead, where the Man was steering the boat. The Man felt Garth's gaze and turned to glare at him. Garth saw vast ugliness in the Man's cold, dead eyes, and was afraid he would be thrown overboard, like the Man's partner had been. Something deep inside the boy refused to allow that. The words burst out from a place he didn't know existed in him: "Stay away from me! Stay away!"

The Man laughed, punched the autopilot, and moved closer. Garth yelled: "My dad's the police and he does Kung Fu! No matter where you take me, he's gonna find me!"

The Man leaned over and ripped duct tape off a roll, plastered it across Garth's mouth. The boy shuddered and closed his eyes, praying for his father to come save him.

# CHAPTER ONE

*Five Days Earlier*

THE BEAUTIFUL COUPLE strolled arm-in-arm through Seattle's Chinatown, talking and laughing past the gift shops, and the plant and bamboo stores created for tourists. It was early and overcast but they looked in love and without a care.

They weren't a couple, they were cops, partners of five years, and they were on alert. Jake Fortune, tall, his body lean, long and conquered, wasn't the kind of man you'd want to meet in a dark alley, probably not even a dark bar. He whispered to his partner: "Two buildings down."

"I can read, Jake." Anya Pashkov was prickly.

He ignored it, knowing she hadn't had enough coffee before they left the station. She was elegant, almost as tall as Jake, and, as usual, wore flats, the better to move quickly. Her perfect skin was emphasized by high Slavic cheekbones, and an easy smile attracted every male she met.

They'd left the squad half hour ago, after Jake had received a fax through his computer. It wasn't just that nobody faxed anymore, it was the third tip in a month with information about a smuggling ring dealing in illegal Chinese immigrants. Even now, he didn't know who his informant was. He had no idea why the snitch had targeted him, faxing the messages to his attention, but they were hand-printed, untraceable so far, from a phone line that apparently didn't exist. The first two tips resulted in only a few stragglers being found near the Greyhound station. But this time was different.

The information identified an address Jake recognized, a sleazy office in the middle of the historic Chinatown district. He'd once busted an unlicensed doctor there who specialized in treating perps who'd been shot or injured. They couldn't go to a legitimate doctor or hospital without the risk that they'd be reported to the cops, so they went to Dr. Zhou or someone like him. Sometimes they'd get better and sometimes they wouldn't.

Jake had parked their undercover sedan around the corner from the target address. He could smell the Baozi coming from the neighborhood restaurant down the block. The area was already crowded with residents and tourists, but none of them gave the pair much of a glance.

Anya drew her parka over her shoulders as the chill wind blew again. She glanced over to where she knew Mount Rainer was supposed to be, and shrugged. "I'm already sick of the dark, and winter hasn't even started. I don't think the mountain'll ever be out again."

Seattleites' eyes lit up when Mount Rainer's towering peak showed through the usual haze. It was like a primal sigh of relief, a nanosecond that augured well for the future.

"You couldn't see it from here, anyway."

"I know where it's supposed to be."

"It always comes out, Annie."

"Hah."

They reached the nondescript two-story building stuck in between a small family-run market and an aquarium and bird shop, alert to any unusual activity. Anya looked around, then murmured, "Appears clear."

They climbed the narrow, concrete stairwell up two flights to the landing. Anya took a position to the side of the door, as Jake knocked.

He used a bit of the Chinese he'd picked up when he was a beat cop in the district. The man Jake assumed to be Zhou opened the door, leaving little room for anyone to enter, but Jake was ready for him. He slammed Zhou back into the makeshift emergency room.

Across the room, a man lay on a cot near the window. The worn, grimy sheet that covered him was stained with his blood, the lumpy mattress soaked with his sweat. He could barely get his voice above a whisper. "Help me. Please."

Anya rushed to him as Jake cuffed the doc.

Zhou squirmed. "It's not necessary to hurt me."

"Who is he and how long has he been here?" Jake asked, pointing to the man on the cot.

Zhou blinked quickly. "Too late. Too much infection."

"I didn't ask you for a diagnosis. I asked his name and how long he's been here?"

Zhou shrugged. "He is Martin Lo. And he's been here for two days." Jake pushed Zhou into a chair, knowing that the call he'd make to 911 probably wouldn't be in time.

As he requested paramedics, he watched Anya crawl next to the dying Martin Lo and cradle his head. Her voice was soothing. "My partner's calling for help. It'll be okay."

Lo whispered to her with scarcely a breath left. "Bastard left me to die."

"Who left you? Who did this?" She hurried because every movement of his chest up and down might be the last. Zhou had patched up the multiple stab wounds as best he could, but the infection was massive and uncontrollable. Martin Lo was barely alive.

"Victor. Don't know his last name. Middle man." He eked out his story, every word an effort. "Seller's rep."

Jake finished the 911 call and stood back as Anya continued to establish a rapport. There was no time for subtlety. "Who's the seller?"

"Don't know. Never know."

"Okay, I understand. Take it easy. What was Victor selling? Dope?

Weapons?"

Lo slightly moved his head 'no.'

"Then what?"

"Labor."

"And you were buying... labor."

He coughed and moaned. "Not me. Only picked 'em up. Please, where's the ambulance?"

It was Jake who answered. "On its way. A couple minutes."

Anya nodded. "See, I promised, didn't I? I always keep my promises. Talk to me while we're waiting. It'll keep your mind off the pain. Tell me where the labor was going."

"I can't. He'll know. I swear he knows I'm here."

Anya shook her head. "If he knows, he expects you to spill."

Lo took this in, then, his voice a whisper: "Minneapolis."

"Did you piss Victor off? Try to double-cross the buyer?"

"Never. One of the workers figured out..." Lo had to stop. His chest heaved in agony. A rumbling cough took over, bringing up blood. "Please."

"Tell me, Martin. You'll feel better if you tell me."

Lo took as deep a breath as he could, trying to get the rest of the story out. "The guy figured out the Snakeheads were shipping him somewhere else. To finish paying for his passage. He thought once he was here, that was it. Victor laughed. The guy had a knife. He wasn't supposed to." Lo had to rest.

"So the illegal laborer stabbed you, right?

Lo nodded. "Yeah. Victor nailed him. Emptied his gun. Didn't have to." He fell silent and closed his eyes.

Anya shook him, gently. "C'mon, Martin. Get it out. It will help."

Jake watched from across the room. When Lo opened his eyes, they were glassy. A death mask hovered over his face. But he tried again, determined. They could hear sirens getting closer.

"Nobody else put up a fight. Not after that. I was out, but I heard hammering. Then Victor rolled me into a blanket and dumped me on skid row."

"He didn't bring you here?"

"He left me to die. But I still had my cell. I don't remember how I got here." Lo grabbed Anya's hand, holding on in desperation as Jake brought in the paramedics.

Anya leaned into him. "Victor's last name?"

Lo started to shake his head, but was too weak to finish.

The two EMTs tried to move Anya out of the way so they could do their job, but Martin Lo wouldn't let go of her hand. There was a look on his face that said he knew he was a dead man, and now it was payback time. In short, agonizing bursts, Lo gave Anya the warehouse location, and a partial description of Victor, which was so generic it was useless, before the paramedics rushed him out.

Jake pulled out his phone. "No point in going to the hospital. If there's any chance of finding these people, we need to set up a rescue op right now." They raced to their car, worried that the time had already run out.

# CHAPTER TWO

THE GLEAMING WHITE ferry cruised through the waters of the Strait of San Juan de Fuca, undulating in the aftermath of the latest storm. At mid-point between Lopez Island and the mainland, the gray sky and the gray water melded together in a seamless whole. Only a few passengers were hardy enough to travel on the upper deck.

Garth Fortune leaned over the green mesh railing as far as he could, captivated by the foam churning in the ferry's wake. He jingled the lucky coins his Grandpa Tony had given him in his pocket and sighed with contentment. When the little boy closed his eyes and let the fine spray envelop his face, he breathed in the cool salt air. It made him feel as if he were floating in the middle of nowhere, in the middle of no time. He had little sense of physical danger: what always worried him were the things he saw inside his head.

He felt Kate Dooley watching him, close enough so she could grab him if she thought she needed to. Garth knew what was about to come.

"Garth! You're too close to the edge! Move away from there, if you please. That sign says to stay behind the red line."

Kate was a mother of two grown boys with families of their own back in Ireland. Garth had asked her once why she lived here instead of with them. He was sure she'd tell him the truth, always. She admitted that after she was widowed and her children settled, she had followed her surprising wanderlust and ended up in Seattle. Garth understood that Kate protected everyone she considered hers.

He looked at her kind face and knew that he wouldn't win this argument. Garth sighed, shifting toward her with reluctance. He loved Mrs. Dooley almost like she was his mother. He only vaguely remembered his real mother, but sometimes a certain scent brought her back to him for the barest moment. He knew her name was Peggy, and she lived somewhere in the East, far away, but he doubted he'd ever see her again. Not if his father had anything to say about it, and his father had a lot to say about almost everything. Garth smiled up at Mrs. Dooley, grateful for her presence.

"Thank you, Garth. One little bump and you'd be shark bait."

"No sharks. The dolphins and the Killer Whales keep 'em away. They can do anything."

"Killer Whales. Sharks, propellers, jelly fish, it doesn't matter. Too close is too close. The sea deserves respect. Believe me, I know."

Garth had already heard the story about Mrs. Dooley's brother Sean and his fishing fleet being lost in a wild storm off the coast of Galway. Several times, in fact. He spoke quickly, before she could take a long breath and get started. "I *do* respect the sea. Dolphins are part of it, and I gotta look for them. It's for my science project."

She practically snorted. "I'm beginning to think everything on God's earth is part of your science project. First it was Bald Eagles on Lopez Island, then it was deer in Moran Park, now it's dolphins. Pretty soon it'll be whale watching off the farthest island."

"Everything *is* included in my project. It's about the flora and fauna of the San Juan Islands. That's why we have to come back. Soon."

"We've had enough flora and fauna for the day, then. Food is next on the agenda. Let's go below and get something to warm you up. The wind's a bit chilly." It was always chilly in October near Seattle, especially crossing the Strait. Windy rain they called it.

Garth didn't much care. A sweet child, smart for his nine years, he was small-boned, the kind of boy who wouldn't reach his full height until his late teens. He loved his San Juan Islands, even though it was a whole day trip from Seattle. Right now he'd rather be on the water than anywhere, windy rain or not. He wished the trip back to Seattle could last even longer.

"How about a nice sandwich and a bit of hot chocolate with whipping cream?"

Garth smiled. Mrs. Dooley had an unyielding sweet tooth, which was severely aggravated by breathing the sea air. Or so she told everyone, along with the claim of how fit she was for her age.

Mrs. Dooley steered Garth past the few other passengers who, despite the weather, preferred the open air to the inevitable smell of diesel fuel below. Garth followed her to the stairs leading down to the coffee shop. "I'd rather have some of your spicy cider, Mrs. D."

Garth, at her request, would have been happy to call her Kate or Aunt Kate, but his father was adamant. He insisted that as Garth's caretaker she deserved more respect than that. Garth had overheard her telling Jake that she thought he was too strict, but he was a good man so she wouldn't argue. "Mrs. D." was hers and Garth's private compromise. Coming from him it sounded as loving as "Mom."

"You do know the way to a lady's heart, don't you, little one?"

He glared at her as best he could with his bronze-colored velvet eyes.

"So sorry. *Young man.* I forget, sometimes. But you must understand that you'll always be my little one. You're stuck with that."

Garth slipped his hand into hers and stood on his tiptoes to whisper. "It's okay. As long as you don't say it in front of anybody."

"We have an agreement, then."

Garth felt how much she loved him. She'd been with him for six years, since right after his mother had left. Mrs. D. put her arm around Garth's shoulder, finding the back of his heavy parka damp through and through. "You're soaked. I'm supposed to be taking care of you. What would your father say?"

Garth shuddered, not from the cold or wet. He always shuddered when his mind touched that place inside that connected to things he shouldn't or couldn't possibly know. Sometimes he could get there by trying, sometimes it appeared. When it happened, it was like a window opening in his heart and showing him pictures in his head. Frequently the visions were like the 3-D movie he had seen at Disneyland, even with music, but they could be fuzzy and without color, more feeling than seeing, like this one.

*What the boy became aware of now was his father, in a terrible mood, angry with himself. Goosebumps on his arm. Watching something.*

Garth relaxed, coming out of his reverie. He thought about Mrs. D's question, about what his father would say. He didn't have to imagine the answer; he knew with certainty how his father was feeling right now.

"Don't worry, Mrs. D. I bet Dad's even wetter than I am."

"Nonsense. He's got more sense than that. He's at the station house or in his comfy car with the heater on."

Garth knew better. But he had learned from the time he was a toddler not to tell anyone what he saw. No one ever believed him and that made him feel bad. So he kept his thoughts to himself. But he had just seen in his head exactly where his father was. And it wasn't in his car, and he wasn't warm. He was wet, mad, and swearing.

# CHAPTER THREE



"Sonovabitch."

Garth was right. Jake was pissed, but then he was frequently pissed, usually about evil, or stupidity, or people who took pleasure in hurting others. This time he was his own target, for the crime of forgetting his overcoat, which he had left hanging on the coat-tree in the office. *Idiot,* he yelled at himself. The garbage bin he was using for cover left him completely unprotected from the sudden deluge. He was a total idiot.

He glanced across the alley at Anya. She had made a little cave amidst soaking wet cardboard boxes. It never failed to amaze him how easily Anya appeared to deal with any situation, and still look serene, no matter the discomfort. But he'd been partners with her long enough to know that she was miserable. He watched her try to fit her slender body behind her disintegrating cover, but it was like trying to shove Venus into a shoe box.

He also knew her looks were low on her list of priorities. Right now, as always, work came first. He figured that her constant battle with what she called the 'demon weed' was getting the better of her. He watched her chew on her lower lip, which meant she desperately wanted a cigarette. Or one puff. He nodded to himself and smiled as she breathed deeply and let it go, her attention never leaving the target in front of her.

The rain came down in torrents as Jake and Anya waited across from the rear entrance to a dilapidated warehouse on Harbor Island, a few blocks from the West Seattle Bridge, and not far from the Port of Seattle's terminal. Jake forced himself to keep his mind blank, to focus only on the impending raid.

The radio in his hand squawked. Jake held it to his ear so he could hear over the driving rain, then mumbled a response. He signaled Anya a one-minute warning.

Jake shook this morning's image out of his head. It was never easy to watch a man die, even someone like Lo, and instead he focused on what was right in front of him now. He checked his watch, then whispered into the radio. "Go."

He knew that by now every entrance and exit was surrounded by the combined squad he was leading: twelve SWAT cops, six County Sheriffs, two paramedic units, and an INS observer.

Jake and Anya worked like a choreographed dance team, each movement leading them closer to the warehouse. They had done this so many times, they covered each other's back without words. It worked ninety-nine percent of the time, and they liked those odds.

A swarm of blue-jacketed cops, vests in place, guns drawn, descended on the warehouse. The two lead men battered the huge, locked sliding doors open, and behind them the battalion of cops advanced into the building.

Inside, the barely lit space appeared empty but for a few wooden crates and cartons. Anya slowed and pointed to a patch of a red-brown stain on the concrete floor. Jake leaned down, touching it with his finger, then mouthed to her: "Blood."

They followed a trail to a door where someone had haphazardly nailed two by fours across it. Anya put her ear to the boards, and signaled to Jake, who grabbed a crowbar from one of the Sheriff's deputies. Jake ripped off the boards and slammed through the door, Anya following him in a crouch.

The stench in the room assaulted them. About thirty Chinese, mostly men but a few women, huddled in fear against the walls. A few were crying; most simply stared at their new captors.

Anya pulled herself upright. "Shit."

Jake lifted his radio, speaking in a flat voice. "Get the paramedics in, and call for two transport buses." He looked around, forcing down his emotions, as his Marine training had taught him. *No. Not now. No.*

Anya held her automatic steady, covering Jake, who was trying to calm the crowd of refugees. He knew they probably wouldn't understand him, but he kept his voice in a soft cadence so as not to spook them.

"Okay, folks, it will be okay. We're going to get you out of here now. Get you some help, some food and water." Then he repeated these words in his minimal Chinese. No one responded, so he walked among the terrified people, leaning down here and there to help someone up.

Anya waited until the backup team came through the door in full force, then holstered her gun and moved to assist Jake. There was a tiny, wrinkled woman who seemed to be staring at Jake, nodding her head as if she were talking to herself. It soon became clear that she was pointing toward the corner.

Jake moved to the spot, and found something hidden under a bunch of crates. It was a makeshift shelter, but in front was a human leg stretched out at a strange angle. Anya helped him pull the boxes off. Jake recoiled and Anya gasped at what lay underneath. He recovered within a moment.

The sight facing them was a young woman, probably in her early twenties, cradling an emaciated toddler. The boy was rigid in death. The Chinese girl was alive, and was rocking her son, humming softly, as if this would bring him back to life. She ignored Anya and Jake, focused only on her child.

"I've got her." Jake's voice came out in a rasp. Trying to disturb the young mother as little as possible, Jake lifted her from her hiding place. Her ankle appeared to be broken. He did not even attempt to pry the child away from her; the young woman was clutching her baby with such fierce determination, Jake knew he would never succeed.

He carried them to a waiting EMT. A large firefighter took the mother and child from Jake's arms, and carried them outside. Jake watched them go. *Only a bride should be carried over the threshold,* he thought.

The cops quieted, cajoled, lifted and ushered those who could still walk to the ambulances and buses outside. None of the refugees attempted to get away; they knew there was nowhere to run.

Jake saw Anya was having trouble catching her breath in the still and fetid air. Jake appeared at her side, his hand grabbing her shoulder. He looked into her eyes, which were almost level with his. It was as if he were infusing her with his strength. She relaxed and he let go.

"Thanks. I thought I was going to lose it." She looked around and sighed. "Jesus, these poor people must have been in here two or three days."

Jake watched the last of the group being led out. "You're taking it personally because it could have been you. You know better than that. We can't take any of it personally."

Anya started to argue, then shook her head. "You're right."

They moved aside for the forensics team to do their job. Jake stopped the lead investigator, Karen Cardoza, grateful it was her rotation. Not only was she extremely competent, but along with her freckles and red hair, Karen possessed a nature so cheerful even this work didn't daunt her. Once in a while someone would push Jake to ask Karen out, but he never did. It would be too unprofessional, or so he said. "I followed a crusted blood trail to the door, Karen."

"We found it, Jake. Ten to one it'll match Martin Lo's blood."

"Ten to one it's mixed with his assailant's blood. And as far as I can tell, he isn't here."

"We'll have 'em all tested, anyway. Jesus, it stinks in here." Karen whipped out a hospital mask and some Vick's, then moved off to comb the scene.

Anya turned to Jake. "I had the troops secure a three-block radius. Victor had an awful lot to do. Maybe he dumped the immigrant's body somewhere close."

"Maybe. Maybe Victor dumped it forty miles from here. Maybe we'll know more about him when we get these people with an interpreter."

"Not likely." Dave Bell, the Immigration Liaison, came up behind them. "Can we move this outside, ya think?"

As Bell guided them toward the fresh air, Jake asked him: "Why are you here? Aren't you supposed to be fishing on the Colorado?"

Dave shook his head. "My wife is determined we get my twenty-five for the pension. Then she'll let me stop. She doesn't understand this gets harder every day."

They reached the open doors and breathed in the fresh air, the blessings of the rain.

Anya sympathized. "I can't imagine."

"You're lucky." Dave had been complaining to Jake and Anya for months now. They all knew his job had become relentless, overwhelming and unmanageable, mired in politics and ego. "It's a damned invasion. There's no good way to make 'em welcome and no good way to stop 'em. And you know none of them will talk. They're lured across the border with fake promises and they'll be too worried about their families back home. Whoever was responsible for this won't hesitate to teach them another lesson."

Jake was impatient. "We can only handle what's in front of us."

Dave nodded. "Exactly. And I know this is officially a homicide, so I'm going to leave this mess with you guys until we have more to go on. And until the higher-ups decide what to do with this group. Obviously INS reserves the right to intervene." He shook his head. "This coulda been worse."

Anya smiled up at him. There weren't too many men she could look up at, being almost six feet in flats. "Bad enough. You sticking around for a while, Dave?"

"Not unless a miracle happens and you actually get a lead to somebody who actually knows something and actually wants to share."

Dave was one of the good guys, so Jake ribbed him. "So, we'll do the work and INS will take the credit. Smart move, Bell."

Dave laughed and shook Jake's hand, then disappeared toward his warm car.

Anya turned to her partner. "Who cares about the damned credit? I don't want to find anymore dead babies."

Jake shrugged. "Dave's used to me."

He put a hand on the small of her back to guide her out, a gesture she would have disdained with anyone else. "Let's follow them in. Maybe we can get the mother to talk."

The Sheriffs were almost finished loading the immigrants onto the buses, men on one, women on the other. Deputy Sheriff Bob Podinsky, trim, attractive and all too aware of it, preened past Anya, eyeing her perfect ass. She ignored him. When he finally met Jake's gaze, Podinksy was full of apologies.

"Sorry, Lieutenant. The translators are across town. Somebody screwed up."

Jake barely contained himself. That allowed an extra hour for the illegals to spend together, terrified, to support each other's determination not to respond to questions. Anya put a hand on Jake's arm. The last thing they needed was for him to explode. His voice was cold and even as he addressed the deputy sheriff. "Get 'em some food and hot water. And wipe the drool off your tie."

Anya looked over her shoulder at Podinsky. "We'll meet the buses down there."

Jake was silent until they got into the car. "You don't trust me."

Anya smiled. "I always trust you. I also know you, and this wasn't the time for a lot of wasted screaming and pissing and moaning. We need to focus on what's happening here, not on asshole fuck-ups like Podinsky."

They rode in silence a few blocks. Jake let out a grunt, then shrugged his shoulders.

"Apology accepted," she said. "You're forgiven."

"I didn't ask to be forgiven."

"You should have."

"I don't get it. Why me?" She knew exactly what he was asking.

"You, because of the Harlin bust. It made all the papers and you got good press. This snitch isn't a pro, doesn't go through the usual channels and clearly has his own agenda."

"Okay, I buy that. Then what's his agenda? That perp today, Lo, was waste material. We have nothing on the organization or who's running it. Nada. We're stuck with a dead baby and more than thirty poor suckers who don't speak English and won't talk to the interpreters anyway."

"You're right. It's screwy. It's all good info, but why tip us off at all? Unless the informant doesn't *want* us to find the head guy. Only the victims."

"Good thinking. Could be." He grinned. "You always surprise me."

"You should be used to me by now. In my world there are grays, Jake. Unlike yours."

The rain clouds burst again as they drove in silence on First Avenue, along the harbor, past Pike Place Market, now teeming with tourists. Anya looked out at the people living their lives oblivious to the dangers that surrounded them. Jake knew better than to interrupt her reverie.

She relaxed into her seat, sighing. "Look at them. They have no idea what's happening in the world while they're watching guys toss fish back and forth. They're lucky."

"That's what we're here for. To keep them lucky."

They worked so well together, he was certain that their thoughts were following a similar path: this was the tip of a deep iceberg. He also knew their caseload was so heavy, they didn't have the time or resources to deal with it adequately. It felt too big, too amorphous, and unless it came together quickly, they'd lose it to another agency or it would disappear into the black hole of the unsolved. That option was unacceptable. The image of the dead toddler was too clearly etched in their minds.

# CHAPTER FOUR

GARTH LISTENED TO the rain dance softly on the kitchen roof. He couldn't wait until it got a little colder and they'd build a fire in the living room fireplace. Mrs. D. was really good at placing the logs and had taught him how. He was very proud of this ability, and he loved it when the whole neighborhood had smoke coming out of their chimneys in the Seattle damp.

He also loved to help Mrs. Dooley snap the ends off the green beans. He didn't much like eating them, but the popping noise was satisfying, like a job well done. The kitchen television was playing with a low drone. Mrs. Dooley always had the small, ancient TV on in the background, *in case*. Garth had never figured out in case of what, but he'd learned to block out the noise. Especially when he was helping her cook. That way he could stare into space while he was doing it and let his imagination relax.

He especially liked to do that at home. The old Victorian was in the Montlake District, a great neighborhood bordering the Arboretum, northwest of Capitol Hill. It was surrounded by elegant, ruby-colored Japanese maples, and overlooked Portage Bay. The view was beautiful, but more important, it was the house where his mother had grown up.

There was no way they could've lived here on his father's salary, but it didn't matter. The house belonged to Garth.

Garth's grandparents had put the house in trust for him after their daughter moved back East, leaving Garth behind. It came to him when they died three years ago, two days apart. Garth knew that Peggy flew in for the double funeral, but his dad said he was too young to go. He missed seeing his mother there, but he could feel her presence in the house. Sometimes he'd go up into the attic and rummage through the trunks his grandparents had left behind. He'd look at everything they'd saved from his mother's childhood, her school books and pictures and music. Then he'd imagine them still alive, living there with his mother.

Once, when he was in the attic playing alone, he felt his father standing in the doorway behind him, watching. When Garth turned around, Jake was gone. He would have liked to go through the boxes and stuff with his dad, but he knew his father would probably never want to do that.

As it was, Jake was always swearing about how hard it was to keep the place going, how much money the big old house ate up in taxes and maintenance, inside and out. Garth hoped he wouldn't sell it. In fact, he often thought, if his father did that, Garth might have to run away from home.

Mrs. Dooley always noticed when he was 'gathering wool,' as she called it. She usually chose not to comment, but she knew when to bring him back. This time she brought him back by turning up the sound on the TV. What Garth saw was his father's face appearing before him on the 5:00 pm news. Jake was soaking wet, herding a group of sad-looking Chinese people onto buses.

It was obvious that his father was angry about the camera's intrusion. Reading Jake's face was never difficult, even for dumb reporters. They knew better than to talk to him, but Anya was there, and she was ignoring them too.

Mrs. Dooley beamed as she watched Jake. "Such a handsome man, your father." She patted Garth's cheek. "You look exactly like him."

Garth squinted at the screen. "Uh uh. I look more like my mom's side, I think."

"It doesn't matter one whit. You're a fine-looking boy, whomever you take after."

Garth finished the green beans and handed the last of them to her. "What's a whit, Mrs. D.?"

She hesitated for a second. "Well, I guess it means a little bit."

"That rhymes."

"It certainly does, my boy. Now, what'll you have on your hamburger? No onions, I know, they make you upchuck. No tomatoes. No lettuce. How about some cheese?"

"Well, maybe a whit."

Garth was very pleased with himself when Mrs. Dooley burst into her cackling laugh. "Good enough, a whit of cheese." She sighed deeply. "Sometimes I think you're too smart for your own good, Gar."

"That's impossible."

"No, I'm afraid it's not. But we are who we are."

A car door slammed down the street. Mrs. Dooley cocked her head, waiting for the footsteps along the front walk. Garth watched her listening. "He won't be home for a while, Mrs. D."

"Now how do you know that?"

"He didn't look happy on the TV. He usually goes out with Anya when he's not too happy."

She threw his hamburger patty onto the pan, over a high flame, its skin crackling and splattering oil drops all over the stovetop. She waited until the sizzle died down, then lowered the heat. "Only a few minutes, now, until all the pink is out."

"I like the pink."

"Too much E coli around, young man. No point in tempting fate."

Garth knew there was no way he was going to win this one. "Then can I make my dessert now?"

"You *may* not until after dinner."

"But if I make it now, it'll be ready for when I finish my dinner."

"I did agree, didn't I? A deal is a deal, then."

Garth didn't wait for her to change her mind. He rummaged in the bread bin for the Wonder Bread. Mrs. Dooley's lip curled in disdain. "That isn't like any bread I grew up with."

Garth smiled. "It's really chewy." He painstakingly slathered butter exactly to the edges of the bread, then added two Hershey bars and arranged them so they were precisely aligned to the crust.

Mrs. D. watched with a mixture of fascination and revulsion. "Where did you learn this, Gar? From some dentist who advertises on a bus bench?" She flipped his hamburger.

"I told you. Gretchen Vanderhall. The girl in my class from Denmark. Her mom makes them all the time. She told me exactly how to do it."

"God only knows."

"You wanna taste? After dinner, I mean."

"I don't think so, dear. Here. Your meat and veggies. Every bit now, or Gretchen what's-her-name can eat that concoction herself."

He dug into the hamburger happily, as Mrs. Dooley puttered around the kitchen, cleaning up. She was a wonderful cook, even with her unyielding fear of e coli, but she seemed to use every single pot and pan. He thought it was a good thing she enjoyed washing dishes.

As Garth watched Mrs. D move around the old-fashioned kitchen, his eyes grew bigger and the color drained from his face. He put his hamburger down. A shudder went through his body, like it did when he was on the ferry thinking about his father. He knew better than to try and hold back whatever he was seeing. This time unbidden tears streamed down his face. Garth felt *a sharp pain in his chest, tight, breathless, I can't breathe, it hurts.*

He forced himself to push back the terrible sensation. Over the last couple of years, he had learned how to move away from the feelings so they didn't overwhelm him. He wiped his tears with his napkin so Mrs. Dooley wouldn't see them.

She was still humming as she rinsed the dishes, occasionally looking over at him to make sure he was eating. She stopped rinsing when she noticed him staring at her intently. "What's wrong, Gar dear?"

"You feeling okay, Mrs. D.?" He knew she wasn't.

"Never better. Don't try to distract me, young man. Eat up or no chocolate sandwich."

"Okay. But I have to check something... in my room... first. I'll be right back." He bolted from his chair into the hallway. Mrs. Dooley watched him go, a puzzled look on her face, then turned back to the sink.

In the small, old-fashioned telephone alcove off the hallway, Garth quietly picked up the phone. He didn't want to do this, he didn't want to expose himself to the disbelief, but maybe they wouldn't figure it out. It didn't matter. He *had* to call or she'd die and it would be his fault. His fingers trembled as he punched in '911'. He whispered into the phone so Mrs. D. couldn't hear him and get worried.

"Uh, my sitter's sick. I think she's having a heart attack. Please hurry. Please."

# CHAPTER FIVE

GALLAGHER'S PLACE WASN'T low-end or rowdy, but it was the kind of bar where carrying a concealed weapon was expected. Sawdust and the husks of ballpark peanuts layered the floor, cigarettes weren't allowed but smoke polluted the air anyway, uncomfortable wooden booths afforded privacy but made the patrons sit so straight they may as well have been wearing whalebone corsets. A jukebox sat in the corner, but its main function was as a frustration barometer – it worked only half the time, and mostly the patrons kicked the shit out of it when they were pissed off. The bar was at the bottom of First Hill, a few blocks from the Courthouse and Seattle PD headquarters, but the owner never let the patrons get so drunk they'd end up in either place.

A cop felt comfortable here, welcomed by the proprietor, a school-marmish-looking woman in her late forties with the mouth of a steel-worker. Megan Gallagher was probably not her real name, but nobody much cared. She served good, cheap food and great draft beer, took care of her customers, never gossiped about any of them, and always knew what was going on in the city. There wasn't a cop in Seattle who wouldn't do anything for Megan, especially since she would never ask.

Jake and Anya sat hunched in a back booth, nursing the last of a half-pitcher of draft Peroni. A portrait of irritation, Jake cracked peanuts without thinking, aiming the shells somewhere near a trash can, mostly missing.

Anya sighed. "Get over it, Jake. We'll work on them again tomorrow."

"Three busts. Perfect description of 'em. We don't know any more now than we did a month ago. We don't know how they're getting here or who's behind it."

"Well, brooding ought to help." She tossed a peanut shell straight at him. "The bad guys should stand there and say here we are, come and get us."

He ignored her sarcasm. He always ignored her sarcasm. "Besides, we know they're coming in by boat."

"We *think* they're coming in by boat. We could've figured that out by throwing a dart. Jesus, you're such a goddamn optimist."

"That's a nasty way to describe a Russian. We pride ourselves on melancholy and dark nights of the soul."

Jake didn't answer, missed another toss.

She prodded. "What else?"

"I don't know."

"Think. Then talk."

"There's something bugging me."

Anya laughed. He snapped out of his torpor and looked sheepish. "Okay. I deserved that. But seriously, there's something niggling somewhere in the back of my brain that feels familiar about all this. And I can't reach it."

"You're trying too hard."

Jake laughed. "No shit."

"Okay, I guess that's a given. Lay it on me. Free associate."

Jake thought for a moment. "I think it's a picture."

"Close your eyes. Can you see anything about it?"

Jake took a deep slug of beer first. "Now I'll close my eyes."

"Black and white? Or color?"

Jake hesitated, then: "Black and white." He opened his eyes and looked at Anya, smiled. "Okay. Sometimes you're right. I think it was a picture of a young dead Chinese woman. Like in an interstate or Federal bulletin. Or international?" He took another swallow of Peroni.

"Was she pretty?"

"Pretty. And dead. That's all I got."

Anya pounded the table, startling Jake and almost spilling her beer. "Not me. I got more!"

"You gonna keep it to yourself?

"Nope. About two years ago. Beautiful, young Chinese girl, missing, found dead. Vancouver BC."

"Our backyard." He sighed deeply. "I think that's it.

"You think it might be connected?"

"I don't know. But there must've been something about it that struck a chord."

"Good. We'll check it out. Tomorrow. Tonight it's hamburgers and beer. And fried clams."

"It's not easy to let go."

"It never is. But…" She was interrupted by an intrusive high-pitched signal projecting through the bar's din.

"Yours or mine?"

"Mine." She reached into her purse, switching off the irritating noise, then checked the number of the text on her phone. Her face remained impassive as she erased it. Jake waited for her to tell him, but instead she picked up her mug and drained it.

Jake questioned her. "I thought you blew him off."

"I did."

"You want me to have a talk with him?" Jake would have been happy to get his frustration out somewhere, anywhere. And Anya's sometime boyfriend was a good place to start. Jake was protective of her, and much more, but the more they hadn't acknowledged in over a year.

"He's not dangerous, Jake. He's only married."

Jake understood this was not a discussion she wanted to have, especially with him.

"That's dangerous for you. He's a nasty habit."

"Don't worry so much about me. Damn — you, my parents, my brothers... it's enough to drive a person over the wall."

"Up the wall. Over the edge." Occasionally she mixed up her slang. He loved to catch her.

"Over, up, it doesn't matter. I can handle my life." Jake knew she believed that down to the marrow of her bones. Especially considering that Anya was only thirteen when she and her family settled in the U.S. He'd prod occasionally, but she didn't want to talk about her life before then. But Jake knew they were from the Ukraine when it was part of Russia, and they'd gotten out in a hurry.

He also knew that when she'd arrived, she had felt awkward and gawky, spoke stilted English, flawless French, and spent her first year in the U.S. rarely saying a word. Then, when they moved to Seattle during the early part of her freshman year in high school, she stalked the scene like a quiet hunter. He thought it was remarkable that within six months she had transformed herself into a new person. Someone who fit in. She had plunged into American life, spoke perfect English, and dressed completely in style. She was a cheerleader, voted most popular, and never looked back. She blazed the path for her parents and two brothers, and her family always told Jake that they still looked to Anya as a beacon, which annoyed the hell out of her. Jake respected that she wanted to live her own life without being a role model for someone else's, that it was too much of a burden. And he understood that she hated being told what to do.

Jake looked at her as if he was about to lecture, so she gathered her jacket, purse and case notes. "Big hurry, huh? You're going to meet him."

She mimicked Jake. "No, I'm not going to *meet him*. Not hungry anymore. I'm going home to soak in a hot tub and think about our case. The more interesting question is, why aren't you?"

"Why aren't I what?"

"Gimme a break."

"Garth's okay."

"He doesn't get enough of you."

"He's fine. He's with Mrs. Dooley. When I'm this distracted by a case, she's better for him than I am. C'mon, have one more Peroni. And the hamburgers and fried clams. You know you want to."

She laughed and challenged him. "They have great local craft beers here. How about one of them instead of Peroni?"

"It's my heritage."

"Ha. Nothing to do with that. You simply don't like change. Of any kind."

"I like knowing what's around the next corner."

"Impossible to control, Jake."

"I'll give it my 'A' game." He gestured to the waitress.

Anya sighed again, and resettled onto the hard wooden bench. She couldn't say no to him, but Jake rarely took advantage of that. He watched her, knowing she'd given in, and smiled, his guard down. He didn't expect that Anya would go in for the kill.

"Peggy's been gone a long time, Jake. It's not Garth's fault."

Jake scowled. "You're right. It's Peggy's fault."

"You can't keep blaming her. She wasn't well."

"Maybe not then. But what about now?"

"So you're still blaming her and Garth's left with no mother and a part-time father."

"I do the best I can. Besides, he can't learn how to take care of himself unless he takes care of himself."

"He's only nine. Just because your dad wasn't there for you doesn't mean Garth has to experience the same thing."

"My dad was there until I was three. If you're going to shrink me, keep your facts straight."

"Excuse me. *Three*. And the *fact* is your dad was a hidden POW in El Salvador for five years, for Chrissake. It's not like he deserted his family. He came back with PTSD."

"Tell that to a kid."

"Too bad for you. Parents are supposed to try to make it easier for their kids than they had it. Not harder."

"We worked it out, Annie. But Tony and I have nothing in common."

Anya laughed. Jake had the grace to be embarrassed by his own denial. When the waitress plunked down a fresh half-pitcher, a different annoying signal began to buzz. Jake's phone. He pulled it out and for a fleeting moment a look of panic crossed his face.

Anya was already up and ready to move. "What's wrong?"

"I don't know. It's Garth's 911 emergency code. He's never used it before." Jake strode to the door and rushed out, Anya right behind him.

# CHAPTER SIX

Seattle residents loved being part of a pioneer city, whether it was computers or coffee or medicine. For years their beloved community had been rated the best place in America, even in the world, to have a heart attack, an unusual distinction that made its citizens proud. Harborview Medical Center sat high above the city on First Hill, only minutes away from any emergency. The quick response time and King County's innovative medical technology, combined with the fact that Seattle fathered one of the country's first paramedic programs, led to excellent medical care in any trauma situation.

Garth did not know or care about any of this. All he knew was that the woman who was like his mother, the woman who protected and loved him, was behind closed glass doors and he couldn't get close to her. Like a little pill-bug poked by the end of a stick, he huddled in the corner of the lumpy couch outside the ICU. Since he was a baby, he always became very still when he was truly upset. He kept forgetting to breathe as he watched the doctors and nurses hustle through the corridors with great purpose.

In the parking lot, Jake's long legs carried him through the double doors, down the corridor toward his son, Anya right behind him. He stopped in front of Garth, laying a protective hand on his son's shoulder. He could see the tear stains on Garth's cheeks. "Are you okay?"

Garth bit his lip to keep from crying again. He shook his head.

"How's Mrs. Dooley?"

"They won't tell me anything. It's 'cause I'm a kid."

Anya gave Jake a gentle push out of the way, slid next to Garth on the couch and enfolded him in her arms. He leaned his head on her shoulder and the tears began to fall.

"What happened, son?" Jake asked. He figured the more he knew, the more control he'd have over the situation.

"Give it a minute, Jake. He's not going anywhere."

Jake knew she was right, but he didn't know how to deal with his son's pain. He hadn't known since Peggy left, and in this moment he doubted he ever would. No matter what he tried, it came out wrong, somehow. Goddamn, he was mad at himself. "Sorry. I thought it might make him feel better to talk about it."

Garth pulled away from Anya's safe embrace, but her arm never left his shoulder. Jake began to pace up and down the corridor. Garth watched his father for a moment or two, then took a breath, his lips trembling, as he told the truth.

"Mrs. D. looked pale. She was making dinner, then she got shimmery lights all around her, some orange, and then this gray cloud kinda came down and surrounded her. I asked her if she was feeling okay and she said she was, but I knew she was real sick. I could feel it. So I called 911... like you taught me."

Stunned, Anya looked up at Jake, who froze. He hated all this talk about shimmering lights, about orange and gray clouds. He'd heard it before. More than that, it triggered half-forgotten memories of his own childhood he wanted to bury. He'd blocked them then, and now they made him want to run like hell. It was a most uncomfortable feeling for a former Marine and a two-time Medal of Valor-winning cop. He could sense Anya glaring at him, her eyes willing him not to say a word.

"Go on, honey," Anya said, keeping her arms around the boy. "She had a heart attack and you called 911."

Garth sighed. "*No.* I knew she was getting sick, but she didn't know it yet. I figured she had to get medicine or…or…" He stopped himself from saying it out loud.

Anya's voice was calm. "Okay. She didn't know she was sick, but you did, and you called 911."

"Yeah. They said they'd send somebody right away. I was real glad, 'cause then Mrs. D. grabbed her heart and fell on the kitchen floor. I knew it was gonna be her heart because I could feel it hurting. But the paramedics got there real quick. They said she coulda died if I didn't call."

Anya exchanged a warning look with Jake. He leaned down and turned his son around to face him. "Garth, you did the right thing. Mrs. Dooley got sick and you did the right thing and it saved her life. You're a hero… but I don't want you to keep saying you saw this happen before it happened."

Garth started crying really hard, gulping for breath. "You never believe me. I saw her. Like I saw Murray before the car squished him. Like I saw Mommy leave before she left. I saw it. I saw it!"

Anya continued caressing the boy's back, ignoring Jake. "Of course, honey. Don't you worry. I know you're scared about Mrs. Dooley. It's okay to be scared." She held Garth while he sobbed quietly against her shoulder.

Jake disappeared around the corridor. He headed for a soda machine, pushing his change in as if it were his adversary. The machine didn't work fast enough for him. He slammed his fist against it, hard, hurting himself in the process. But he won: a can of Coke slid out. He carried it back down the corridor as if it were an offering, and handed it to Garth. "Here. Drink some. When you were a baby, this always settled your stomach. Maybe it'll help."

Garth accepted the Coke, sipping between deep breaths. Jake felt better for a moment.

A doctor in scrub greens strode into the waiting area. Char Sassoon, looking barely old enough to shave, approached the waiting group. "Mrs. Dooley's family?"

They all nodded. "I'm Dr. Sassoon. She's doing better, for now. I don't want to kid you. The attack was pretty severe and we're going to have to go in as soon as she's stabilized and do an angioplasty to clear out the blockage."

Jake and Garth both looked as if they'd been punched so Anya who took charge. "You're going to do a roto-rooter job?"

"Yes, precisely."

"And then?"

"And then, all things going well, she should be up and around pretty quickly. She's not going to be kayaking on Lake Union, but most other activities should be okay in a few weeks."

Jake, relieved, looked down at Garth. "We'd better call Matthew."

"I called him already, Dad. He's going to catch the first plane from Shannon." Garth hesitated, then: "I used your credit card at the nurses' station. I remembered the number."

Jake's solar plexus contracted. He was thrown by how grown-up his son had become. "Good thinking," he said, though what really struck Jake was the fear that very soon Garth wouldn't need his father for anything.

"Can I see her? Please?" Garth asked the doctor.

"If you're Garth, she's been asking to see you for the last fifteen minutes. She said if I wouldn't bring you in, she'd march out of the bed herself. She's pretty tough. I guess I'd better do what she says."

Garth smiled for the first time since his vision. "That sounds like her. She's gonna be okay." He looked up at Jake. "You wanna go in with me, Dad?"

"Sure. I'll be right behind you." Jake noted how mesmerized the doctor became as he watched Anya stretch and lift her long body off the couch. Had he been less tense, Jake might have smiled as the young man's eyes flickered to check out her ring finger, which was bare.

Anya seemed to not even notice. "I'll let you guys visit. I need to do a few things, then I'll meet you at home later. Okay, Gar?" She and Garth hugged.

"You've got a good kid here," Dr. Sassoon said to Anya, clearly eager for more intimate conversation.

"He's my godson. And he is a good kid." She turned away and loped toward the exit. The doctor watched her leave, disappointment on his face.

Jake was used to Anya's effect on men. It didn't bother him with this guy, only with the ones he considered assholes. Most of them. Including himself.

"Whenever you're ready, Doc." Jake said it without malice. The doctor blushed, then led them through the double glass doors, past several draped-off cubicles. The place had hospital smells no antiseptic could disguise. He heard people moaning behind the privacy curtains. Garth did not seem aware of any of it as he followed behind the doctor. It was clear that the only thing on his son's mind was getting to Mrs. D.

Mrs. Dooley had wires attached everywhere. Oxygen through a nasal cannula. Electrodes leading from her chest to a monitor that beeped every few seconds. Saline and other meds dripped through one IV in her arm, while another on her hand carried the pain medication. Garth gulped when he saw her. There was no way he'd let her know how scary she looked.

"Don't worry, young man, I won't always look like this." Her voice was low but strong.

Garth grabbed her right hand, the only thing that didn't look like it was attached to anything except her body. "You look a lot better than you did. They'll fix you up."

Jake inched toward the bed, his gut churning. He hated hospitals and illness, possibly from watching his mother die over two long years. Give him a brawl and he was fine, but seeing someone in pain threw him. "You're doing fine, Mrs. Dooley. And Garth had the presence of mind to call Matthew. He's on his way."

"That's not the only thing Garth had the presence of mind for, Jacob.

He saved my life." She was the only person in the world who could call him Jacob and get away with it.

"He told us what happened. We're all grateful the paramedics got there in time."

"Not in time. Early. Garth saved my life. I don't know how he knew, but he did. He has the gift, the gift of sight. Bless him. You have to protect him, they're so innocent, these people."

"You need your rest, Mrs. Dooley. We'll come see you tomorrow."

"Don't you ignore me, Jacob Fortune. The paramedics got there one minute after I collapsed. Sixty seconds. Garth called them before I got sick. You tell me why."

Jake had no answer, and he didn't want to upset her.

Her voice was raspy as she raised her head off the pillow. "Go on, you can't tell me, can you? You'd better learn to believe him. He's an old soul. I'm not so sure about you."

"This isn't the time to get worked up about anything. You get well. We'll take care of everything."

She glared at Jake. "You take care of your son. He's the only thing that matters." She squeezed Garth's hand and lay her head back down, exhausted.

# CHAPTER SEVEN

FENG WAH HUNG up the phone. It was a landline because they had only intermittent cell service, which was better as far as he was concerned. Victor was almost to the island, but it had not been a satisfying conversation and Feng was irritated. He would take care of it in his own way, as he always did.

He strode into the dining room and returned to his seat at the table, ignoring his wife completely. He moved the soup to the side of his place setting. It was beautifully presented in a Limoges bowl, but Cook had salted it too heavily. Feng watched his sodium intake diligently, and this recipe displeased him. Charles noticed and removed the offending dish. Feng Wah acknowledged him with the most minimal nod. "Too salty."

Charles bowed and left the room. Feng Wah knew the butler was wondering how long this cook would last. He also knew the man would never say anything, would never cross the line Feng had set. He hated the English, their arrogance, their inborn sense of superiority. It gave him enormous pleasure to own a proper English butler.

His wife kept her eyes downcast; he'd let her stay for almost twenty years because she was beautiful, properly terrified, and had made herself obedient. With great politeness, she asked him: "May I see to your dinner?

Feng Wah was abrupt. "Unnecessary."

She remained silent, at the far end of the table, away from her husband. Feng claimed it was a traditional arrangement, as it should be, but in reality it was easier for him not to interact with her.

No Westerner could understand how this refined, educated beauty could be married to the man of stone, the one who looked like a toad. Feng Wah didn't care. It was important to him only that *he* knew. He had risen from less than nothing, from a mother who brought him up in the back room of a brothel. But he had a will of iron and a brain better than anyone he'd ever met. What he lacked was a conscience. His mother had given him a name that had more than one meaning, one that was usually given to a female. The yang version was the wood element, the wind, powerful enough to blow things down. He liked that well enough. But he preferred the yin meaning, that of the phoenix, which meant wealth. He didn't know where he'd inherited his gifts, nor did he care. When he was fifteen, he decided he would own the brothel. It took him a year. He left his mother there to earn her keep, and moved on to bigger deals.

He was living a prosperous life when he saw his future wife for the first time, and he knew he would have her. China had been celebrating the millennium, and the streets of Shanghai were crowded with revelers, many of them foreign. It irritated him because this was the Chinese year 4698 and had nothing to do with the Western world. But he knew if he wanted to grow his business he'd have to transform himself into someone who was flexible in the ways of others, and he was determined to do so. At least it was a Dragon year, which gave him enough power to succeed. That's what he was thinking about when he saw the woman who would become his wife across the street at a café table with a group of friends, laughing and happy.

He stared at her long enough that she turned around to see him watching her. She was exquisite and had kind eyes. He didn't care that she would have smiled at anyone.

He stalked her from that moment. Her name was Shi Mingzhu, and he discovered where she worked, where she lived, and that she was supporting her proud and once-successful family by herself. He followed Mingzhu home from work each night. Even in the very crowded streets, she must've felt him. She would turn to see who was near her, but he was good at hiding. Feng researched her family, and discovered they had fallen far from grace when her father had angered a party official, and they'd lost everything. Five generations a proud Shanghai family; now they were reduced to this, a small place three flights above a bao shop. He paid the landlord to tell him what happened in their apartment, and knew she was met each night by the relentless litany of her family's complaints. Not enough heat. Not enough food. Everything was tasteless. Why had this happened to them? Mingzhu didn't have a room, so she and her younger brother slept in the living room after her parents would retreat to the one small bedroom.

Then, finally, five months after he'd first seen her, he knew everything he needed to know. He knocked on the door, and she opened it. He saw recognition in her eyes. "You."

"Yes, me. Good evening, Shi Mingzhu. I am Wah Feng. May I come in?"

"Why?"

"I need to speak to your parents."

Everything was different after that moment. Feng didn't care that her parents were horrified by him. At least until he'd offered them a new house and a stipend for the rest of their lives. All if they'd allow him to marry their daughter.

They resisted him at first. Despite their complaints and their fall from grace, he knew they loved their daughter. Then two thugs had waylaid Shanyuan, Mingzhu's younger brother, on his way home from school. He was bloodied and beat up, so when Wah Feng appeared at their door that night, they realized he'd been responsible. It served his purpose. Fear always did. He looked at Shanyuan, spoke his condolences for their troubles, and then reiterated his offer. This time Mingzhu accepted before her parents could refuse.

They were married in a spare ceremony with no celebration. Wah Feng was true to his word, and her family was taken care of, but she never saw them again. He took her to Hong Kong, where he made the first six months of their married life hell. On their wedding night, he slapped her across the face so hard she slid across the floor, because he could, and he wanted her to know that. After that, he would beat her with a belt if she annoyed him, distrusted his decisions, discouraged him, or did nothing at all.

He taught her how to satisfy him. One night, several years after their marriage, she told him she was pregnant. He never hit her again, but when his daughter was born, he took the baby from her. He would take her whenever he wanted, he said, and there was nothing Mingzou could do about. It was clear he was telling the truth. This was much worse than being beaten. Also, she had given him a daughter, Li Li, but no sons; he held that over her head as well.

What he thought no one knew was that the only living thing he cared about was his child. He saw the better parts of himself in her, though intellectually he knew the attachment he felt was irrational. This could turn out to be a dangerous lapse, but so be it.

Now, at the dinner table, his wife remained stoic, as always, with deliberate invisibility. The room was opulent, perfectly lit by candles and a rare Waterford chandelier. The oak rectory table had been imported from a long-ruined Abbey in France. Feng Wah had nothing to do with the ruination of the Abbey, but if he had wanted the table and they wouldn't let him have it, he would have destroyed the Abbey to get it. He liked that his wife understood this.

They had moved to this private island in the San Juan chain a little over a year before. Feng had prepared long and well for the return of Hong Kong to the "stupid hordes," as he called the Chinese leaders. Much of his business was done in Vancouver, some in Seattle, and elsewhere along the coast.

Feng Wah had given nod to his new countries, Canada and the

United States, and reversed his name from Wah Feng to anglicize it to fit their custom. He thought the Chinese naming tradition was much too complicated and was glad to be rid of it. Mingzhu meant pearl in Chinese, so she became Pearl, as a nod to being a real citizen. He'd paid for it, of course, with a great deal of cash, but changing their names was as far as he was willing to go to 'fit in'. The truth was, he fit nowhere and was proud of that.

They had moved to Vancouver BC before the changeover, but Feng wasn't satisfied. It was too cold and Seattle was too friendly. The island was a perfect location. Feng had designed the compound himself. The house was sprawling, large enough to keep the family and the business separate. And it was easily defended. A small airfield gave him the flexibility of travel. Their only neighbor was the convent on the far side of the Island. They had a ninety-nine-year lease, and Feng Wah believed they neither knew nor cared what happened in the rich man's compound. If he thought they did, Feng would have found a way to deal with them.

As it was, no one bothered them. Nor did anyone bother the dozens of Chinese slaves he kept in the compound a quarter mile from the main house. They flowed in from Asia with no detection, and, until last month, they were moved out to the mainland in the same way. At approximately $50,000 per head, more for a sturdy child, even more for a beautiful whore, it was a very profitable operation. Yet suddenly his business was compromised. It annoyed him. He hadn't figured out who was betraying him, but when he did, punishment would be immediate and lingering.

The butler approached with trepidation, again interrupting dinner. He whispered to Feng Wah. "You have a visitor, sir." Feng rewarded him with a simple nod. Charles, relieved, backed away.

Feng Wah got up from the table, moving with more grace than one would expect from his squat body, perhaps due to his early martial arts training in the streets, a most vicious way to learn. He turned and looked at Pearl. His small eyes seemed to disappear into his face. "Enjoy your dinner. I have business. I will see you in the morning."

He turned his back to her and left the room.

Pearl bowed her head with relief, grateful she had been dismissed for the evening. Perhaps, once they left this isolated island he would be in a better mood, she tried to reassure herself. She doubted it, yet held onto hope. It was rare that he beat her now, but when he did she would react whatever way she thought might satisfy him quickly. But that wasn't her worst fear; what really terrified her was her awareness of how important their daughter Li Li was to him. It would be safer if he were indifferent. With no possible way to escape, Pearl promised herself that if she suspected Li Li was in any danger from him, she would kill her husband. It would have to be death; if she only injured him, he would find them. He had tentacles everywhere.

When Feng got to his study, Victor Kasun was waiting for him. If the man looked vaguely as Martin Lo had described him, the reality was worse. His arms and legs were much too long for his torso, but it was his eyes that were the most startling. They were like opaque marbles that stared out from a dead world. He blinked half as often as normal, as if he feared closing his lids more than a nanosecond. Feng had heard of him several years ago and searched him out, letting Victor think it had been a chance opportunity. Kasun was a Croatian Serb who'd learned his trade as a member of the Kosovo Liberation Army. Feng understood it was not out of any political loyalty but because Kasun was sure they'd win. He timed it exactly right to get out without a trace, despite the crimes he'd committed. When he forged his way into the United States through Colombia, he moved up in his profession.

Feng didn't care that Victor was a sociopath because he was very good at his job. And so he allowed Victor to tread a fine line between being amusing and tiresome.

Tonight, Victor had waited, slumped in a burgundy leather chair, his feet up on the matching footstool. He was a chain smoker, which didn't bother Feng, though Feng himself had quit smoking after a minor coughing spell. He'd never looked back.

Feng sat behind his partners' desk. It amused him because he knew there would never be a partner. He faced the door, his back to shelves of first editions. The office was set up with perfect acquiescence to the art of Chinese environmental design. Feng considered it a good omen that it was called feng shui. He was not overly superstitious, but he was Chinese, and he saw no point in disobeying the ancient laws of Chinese energy. He had lush flowing plants and gold in the wealth corner, to ensure money; a mirror facing the door to ward off evil spirits; stacks of books in the knowledge corner; and a crystal in the health position. He never discussed this with anyone lest it be considered a weakness, something to be hidden. Pearl probably knew — she was very learned in that area — but his wife's perception didn't count unless he wanted it to.

Feng demanded that Victor show him respect, but he was amused by the enjoyment Victor derived from his work as well as by his irreverence. Feng was aware Victor was in this for the money, and to learn how an expert ran a successful operation. He didn't care that when Victor absorbed enough to start his own business, he planned to leave. That wouldn't happen.

But right now, Feng was annoyed and it showed. "How did this happen?"

"Like I told you before, I was careless." Feng appreciated that Victor followed his own code of honor and, unlike other psychopaths, he was willing to take responsibility for his mistakes. Besides, part of the thrill was rectifying them. "I dumped Lo. He should have died, but he didn't. I should have made sure. Somehow he made it to Doc Zhou's and it was reported to me. I figured I'd leave it alone, he was gonna die anyway. The merchandise was locked up tight and the buyers were sending another rep. But the cops were tipped about the shipment or maybe about Lo. The rest you coulda watched on the news."

"The merchandise will not be a problem. None of them will give the police any information. There are too many family members left behind."

"It's the third time the cops got inside info from somewhere," Victor reminded Feng. "And it's not from my side."

"That remains to be seen. Wherever it's coming from, we will find out, I assure you. These shipments have been small, but my losses are still above the percentage I allow for breakage. I do not want this to occur on the next trip. It will involve three times as many heads, and a great deal of money."

"How're you gonna plug the leak if you don't know where it's coming from?"

"A diversion. The same police detective was at the scene?"

"Same guy. Same partner. More cops. INS, sheriffs. But this guy was the lead."

"He needs to be discouraged."

"I can get to him easy. But that won't give us the snitch."

"Of course it won't." Feng looked at Victor as if he were dull-witted. "That is my responsibility. Whoever the snitch is has to be made aware that informing does no good. Kill the detective."

"No problem. His partner?"

"Not necessary yet."

"Too bad. I'd like to do her."

"I don't care who or what you'd like to do, it's a waste of energy and opens us to more possibility of error." Feng could see Victor react to the deliberate jab. He didn't mind admitting his mistakes, but he didn't like being reminded of them. Feng deliberately relented. "If and when it becomes necessary, then you can do what you wish with her."

"Okay."

Feng Wah rose from his seat, pushing up the sleeves of his cashmere sweater and making the coiled serpent tattoo that covered his right fore-arm visible. He knew Victor thought it was the symbol of a powerful Chinese Tong. It wasn't, but Feng Wah enjoyed using it to intimidate. "Did you bring me the package?"

"Yeah. She's waiting in the guest house. You had her a couple years ago. She's better now. Prime."

Feng Wah half-smiled for the first time. "I'll be the judge of that." Feng looked to a corner of the room and stared into it, as if he were consulting some unseen master. It was one of the few things about him that made Victor uncomfortable. No, more than discomfort; it gave Victor the creeps.

"I've changed my mind. Don't kill him. It won't deter anyone. I need to teach them a lesson. I want them distracted, not on a hunt for a cop killer. Find out more about this man. Then I'll decide how to handle him."

"When's the next shipment?" Victor sounded very casual; Feng knew he was probing and didn't care.

"Soon. I won't keep the groups here longer than five days. Less potential for trouble. Do research on Detective Fortune and get back to me tomorrow morning. I am going to make his life hell."

# CHAPTER EIGHT

THE EVEN RHYTHM of Jake's breathing filled the dimly lit garage. AC/
DC blared through his headphones, drowning out any thoughts that
might sneak through. Sweat poured off his face as he jumped rope without missing a beat.

Jake had cleared enough space to house his car, a few storage boxes,
a washer and dryer, and a workout area. He'd been at this almost an
hour, and now was slowing his pace, continuing a brief warm-down.
When he finished, his Marine sweatshirt was soaked. More relaxed, he
grabbed a threadbare towel, wiped his face, turned off his old iPod, and
ambled through the connecting door into the kitchen. He stopped cold,
surprised to see Garth there. His kid should have been in bed an hour
ago. "Why're you up?"

Garth pulled a loaded sandwich out of the refrigerator, his version of
a sub. It was messy, had practically every leftover imaginable on it, and
looked delicious. "You didn't eat yet, Dad."

"I'm not hungry, Garth. You should be in bed."

Garth pulled out a glass of milk for himself. "You're always telling
me I should eat."

Jake pulled out the chair in front of the sandwich, stared at it. "Did you leave anything out?"

"Nope."

"I didn't think so. Okay, I'll have a little." His son had suffered another major blow, one he hadn't been able to protect him from. It was good to see Garth's chest swell with pride as Jake reached out for half the sandwich. The boy plopped down, ready to watch him eat. "Why don't you get ready for bed while I finish this?"

"In a minute, Dad. Okay?"

"Okay."

Garth grabbed a graham cracker from the bread bin to dip in his milk. "She's gonna be okay, isn't she?"

Jake realized the boy had been drumming up the courage to ask. "I won't lie to you, Garth. I never will, you know that." It was a promise Jake had made to himself and to Garth right after he was born.

Garth held his breath. Jake put his hand on Garth's arm. "It looks like she'll be okay. It was pretty bad, though. We can't ever be sure about these things."

A sharp knock on the door startled them both. Jake reached over for his gun, forgetting it was in the lockbox. He relaxed when a key turned, and Anya bustled in. She carried a large pizza and a six-pack of beer. She looked at the two of them at the kitchen table, sizing up what they were eating.

"That's quite a creation, Garth Fortune. Very impressive. But what're you doing up?"

"That's what everybody wants to know." Garth sighed, stalling a little longer. "I wanted to have dinner for my dad, that's why I'm up."

"Well, that's fine. You did that. Now you can go get ready for bed. Then I'll give you a story."

"Do I have to?"

"Yes."

He rinsed his glass in the sink. "That pizza sure looks good," he said as he started out of the room.

"Not before bed. You can warm it up for lunch tomorrow. And it may not even be here, anyway. Looks like you took care of your dad and I can take the pizza for myself."

"Nah. You'd never eat that. Too fattening."

"Wanna bet?"

Garth smiled. "Nope. You'd do it so you could win. I'll be ready in a minute."

"Okay. I'll be right there."

"You know, Dad was gonna shoot you coming in." Garth sounded solemn, but Anya rolled her eyes. Garth grinned.

"Upstairs."

This time he obeyed. Jake watched this exchange with awe. "How do you do it?"

"Do what? Talk to your son as if he's a normal human being?"

"He's not. He's a kid."

"Jesus, Jake." She sighed. "For a smart guy, you're so... stymied. What're you doing letting him take care of you? He's the one who needs taking care of."

"It made him feel good."

She put the pizza on the table. "Here. Have dinner. Have a beer. I'm going to tuck your son into bed. It would be nice if you came up in a few minutes and said good-night." She turned back before she got out the door. "You were gonna shoot me?"

"He's exaggerating." Jake wished he could argue with Anya's perception, but he struggled to relate to Garth. It didn't start out that way, but he'd been a wreck since Peggy took off. He still couldn't understand what went wrong. They'd been great together. Or so he'd thought. The first few years they were married, and then when Garth was a baby, were the happiest of his life. They were a *family*.

He remembered the day Garth was born. When he held his son, his heart opened in a way it had never done before or since. The connection was so powerful it scared him. He hadn't realized he was capable of feeling so much love for another human being.

Then everything changed. Peggy wanted more. Peggy always wanted more. When they'd met at school, their goals and plans seemed so in sync. But it stopped being enough that she was a lawyer, an assistant D.A. It wasn't enough to be married to a cop. When the offer came from the Senator's office in D.C., she jumped at it. Jake knew it was partly his fault. He'd stopped listening to her, then balked at uprooting their lives. She left without him. And without Garth. She had accused Jake of sucking her dry, of being so closed that she had to create an emotional life for all of them. She was tired of it, tired of being a cop's wife. She'd had enough.

His jaw clenched as he remembered. Okay, leave him. But he never could understand what kind of mother could leave her child. She told him he should be the single parent for a while, like she'd been, then he'd understand it was too big a price to pay. As far as Garth was concerned, she'd be so busy in the beginning of her new job, she'd never see him anyway. He'd be better off in a family setting with Jake, with her parents as support. When Jake came to his senses, he'd bring Garth and join her in Washington. At least that's what she said then.

That was before she'd been diagnosed with a "mild" bipolar disorder. Cyclothymia is what she called it, when she phoned him one night, hysterical. It didn't sound mild to him. He understood then that she was going through something major, and finally why she had been able to leave everything behind. Including Garth.

At least he said he understood, but he didn't really. Even his dad had never left him, despite his PTSD; okay, theirs wasn't much of a relationship, but at least his father had *stayed*. Peggy's inability to maintain any relationship with Garth was beyond reason to Jake. She kept saying she wanted to be part of Garth's life, but she couldn't handle it yet. The 'yet' had never come, and after four years she'd stopped asking.

The first year Peggy was gone, Jake thought he saw her everywhere he went. He felt off-balance, without an internal compass. Bitterness and rage crowded out his normal emotional responses. He was still a great cop, he'd always been a great cop. It was fatherhood that became hard. He could've blamed his uneven relationship with his own father, but wouldn't allow himself that excuse. Anya's presence in their lives helped, but as the time passed, he felt more and more inept.

There were sounds of giggles from upstairs, and a stabbing envy blindsided him. He opened the Peroni Anya had brought. Two, and that was it. It was already late and he didn't want to get out of control. He didn't like anything out of his control.

Upstairs, Anna took in Garth's chestnut hair, still damp around his ears, his face scrubbed and shiny. He was wearing his Seattle Mariners' pajamas, which he loved more than almost anything in the world. "Did you brush your teeth?"

"Yes. A whole two minutes, promise."

She straightened his sheets with authority, then tucked in one side.

"Leave this side open, please."

"I know that, Gar. How many times have I done this?"

"About a gazillion. Maybe a few more."

"At least a gazillion. One side open, night-light on, a kiss on the forehead and each cheek, after a story. And the music. Enya. I don't get her, but is that about right?"

"About exactly right."

"Okay, which story do you want? The Loch Ness Monster, Big Foot, UFOs, or Bossy in the Village?"

"You know which one, Anya."

She pretended to sigh. "Oh, okay. I guess it'll be Bossy in the Village."

He snuggled under the blanket, contented. "Yep."

She teased him. "I'm not sure I remember it all, but I'll try."

"Ha ha. You remember!" He curled up so he could watch her tell the story. Everything Anya felt showed in her eyes and smile.

"Once upon a time, in a small *shtet'l* in Ukraine called Sadiba, near the town of Zhitomer, lived a woman named Bossy. She came by that nickname honestly. Bossy wasn't afraid of anything and told everyone else what to do. Her father, her brothers and sisters, her husband and children, Bossy knew best."

Garth interrupted. "Who was Bossy?"

Anya smiled. Garth asked this every time she told the story. "She was my great-great-great grandmother, darling. Her legend has been handed down in my family for generations. Anyway, Bossy was walking through the village one day, checking up on everybody, when she encountered a snake. Not any snake, mind you, but a huge serpent. It terrified her. She ran far away from it, as fast as she could, but the serpent was simply too big for her to escape. It swallowed her whole."

"In one big bite?"

"In one big bite. And everyone in the village went looking for Bossy. They couldn't find her anywhere. Not until Shlomo the shoemaker came running in to tell them he'd witnessed this horrible event. A snake had eaten Bossy and then disappeared. Well, Bossy had always been the one to tell everyone what to do, and now no one else could decide how to save Bossy and the rest of the village from the serpent. They argued and argued and finally Bossy's husband, Menachim, came up with the plan: they'd fill the big tub in the center of town with milk and honey, and lure the serpent out of hiding. Everyone knew that snakes loved milk and honey. He'd smell the concoction and not suspect a thing. When the snake wasn't looking, they'd kill him and cut him open and save Bossy. They all thought this was a great plan. They milked every goat in the village and filled the huge *mikvah* with milk, sweetening it with the honey from the beekeeper's hives."

"What's a *mikvah*, again?"

"It's where the ladies of the village bathed together. They filled the tub with milk, and lo and behold, Menachim was right. The snake came up through the ground, into the milk. This huge serpent slithered into the bath and lapped up its food. All the villagers sneaked up together and hit the snake over his head with the only weapons they had, sticks and rocks and brooms, until the serpent was stunned. They slit his belly open and dragged Bossy out..."

"Wait! My turn!" Garth always wanted to tell the rest of the story.

"Go ahead. Let's see if you can remember."

"Bossy was okay! She was so surprised that they did this without her telling them, and she was so grateful, she promised she'd never be bossy again. Then they chopped the huge snake into pieces, enough food for the whole cold winter. They feasted on the meat of their enemy."

"That's it, Garth. Word for word."

"Wait, I'm not finished. Don't forget 'And they lived happily ever after…'"

"Well, darling, as happily as Ukrainian Jews could live." She laughed. "Mrs. Dooley's going to be fine, Garth. You have sweet dreams, okay?"

"I will. Don't forget to leave the light on, please."

"I won't forget." She hesitated, then couldn't help herself. "Garth, I'd like to ask you something, okay?"

He looked into her soft green eyes and turned his head away. "Dad doesn't believe me. You don't either."

"I don't know what to believe."

His voice was muffled in the pillow. "It's okay, Anya. Grandma and Grandpa used to think I was pretending. Nobody's ever believed me, except maybe Mrs. D. It doesn't matter."

"Yes, it does matter. I need to understand it a little better. Come on, honey, look at me." He turned back to her reluctantly. "You've done this before, huh?"

"Uh huh."

"A lot?"

He shrugged. "Come on, Garth, give me some help here."

"I don't *do* it, Anya. It just happens. When it wants to happen. I can't make it come. Not always, anyway."

"Tell me about it.

"I know things. I see things. I can't help it that it's before. I know them. Doesn't that ever happen to you?"

"I honestly can't say that it has or hasn't happened to me. I don't remember it happening."

"Dontcha ever get a feeling about something?"

"Sure, a feeling. Sometimes. But I think it's usually because my mind has had some clues I haven't noticed, and then my subconscious works on a problem and presents me with an answer."

"It's not the same, Anya. It's like… like a window that opens up and I look through it and I see something happening. I don't ask the window to open in my head. It just does. Then it closes. Sometimes the pictures are real clear, sometimes it's like when the cable is bad, and sometimes I don't understand them." He was done. "That's it. Okay?"

"Okay. And I do believe you, honey. It's only that I've never encountered anything like it in somebody I know. I've heard about it, but it's happening to somebody I love more than anything, and that makes it really different."

Garth threw both arms around her neck, tight, and nestled into her. "I love you, too. You're the best Godmother. I wish you could move here and take care of us."

"Thank you. Coming from the source, I take it as a great compliment."

"Who's giving compliments?" Jake hovered in the doorway.

"Your son. He thinks I'm a terrific godmother."

"He's right. You're almost as good a partner."

"I think I'll leave while I'm ahead and let you two say goodnight." She kissed Garth on both cheeks and his forehead, like he always wanted, then pushed the button on the iHome to listen to Enya. Anya waved and slipped out the doorway.

"You okay, pal?"

"Yeah, Dad, I'm okay."

"I talked to your Grandpa Tony. He said he'd be here in the morning, and he'll take up the slack while Mrs. Dooley's recovering. That's okay with you, isn't it?" Grandpa Tony wasn't Jake's first choice, but his only choice. He figured even though his father had done a lousy job, he turned out okay. A few days with him would be fine.

"Sure. Grandpa's fun."

"Fun?" Jake half-smiled. "He must've changed a lot."

"Well, he's a lot older than when he was your dad. Will he take me to visit Mrs. D.?"

"Ask him. My guess is he'll do pretty much anything you want." Jake mussed Garth's hair. "I'll see you in the morning." Jake bent over to switch off the light.

"No, Dad! I need the nightlight on."

"We've talked about this before, Garth. You're getting too old to use this as a crutch."

"What if I have to go to the bathroom?"

"There's enough light in the hallway. That's an excuse."

"Please, Dad. I'll have bad dreams."

Jake looked at his son. He wanted to reach him, to make the right choices, but all he knew was what he knew. Did he give too little or too much? So hard to figure out what enough was. "Okay. This time. You've had a long, rough day. But we've got to try... never mind. We'll leave it on. Goodnight, son." Jake turned off the overhead. The little Pooh nightlight cast a gentle shadow across the wall.

As soon as his father left, Garth let the tears come.

Downstairs, Anya paced the kitchen. With her long legs it was only three steps. When Jake came in, she stopped, furious. "Goddammit, Jake, you've got to stop bullying that child!"

Her words assaulted him like a slap. "Jesus, Annie, give it a rest. It's been a long day. I don't want to hear it now." Jake was the only one who called Anya by a nickname, but right now it didn't sound affectionate.

"You never want to hear it. You walk around pissed at the goddamned world because your wife left you, because your father had the nerve to be at war when he should have been going to your Little League games, because you can't solve every goddamned case. You're a pain in the ass. A mess. Stop taking it out on Garth. It's not his fault."

"You keep saying that. I never said it was his fault."

"It's how you act. It's not what you say to kids that counts, it's how you treat them." She was sputtering. "And you treat him like... like you don't know him. Like he's a kid from down the block."

"If you're not finished, take it home with you. He's my kid and he's fine and I don't need to hear any more of your touchy feely crap."

She refused to budge. "Your kid thinks he can see the future, for

God's sake. He thinks you never believe him about anything. What are you going to do about that?"

"Nothing. Kids have imaginary friends. It's common. So Garth thinks he can see things. He'll grow out of it."

"Well, maybe he can see things. And maybe he can't. And maybe he'll grow out of it and maybe he won't. We're not dealing with *maybes* here, we're dealing with a child. What if he can see more than you or me? So what? Is that a reason to punish him?"

"I'm not punishing him for anything. Go home before I get pissed and we have a real fight."

She got right into his face. "I will. But you'd better look at what you're doing here. I mean really look. Maybe you're worried that he has a sickness like Peggy, I don't know. But figure it out. It's time for you to grow the fuck up, partner."

Anya slammed out of the kitchen. Jake looked after her, ignoring his usual impulse to grab her and hold her in his arms. And he tried to brush aside the thought she could be right. Maybe he was worried Garth had inherited Peggy's problems. But his heart started pounding as a flash of memory hit him from when he was three and saw his daddy in front of him... but that was impossible, because his daddy was at war in a jungle someplace. His daddy was crying, but waved at him to assure Jake everything would be fine.

Jake tried to shake off the memory, but he couldn't. It was exactly what Garth described. Jake grabbed his jump rope and headed out to the garage once more to welcome oblivion.

# CHAPTER NINE

*Two Days Earlier*

JAKE WATCHED AS Tony Fortune ladled exactly the right amount of batter onto a perfectly heated griddle. The pancakes were all the same size, color, and shape. The former Marine Sergeant would have it no other way.

His son sipped coffee, reading the paper intently. His father always had an unsettling effect on him. Tony had been there for three days now, and Jake still wasn't comfortable. He felt guilty that his father had to stay here instead of his comfortable downtown loft. It had big rooms, which Tony had longed for during his time as a POW captive in a tiny hole. But Tony said of course he didn't mind the sacrifice for his only grandson.

"Sure you don't want some, Jake? There's plenty to go around."

"I don't like breakfast."

Garth put his hand on Jake's arm. "But Dad, it's the most important meal of the day. You're always telling me that."

"For a growing kid. I'm all grown. I only need coffee."

Garth poured syrup over the hotcakes. "Grandpa's a great cook."

Jake couldn't help himself. "Something new he learned."

Tony sat down with his beautifully constructed pile of pancakes, melted butter dripping over them to the edge of the plate. He tucked his napkin into his shirt collar so he wouldn't get messy. Jake thought it was so odd that his dad knew how to kill a man fifty different ways, but sticky hands could send him screaming into the bathroom. "You learn lots of stuff when you're my age. If you're lucky enough and willing."

Jake put the paper down. His father made him feel like a recalcitrant child. He knew that he was being petulant, but it was what it was. He had to get out of his own house, to his job, where he made a difference. Where he could accomplish something.

Not like his father, who'd spent most of his life being a good Marine. Now all he did was watch soap operas or reality shows on television. Tony had explained to Jake that it was a business, a very successful one. Even though the number of shows had shrunk in the past few years, his father wrote a newsletter, a digest of soap operas, reality television and daytime talk shows, and distributed it to current and retired military personnel. Jake couldn't understand that Tony took his job seriously, that he loved it, and that soldiers deployed on duty found solace in the connection to home. Jake was blind to Tony's dedication. He thought it was a ridiculous occupation and had long ago given up trying to understand it.

"Gotta go." He patted Garth's head. "Be a good kid."

"Be careful out there."

"Garth, you've gotta stop watching those *Hill Street* reruns."

"That's how I know you gotta be careful out there. Promise."

"I promise." Jake looked at Tony. "You need anything, text me. I may have to work a double shift." He didn't want to admit to anyone, let alone his father, that he was frustrated they'd made virtually no progress in their investigation.

"We're fine." Jake left quickly, grateful to be out of there.

Garth finished the last bite of his breakfast, and took his plate to the sink. "Thanks, Grandpa. The pancakes were even better than yester-day." He saw his Grandpa's face, which looked sad. "You okay?"

Tony shook it off and turned to Garth, smiling. "I'm fine, Garth. I think your dad's an old worrywart, that's all. Sometimes I think I'm younger than he is."

"That's impossible, Grandpa."

Tony tweaked Garth's nose. "Nothing's impossible, Gar. Don't you forget it. Now let's get you off to school so you can see your little girlfriend."

Garth blushed at the thought of Gretchen Vanderhall. "Will you be here when I get home, Grandpa?"

"Nope, I'm going to pick you up at school, and then we'll go right over and visit your Mrs. Dooley."

"Will you miss some of your work?"

"That's what DVR was created for, my boy. Don't you worry about a thing. Let's go, let's go."

Garth picked up his lunch and his backpack, then turned to his grandfather. "She's not only my Mrs. Dooley, Grandpa. I think she likes you a lot."

It was Tony's turn to blush. "Sometimes I think you're too smart for your own good."

"See, that's exactly what Mrs. D. said!"

"Let's get you to school before you have me walking down the aisle in Shannon, okay?"

"Okay." Garth slipped his small hand into his grandfather's large, rough, man's hand. It felt good there. Garth felt a huge sense of relief flood over him. Now he was ready to go to school.

# CHAPTER TEN

ANOTHER GODDAMNED HOSPITAL room, Jake groaned to himself. He stared at the tiny body in the bed, covered by white institutional sheets. She looked not much more than a child herself, and they still didn't know her name. Jake flashed on the image of a baby bird who'd fallen out of her nest and hurt her wing, then pushed away the thought as irrelevant.

The young woman lay on her side, staring at the stark white wall, barely blinking. They'd kept her isolated in a private room for the past several days, in hope she could be persuaded to talk to someone, but she had isolated herself in her own way. Eight other illegal immigrants, also under guard, were being treated for their health problems in another wing of University Hospital. Interrogations were at a dead stop. They were all too scared to speak.

Jake approved of the young Deputy who had carefully vetted him and Anya, even though he recognized them on sight. He knew the guard wasn't simply covering his ass. He was a good cop and in this instance there was no such thing as being too careful.

The other twenty-three illegals were being housed dormitory-style at a safe house on Bainbridge Island. Interrogators from both the INS and Seattle PD had gotten nowhere, despite threats of immediate deportation back to China. Not one would respond to their questions.

Jake didn't want to waste time duplicating the effort. He decided to go right for the jugular, although if this didn't work out, he'd interrogate the illegal he had privately named 'The Old Woman'. He didn't know what else to call her, because no one had given up a name. Jake was sure the Old Woman had made eye contact with him in the warehouse, and he'd push her hard if he had to. But he figured their best bet was the tiny young woman with the broken ankle and the dead toddler.

Anya had visited twice in the past few days, but reported the woman had responded to nothing and no one. She was still on an IV for severe dehydration, and they'd given her a pain shot when they'd set and cast her ankle. She had a compound fracture and the orthopedist had to put a pin in it. She'd probably always limp a little, but clearly that was the least of her worries. The shot had knocked her out; it was the only way they could pry the child from her arms.

The toddler had suffered from severe dehydration as well as malnutrition, but it was the pneumonia that had killed him. His little lungs had given out. Wherever they'd been held before the warehouse had been malignant. Jake wanted to know the location of that hellhole, so he could make sure no one else would suffer as they had.

The psychology of the people running the operation eluded Jake. If he were importing labor, he'd want them as healthy as possible; certainly they'd get bigger bucks for healthy slaves than for sickly ones. Maybe they split them into groups somehow, unless they only got rid of the ones they thought couldn't cut it. It was too horrible a thought even for Jake, and he figured he'd seen it all.

Anya slipped into a chair in the corner of the room out of the girl's eye line. She didn't acknowledge Anya's return, nor did she seem to pay attention to the roly-poly man seated next to her bed.

Max Woo had been trying to get through to her for half an hour before Jake and Anya arrived. He sat calmly and quietly next to her, speaking in soothing tones, segueing through six different Chinese dialects. Max was an extroverted, brilliant Professor of Psychology at the University of Washington. He and Jake had been friends since their college days, when they'd found out each was a Kung Fu addict, both the art and the old TV show.

Jake glanced at Max, who raised his eyebrow in greeting. Max hadn't changed in the last twenty years, except he'd gone completely bald. Jake watched him gently coax the patient again. If Max couldn't get through to her, Jake would have no choice but to dive in, and he wasn't looking forward to it. This wasn't Max's usual gig, but he was a linguist, he was a shrink, and he was doing his old friend a favor.

Jake had a reputation in the department as the best interrogator of victims and perps. He was frequently brought in even on cases he had nothing to do with. He had an intuitive ability to find and push the hidden buttons in another person, and ferret out the truth, something no one would guess from his tough demeanor. He took this gift for granted, thinking of it as part of the job, without recognizing he was operating from empathy. It wasn't a quality he was able to accept in himself or apply to the rest of his life, nor had it helped forge a bond between him and his son.

Jake turned his attention to the woman-child in the bed. He motioned to Anya, who flipped on a directional recorder, taking notes on a yellow pad as back-up.

"Nowhere, Max?"

"Nowhere. She appears to be in a self-induced altered state. She's completely psychologically unresponsive."

"Did you talk about her baby?"

"Not yet. I stuck with her family back home, wherever home is, and with the trip here. I suspect Cantonese is her native dialect."

"Okay, it's my turn. Translate for me. Don't hesitate, no matter what I say, translate. She'll hear me."

"I don't like the sound of this, Jake."

"You don't have to. I'm the inquisitor, not you." Max moved behind him, ready to interpret almost as fast as Jake talked. But in the end, it would be the melodic rhythm of Jake's voice that crept into her consciousness more than the words.

He started out softly, asking her name. She ignored him, as she had all the others. He reminded her that he had pulled her out of the warehouse. He spoke again and again of how they needed her help, anything she could give them, anything, so they could bring to justice the people who had imprisoned her and the others. His voice was like a lullaby, but still she didn't respond. Jake moved in closer, his face only inches from hers.

Max objected. "She's suffered enough, Jake. Don't push her over the edge."

"Back off, Maxie. Just repeat what I'm saying."

Max sighed, and nodded reluctantly as Jake and the girl stared at each other. Soon it felt as if there was no one else in the room but the two of them. Max's translation became only a narration of their connection.

"Your son is dead. I'm sorry about that. We are all sorry."

No response.

"You couldn't save him. I know you tried, but it was hopeless. I wish we could have helped him, but it was too late. His soul is at rest, you know that."

Then he fired his next words at her like bullets. "Your son was murdered. Cut like fish bait before he had a chance to live. It wasn't fate, he didn't deserve to be killed. He deserved to live, to fulfill his potential, to love you and take care of you in your old age. He can't do that now. But you can help other little boys like him. Then maybe his life will have meant something. No, I'm sorry, not *maybe*. His life *will* have had meaning. He won't have died for nothing."

A tear slid down the girl's face. Jake suppressed a sigh of relief and kept up the pressure.

Anya sat against the wall, tensing. She automatically reached for the cigarettes in her purse, then stopped, her attention riveted on Jake and the small figure in the bed. "We'll give him a peaceful resting place, if you let us. On a hill, overlooking the ocean."

The girl shifted slightly, as if he were rousing her from the bottom of an abyss.

"I know how important it is that he have a proper grave, one where he can see the waves lapping against the shore, from the same water that touches his birthplace. With the right feng shui energies, his spirit can move on."

Anya held her breath, waiting for her response. Max quickly translated the words the young woman was now completely focused on.

"What was his name? Your child? So we can mark his grave with his name. He deserves to be seen, don't you think? If it were my little boy, I'd want his name to be known."

She opened her mouth to speak, but no words came out.

"Tell me how you spell it. Dr. Woo will make sure the headstone is done exactly right. Tell me."

A low-pitched, raspy voice answered him in halting Cantonese. Jake put a glass of water with a straw to her lips and let her sip, soothing her parched throat. Jake leaned in ever closer so he could hear her whispers. "Wei Xian."

"Did you get that, Dr. Woo?"

"Yes. It's Xian."

Relentless, Jake moved his face closer so they breathed the same air. "We should say he was your son, shouldn't we? So all will know that Xian was your son."

She nodded, still looking mesmerized. "Ling. I am Ling. Xian is the son of Wei Ling, village of Shuangshui, province of Guangzhou. He was a blessed child. His marker should say that. He was a blessed, loved child."

Max repeated her name to Jake. "Ling."

"Okay, Ling. We'll do that. We'll make sure your baby sleeps well in his resting place. But you have to tell me what happened. You have to tell me so no other babies will have to be buried alongside Xian."

Ling began to speak slowly, then so rapidly her words tumbled over each other, fighting to be heard. So fast Max could barely keep up, and Anya's hand cramped taking notes from his translation. "We had to leave our home. I saved and borrowed and paid the Snakeheads

$10,000 American dollars to show good faith. A lot of money, yes, but I knew we were expected to work for the rest of the passage after we arrived in America. We left my small town late, we traveled only by night, over many rivers. A man I never saw before or after led the way, but it took almost two weeks to reach the port. I think it was Luzhov Harbor, Sichuan Province. I wish I had listened to my instinct to run before we boarded."

She reached for another small sip of water. Jake steadied the cup for her. She indicated she'd had enough, determined to go on now that she'd started. "We met with a group from other villages, from all over. For endless days they closed us into the hold of an old ship, encrusted with rust and filth. No toilets, only buckets. No windows. Even if we had wanted to turn back, it was too late. We had too much hope for the future, too much fear for those we left behind. The travelers tried to be kind to each other, but the sea was rough and even the sturdiest and youngest among us became ill. We managed with very little food or water through much of the journey, but the last few days, we were rationed only a bowl of rice and a cup of water each day. We suspected Captain Bohai took most of the money paid him to feed us, to line his own pockets. He was a pig."

She trembled, remembering all she had been willing to do to save Xian, then went on. "I lost track of the days, until we docked somewhere in the middle of the night. It was an island, I think, I don't know, but the air smelled of the sea. They put us on another vessel, one a little sturdier. The rumor spread that Bohai had been shot for starving us, but I don't know if that was true. I hope it was. I hope he suffers the torments of hell in every rebirth."

Ling began to choke on her curse, then cleared her throat and once again found her voice. "I remember very little about the second journey. Xian was so sick, and then I fell and my ankle pained me so much... I had to hide him so they wouldn't take him from me. I couldn't give him up." She looked at Jake, beseeching him to understand.

"I know. You did your best."

"No, I didn't help him. I was delirious for the rest of the trip. Others tried to help, especially Yao Gen, who was killed by that demon. But Xian had already suffered too many indignities. When we finally arrived, he was barely alive."

"What happened in the warehouse? Do you remember?

"At first I thought it was a nightmare, but it was real. Yao Gen had hidden a knife. He knew our patrons were not trustworthy. All he wanted was to live with his brother here, without worry the authorities would punish him for liking men. When he realized what was really happening to us, after all we suffered, I think he attacked another man. I'm sure it was deserved. A man, no, a devil, shot the poor boy. I hoped the man would die too, but he was in no danger from us. We had no strength to fight. He locked us in that room with no food or water or toilets. I don't know how long we were in there, but there was no way out. The others tried. That's when Xian took his last breath. Xian is dead and that's what I wished for myself. But the Old Woman wouldn't let me die."

Jake hid how startled he was that Ling described the woman that way, the same way he thought of her.

"The Old Woman tried to protect me. Every step of the journey. I don't understand why. All I wanted to do was die. I still want to die."

"No, Ling. You need to live, so others will know that Xian lived. So those people won't have stripped you of everything. If you die, they win. You can't allow them to win."

"They have already won. They warned us. My family is in danger at home. And those who have families in this country have much to fear. These are bad men who will keep their promises."

"No one outside these walls will know that you've spoken to us. No one. You have my word."

She took his hand and searched his eyes. She let go only when she was satisfied he was telling the truth. She stared at him.

"When you're stronger, we'll be back. You might be able to remember more that will help us." Jake hesitated, then had to know. "May I ask why you made this difficult journey?"

Ling nodded, sad. "My husband... my husband was involved in politics. He wasn't very careful. He disappeared and never came back. I feared I was next. And then, who would Xian have?" A tear rolled down her cheek.

Jake nodded. "I am very sorry." In halting Chinese, Jake thanked her and wished her luck. Gratitude swelled in Ling's eyes before she closed them, and finally she slept.

The three of them left Ling in the room to rest. Jake was spent. He felt victims' pain; it was the way he communicated with them. But it also made him harden his boundaries even more, pushing his rage deeper within. He turned to Anya. He was brusque.

"Take the notes down to the station and start working on them. The sooner we have them the better."

"Yes, sir, partner, sir," Anya answered.

Jake stopped, shook his head. "Sorry. That was... intense."

Anya agreed. "I know."

Jake was distracted. Max watched their interaction and intervened. "Too close to home, Anya?"

She shrugged it off. "Long time ago, Max."

"Some things don't disappear, no matter how much time has passed."

Anya smiled. "Go have lunch with your pal, Max. I think he's got other stuff he needs to talk about."

Jake started to react, then stopped himself. "Drive carefully. That wasn't easy for any of us."

"Thanks for your concern, pal." She turned to Max. "Take care. He'll forget to thank you, so I will." She kissed Max on the cheek, and left without another word to Jake.

# CHAPTER ELEVEN

GARTH'S SCHOOL, MONTLAKE Elementary, had been built in a residential area, a two-story brick structure surrounded by Victorian and Craftsman-style houses, all vibrant colors. The main building was surrounded by green and red much of the year when the red alder and big leaf maple were in bloom. The fine mist, which escalated to a light rain, was not enough to keep the kids indoors. It looked like a peaceful neighborhood, but that proved to be a mirage now.

Victor reclined in the passenger seat of a sedan parked across the street from the playground. He was comfortable, reading the *Wall Street Journal*. Victor's partner, Tom, no neck and no brains, kept a careful watch on all the kids through small binoculars. Gotta love Google: they'd found a picture of the detective's kid in a *Seattle Times'* feature article on Garth's first-grade field trip to Snoqualmie Falls. It was a couple of years old and kids changed fast at this age, but Victor thought he had spotted Garth Fortune. He couldn't be sure, but this was only a recon job. The rest would come later.

Garth had no idea he was being tracked. He was too busy watching Gretchen from across the playground, even with the distracting scents of the macaroni and cheese and chocolate pudding coming from the cafeteria kitchen. He didn't mind recess, because after he let himself be pulled out of the soccer game, he could find a quiet place and stare at Gretchen without anybody noticing and teasing him.

It was too hard for him to approach her. He'd had a crush on her since the first day of the third grade, when Miss Greenwood introduced her to the class. The longing to be part of her awareness seemed to be getting more intense rather than less. He loved listening to her talk to the class about living in Denmark. Her differences and her similarities fascinated him. It didn't hurt that she had beautiful golden hair and a sweet face. Gretchen knew Garth's name and smiled at him sometimes, but she was usually busy with all the other little girls who chased Ben. Ben was loud and funny and seemed to know how to do everything right to get Gretchen's attention, but Garth didn't think Ben cared very much about her. Maybe there was some secret to this he didn't know yet.

The only time she'd really noticed Garth was when he brought his Orcas Island shell collection to show everybody. She thought it was cool. That made him feel really good.

For now it was okay. Even fourth grade was okay. He liked his teacher, reading was fine, but it wasn't the same as figuring stuff out. Besides, his mind's images were so much more vivid than any book he could read. *The Hardy Boys* was boring, and *The Little Prince* was too sad. He looked for books that sparked him like Anya's stories did.

He loved doing the math and science stuff. Everything was neat and logical and fit into its prescribed place. So unlike his real life. He caught Mrs. Stone watching him, and sighed. It was time to run towards the bars over the sand pit and do something noisy so she wouldn't bug him about joining in. Garth did pretty well on the parallels. His Grandpa Tony had taught him how to lift himself up and swing across from bar to bar, like they did in Marine training. Garth was stronger than he looked, agile and quick, and though sometimes he liked to play soccer and volleyball, after he saw things in his head he got kind of tired and drained. It usually hit him even more the next day, and took him a while to replenish his energy. Especially when he had nightmares like he did last night.

He pulled himself over the bars, still caught in his own thoughts. When he dropped down into the sand, Ben jumped him for some good-natured wrestling. Ben wasn't so much a bully, but he had too much energy and couldn't stop himself. He finished pounding on Garth and jumped up. "Hey, Gretchen, watch this." Ben started doing cartwheels across the grass. Garth retreated to the drinking fountain.

He bent over the cold stream making a squiggly arch into the concrete bowl. It felt good trickling down his throat, which was a little scratchy. His head was pounding He wondered if Mrs. D. had been right, he'd been up on the ferry deck in wet clothes and now he was going to pay for it by getting a cold. Then he realized that wasn't it at all. The pounding in his head was different. He looked around wildly for a refuge. The pain over his eye was getting worse.

Garth stumbled into the boys' bathroom. Thank God this year they'd put doors on the stalls. He slammed the door behind him and locked it, then sat down and leaned over, holding his aching head. This was the worst he could remember. His temples felt like they were straining to contain an over-ripe melon that was about to explode. Garth remembered to breathe into it, and calmed down. Then the window in his mind opened and the pain disappeared. The pictures were fuzzy, like there was interference.

*A little girl, a few years older than him, was running in the jungle, along a ledge. She was barefoot, long-limbed and slender, with dark hair. She moved quickly on the dirt. It was a long, long way down, but she didn't seem to care. He didn't recognize her face, which looked vaguely Chinese, but felt like he knew her. She turned a corner and ran into a dead end, slamming against a tree. When she turned around, her face was Gretchen Vanderhall's and the tree became the monkey bars. She fell, hit her head and slipped down, down, down, into a bottomless pit, unconscious.*

Garth wrenched himself out of the reverie, feeling nauseous. He leaned his head against the cold metal stall, his heart pounding loud and fast. He thought he heard someone come in. He flushed the toilet, to make everything seem normal, then went to the sink. There was no one else there. He'd imagined it. He threw water onto his face, then saw himself in the mirror. He looked very pale and really scared.

Garth ran outside to the schoolyard, terrified that his precious Gretchen was hurt or dead. His eyes roamed the yard and he spotted her across the way, perfectly fine. She was giggling and running. He had missed the bell signaling it was time to go back to class. Relief spread through his body. It didn't happen often, but he was so glad he'd been wrong. Gretchen was fine, and nothing bad was going to happen to her.

Across the street, as the kids ran back inside, Victor put down the binoculars and smiled.

# CHAPTER TWELVE

"C'MON, TALK TO Papa." Max and Jake were sitting at a corner table in the hospital cafeteria, which was only half full. Jake looked down at his tray. It was too early for him to eat, and the hamburger on his plate was unappetizing. He glanced over at the pile of food on Max's tray, unable to decide if he was amused or repulsed. It was laden with a quesadilla, a huge cinnamon roll and a foamy cappuccino. Coffee was ubiquitous in Seattle, even in this impersonal hospital cafeteria. There were only a couple of people near them, and Max had flirted innocently with the bus girl before he turned to Jake. It was as quiet as it was going to get over the clanging of silverware and buzz of people talking so they'd forget where they were.

Jake picked at his hamburger and watched Max drop three sugars into his cappuccino. "Why don't you shovel it into your mouth straight from the bowl?"

"Screw you. I've got low cholesterol, my blood sugar's smack in the middle of perfect, there's no cancer in my family, so I'm genetically low risk, and I think all this low-fat nutrition stuff is a crock perpetrated by the multi-national drug companies. I'm gonna end up standing over your grave laughing."

"If you say so."

"Want to go to the dojo and check it out when we're through here?"

"Not with you. I won't contribute to your heart attack. Lose twenty pounds, wait a couple of hours after you eat, then I'll take you on."

"I don't need your charity, asshole. Any time is fine with me." Some of the cheese dripped out of the quesadilla, running down Max's chubby chin. Jake watched him wipe it off fastidiously.

"You haven't been working out anyway, Maxie. I haven't seen you down there in months. Sensei wanted to know where you were."

"Bullshit. That's not what this lunch is about. I know that look, Jake. What's going on?"

Jake hesitated.

"C'mon. We're not here so you can rag on me about my pathetic eating habits. They haven't changed in the last twenty years. What's the problem?"

"What do you think of a kid who claims to be able to see the future?" He could barely get it out. "How would you deal with it? As a shrink, I mean."

"Any kid, or your kid?"

"My kid."

Max whistled. "Garth? Talk to me."

Jake stumbled through an explanation, trying to keep all judgment out of his voice. He laid it out, step by step. He forced himself to look into Max's kind eyes and tried to keep his voice steady. But he was shaken and Max saw it. "So what's the diagnosis, pal?"

Max was blunt. "You're worried he's bipolar like Peggy and this is how it's manifesting."

"It crossed my mind. A lot."

"Highly doubtful. Peggy manifested late, after she had a child, and she has a mild diagnosis. What you're talking about doesn't match the symptoms for manic depression. Garth is an even-tempered kid."

Jake signed. "That's a relief. But then why?"

Max shrugged. "Could be anything. Most likely it's a type of magical thinking."

"Is that serious?"

"Depends. It happens when a person believes he can affect his environment simply by using his mind, his wishes, or some kind of ritual, like lighting candles of a certain color to achieve particular goals. It usually happens with people who are vulnerable, or deeply religious or spiritual, or those who feel abandoned, completely alone."

Jake looked stunned. "I never thought of him that way, but all of that could be Garth. All of it."

"Don't take it personally. It happens all the time, especially with kids. Like having an imaginary playmate."

"That's what I told Anya."

"It doesn't mean you shouldn't pay attention. But there's something else, Jake." Jake knew he was not going like this. "There's another possibility. He could truly have some kind of psychic gift."

"I don't want to hear that shit."

"Why am I not surprised? You wanted me to confirm your opinion and give you a quick fix."

"Go to hell."

"Sorry, friend. No can do. That narrow-mindedness is going to get you into trouble, believe me. From what you say, Garth could have a predilection for psychic impressions. If you'd paid attention to Sensei's philosophical training instead of only the physical, you'd be more flexible. Besides, there have been hundreds of legit studies at Duke, which is the most famous. Then at UCLA, they're big on researching psychic healing, and the Russians have been playing with various applications for years. Hell, even the CIA admitted they spent $20 million on psychic spies, and that's what they *admitted*."

"Those tests prove nothing."

"What they prove is there are some people, a few people, who have an ability most of us either don't have or don't know how to access. I've never personally encountered anyone with a visible gift, but that doesn't mean they don't exist. Hell, when my granddad went to high school, he was taught you couldn't split the atom. We know how accurate that scientific information turned out to be."

"You think I'm narrow-minded, huh? Well, I think you're so open there's a wind tunnel running through your brain." Jake shook his head. "Hey, you're a goddamned shrink."

"I'm a psychologist, not a psychiatrist. We have more inferiority complexes, fewer God complexes. That tends to open us up to more possibilities."

"Great. A joker shrink who believes my kid is psychic."

"For a detective, you don't listen so well. *Might* be psychic, Jake. Big difference. If you want, I'm happy to talk to Garth. Or I have a friend who works with gifted children, if that's better. He's a good kid and whatever's going on with him, he should have an objective person to hear him out."

"I'm not objective?"

Max laughed. "Not even close. You're so freaked by the permutations in this, I won't even begin to explain it."

"Thanks a shitload."

"What're friends for?" He started in on his cinnamon roll with gusto.

Jake hesitated. "I'll think about it, Max."

"Sure."

"No, I really will. Thanks for listening." He started cleaning up his half-eaten lunch. His laser focus had disappeared, leaving him distracted, an uncomfortable feeling for him.

"Any time, friend."

Jake dropped a couple of dollars on the table. "Here. The apple pie looked pretty decent. Have it with ice cream, on me."

"Schmuck. I'll meet you at the dojo next week and beat you two out of three rounds."

"You're on." Jake picked up his tray and turned back. "I'll let you know about Garth."

"Deal."

Max pushed his chair back and followed. Jake was puzzled. "Where are you going? You're not finished."

"You bet I'm not. You take my advice, I'll take yours. I'm going to check out the apple pie." Max grinned at Jake and headed back to the counter.

Jake couldn't help but smile. Thank God for Max.

# CHAPTER THIRTEEN

"I HATE THIS case. There are no winners." Jake and Anya watched Captain Stan Thackery pace the perimeter of his small office, on the third floor of Seattle Police Department Headquarters. If he'd been a higher rank, he would have had a perfect view of the harbor, but now it was only a minimal downtown view. They admired Cap, but his roaming was like a nervous tick, the stuff of several skits at the last few Police Benevolent Society Dinners. He swore it helped him think.

Not that he wasn't smart. He was, but he didn't fit in anywhere, like a piece of a jigsaw puzzle that's cut a little bit higher than the rest. He confused people, which had worked to his advantage when he was a cop in the field. Now he ran three squads in CID and was respected by every person under his command.

His mother was a Jamaican dancer who had married a Merchant Marine. They'd moved from port to port when Thackery was a child, but they'd never received a hero's welcome. It wasn't easy being a half-breed, which is what the other brats called him.

Today he was comfortable in himself, a meld of half-black, atheist computer-phobe who lived in Microsoft-Starbucks country and drank tea. He loved being a cop but it was political, and his detectives always gave him grief of one sort or another. He was way too sensitive for the job, and anything that smacked of people using their power over other human beings for their own greed or satisfaction drove him to distraction. It was what made him a great investigator and also gave him a bleeding ulcer by the time he was twenty-four. Tums were his constant companion. When Anya caught an article describing the use of antibiotics to cure ulcers, she brought it to him. It seemed to work, but he reached for the Tums just in case.

Thackery popped four in his mouth and finally sat down in front of his two most talented detectives. "At least your little Chinese girl gave us a few things to work."

Jake nodded. "It's a beginning. Soto's checking out the possible routes. All small craft, commercial boats, ferries and traffic into and out of our area, and up to Vancouver BC. He's researching the sea conditions, trying to zero in on where they changed boats. Problem is, Ling's time perception is completely off, so we can't backtrack accurately to figure out the distances. No one else has cooperated, so we don't have data on boat speed or direction. There are probably hundreds of possibilities."

Everyone knew that Detective Randy Soto, the twenty-eight-year-old office computer geek, made Thackery nervous. Cap tiptoed around him because he didn't have a clue what Soto did, but believed it was important. Soto took advantage of the Captain, who blew up at him every once in a while only to keep him honest. Soto would give them enough permutations to investigate for the next five years.

"Who's working the other injured illegals?"

Anya interjected. "Harding and Moore, with help from two translators brought in by the County. But they're overwhelmed. I'll go back tomorrow. Jake thinks they'll respond better to a woman's touch and I agree. We figure the longer they stay in the hospital, being well-fed and taken care of, the safer they'll feel and the less cautious they'll be."

"Or all of them there together could backfire. It could make 'em more insulated."

Anya agreed. "It could. But if we treat them decently, then maybe they'll do us the same favor and trust us."

Thackery was realistic. "Pretty soon this is going to start costing the County a fortune. We only have a few more days before the money managers start screaming, and the INS starts deportation."

"Fuck 'em." Jake had no patience for money men or the Feds. Actually, he had little patience for anything outside of his criteria.

Anya stayed calm, as always. "We have to be careful there are no leaks on the information Ling gave us. She's worried about her family, and not only because of the Snakeheads. She's going to need asylum."

"That's not our call." Thackery sighed. "She's had some bad luck. But she's young."

Anya's face remained impassive. "I'm not sure you ever get over an experience like she's been through."

Jake shifted in his chair. Anya never shared her own painful memories, but he knew this case had touched an old wound. He moved on. "The other angle we're working is where the labor is being recruited. Ling speaks Cantonese, but we don't know about the others. INS offered to send over two more translators to track the dialects. And Dave Bell has his Minneapolis office checking out the end of the line destination. Whatever they find, they say they'll let us know. We'll see. One way or another, we gotta figure out what ground the railroad covers."

Thackery was thoughtful. "It'd be too hard for someone without an efficient organization to move so many people that distance, then through here. It feels big, Jake."

"It is big, Cap. Bell figures by the end of the operation, each worker clears $50,000 bucks to the importer. Forty thousand from the buyer, $10,000 from the illegal."

Thackery whistled. "So the laborer pays big for the passage to freedom, then ends up working the rest of his life on a farm or in a factory, and all it costs the buyer is the initial payment and food and shelter."

Anya agreed. "Sweet deal for everyone but the refugee."

"And it was going smooth as silk for God knows how long until your mystery informant showed up. We may be in over our heads, but the Chief made it clear that if we lose this to the Feds she'll be a very unhappy camper."

"Is she ever happy?" Jake smiled.

"Ha. Look, we're spread too thin as it is, and last night we had two more follow-home robberies, a stockbroker beaten half to death on the docks, God only knows why he was there, and that's not counting the usual mix. Jake, play nice with the INS. Make friends and use 'em. Okay, that's it until Soto gets his homework done. Give that twerp a deadline or he'll be here every night putting in for overtime for doing whatever it is he does."

Anya stretched and eased off the hard wooden chair. "Good. I'm outta here. I've got a family dinner." Anya laughed at their surprised reaction. "I know, I know. I was there a couple days ago. But it's Sukkot." She looked at them and sighed. "Don't ask. It's one of those esoteric holidays my mother loves to bake for. So I go."

"You're a good kid, Anya."

"It's no less than my mother wants or deserves."

Jake agreed. "That's the truth. Grab some kugel for me, will you? I'm going to stick around and lean on Soto. And there's a couple of things I need to check."

Thackery pushed his chair back to begin pacing again. "That's what I like to hear. Any more input from your mystery informant?"

"Nothing since the bust at Doc Zhou's. I wanted to put another trace on the fax line, but Soto says it's a waste of time. Communications are sent from a computer and bounced around the world. But it doesn't cost anything to try."

"That's probably why Soto's not interested in doing it. Not expensive enough."

Anya smiled at Thackery. "See you tomorrow. I'm late."

Through the glass that partitioned his cubicle from the grunts, Thackery watched her walk through the squad room. She waved a little wave at them, something men always found charming. "Great looking woman, Jake."

"So everyone seems to notice." He knew what Thackery was thinking. He also knew Cap was wrong.

Thackery clapped him on the back. "Go find something. Anything."

"Will do, Cap." Jake moved through the squad room to his desk, which was surprisingly neat, especially compared to Anya's controlled chaos next to him. He liked to know exactly where things were.

He opened his computer and began a search of past bulletins, starting with two-and-a-half years prior. He would have narrowed the search parameters, but he didn't want to miss anything. Scanning through the notices for missing women or children, young people, old people who wandered away, mentally ill souls, always hit Jake directly in the gut. Even after being a cop so long, it was difficult for him to reconcile how the loved ones left behind coped. As he watched the pictures scroll by, he used his long-honed skill to distance himself from the misery each of those images represented.

He almost missed it. It flew by so quickly, it was only a flash. He slowed down the scroll and went back one by one, until he found it. Anya had been right – it was close to two years ago.

Once he saw it, he realized why it had come back to them. Three Chinese girls, undocumented, beautiful and poised in their pictures, went missing in the Vancouver BC area. He delved as far as he could online, which wasn't very far. There'd been no updates. A Vancouver detective's name was near the bottom of the bulletin. Jake squinted to see the small print, jotted it down, mumbling to himself. "Damn. Gotta get my eyes checked."

He picked up the phone and got through to the Vancouver Police Department operator. "Senior Detective Howard... Sharon? Sharrone?

"Hold on, please." Jake waited through the canned hold music. It took so long, he started drumming his fingers on the desk, becoming even more impatient. "Give me a damned voice mail if he's not there," he muttered under his breath. He was startled when a voice answered back.

"He's here. He was in the loo. Sorry to keep you waiting."

"Sorry. This is Detective Jake Fortune, Seattle PD. I'm calling about a bulletin from a couple of years ago, about three young Chinese women who disappeared... Detective Sharrone?"

"Howard. It's pronounced 'Cheron.' It's ancient something or other so shut the fuck up before going down that rabbit hole."

"I didn't know Canadians said fuck." Jake laughed.

"This one does. I know that case. We got an anonymous tip and pix. The three girls turned out to be high-end call girls. Two we never found. The third, we found her body. In a fucking ditch off a fucking mountain road. I almost killed myself climbing down. Her name was Lihwa Wong. It meant a Chinese princess. Not quite."

Jake understood. "She got to you."

"Yeah. I'm a fucking bleeding heart."

"Did you get the perp?"

He could hear Howard's hesitation. "Yeah."

"You think."

"Her pimp did it. He confessed."

"Chinese?"

"Chinese call girl, Chinese pimp in these parts."

"After interrogation?"

"After five fucking minutes."

"Oh. Too easy." Jake was relieved that talking to this guy was uncomplicated. That wasn't always the case.

"Yeah. There was something hinky about it."

"So Canadians still say hinky. Eh?"

"Nothing you can say to me I haven't already heard, Fortune. How's your bank account?"

"Piss poor, Howard. I'm a cop. And Fortune comes from a Sicilian village."

"Okay, Don Fortunato. What's your interest in our Chinese princess?"

"I'm not sure. They were definitely undocumented?"

"Yes. The pimp said the girls were 'imported'."

Jake felt that he was on to something. He explained the situation, including that the memory of the bulletin had surfaced when he was investigating the group of illegals they'd found.

"Good 'ol gut instinct. It's possible. Why don't I send you the file and you can see if there might be a connection?"

"Great idea. Much appreciated."

"Tomorrow. Now I'm taking my gorgeous wife out to dinner. It's date night. With four kids at home, that's sacred. And I'll get fucking killed if I'm late."

"Tomorrow's fine. I'll get back to you if I spot anything." Jake hung up, optimistic that he might be making progress for the first time since this thing started. He looked at his watch. Shit. He was late for his own solitary date.

# CHAPTER FOURTEEN

JAKE TURNED HIS key in the lock and slipped into the darkened room. He moved across it from memory, then turned on the overhead lights.

The dojo was closed because Sensei was playing golf, but as far as Jake was concerned that made it the best time for him to train. He threw his stuff on a bench and took off his shoes and socks. He was wearing loose sweats, an extra pair he kept in a locker at the precinct. The scuffed wooden floor felt solid under his bare feet as he walked toward the heavy bag. There was a chill in the air, but he knew it wouldn't be long before he was hot and sweating.

He stretched for a few minutes, then began punching the ninety-pound heavy bag. The more he hit, the harder he needed to hit it. He'd left the precinct in a good mood after his call with Sharrone. Halfway to the dojo he started to get a familiar chilled feeling in his bones. He refused to give in to it. He would never admit even to himself how like his son he really was. *A cop's instinct,* he told himself, hitting the bag furiously. *That's all it is.* But he was cold down to his marrow, like something bad was about to go down, and he'd have no control over it. It was like riding the wind, with a hurricane blowing at his back. He pounded the bag faster, until the sweat rivulets poured off his hair into his eyes.

The salt stung but he ignored it, along with the bruising of his knuckles.

The floor creaked behind him. Jake whirled, ready to defend or attack as necessary. A beaming Max Woo threw his old denim bag on the bench. "I thought I'd find you here."

"I'm surprised you remembered the way."

"That's not all I remember, friend. I remember the last time we fought I creamed you. I figured you needed a rematch that wouldn't wait 'til next week. How about it?"

"I'm ready, Maxie. You're gonna be weighed down by that lunch, I guarantee." Jake grinned at him, relieved to have company.

They pulled on their fighting gear. Max's mouth guard made his reply sound like mush, but the intent was clear. "Wanna put a little money on it, Jakey?"

"$10 bucks. Two minute rounds, three points, heavy contact's a foul."

"Deal. Let's do it."

The two men circled each other, feinting, punching and kicking. Max moved in quickly and tickled Jake's jaw, Jake responded with a side-kick to his ribs. They fought, both scored, and Jake felt freer than he had in days.

# CHAPTER FIFTEEN

THE RAIN HAD abated, but the night sky was still blanketed by threatening clouds as Anya pulled up in front of her parents' home. The Pashkov house was like every other two-story on the pleasant, middle-class block in the hills of Ravenna, above the University of Washington. Her parents could have afforded better, but they were comfortable in their yellow clapboard with flowers in front and a vegetable garden in back. They liked that nothing set it apart from all the others. That's what they had wished for when they moved here. Not to be different, not to be noticed. It was an intuitive reaction to the discrimination and worse they faced before they escaped from Russia.

Anya turned off the engine and sank into the soft leather seat. She could see the warm lights beckoning through the curtains, and the shadow of her mom through the window, bustling around the kitchen. She wasn't ready to go inside. She usually needed to decompress before she entered her other world. And she had to figure out what she was going to do about making Kris understand they were really done.

The relationship had suited her needs. Kris was a criminal defense attorney, smart, funny, sexy, and best of all, unavailable. He demanded no commitment from her, which was exactly how she wanted it. She was devoted to her work, and he had to respect that. He was a family man who loved his family, and she appreciated that. Sometimes he accused her of choosing him simply because he *was* married, which she never denied. They managed to be together when they could, and she never had to feel guilty about not being able to — or wanting to — see him. But she'd broken off the relationship when she felt him crowding her, when it became more demanding than fun. When she felt sad around him all the time. And he wasn't taking it well. She sighed. She would deal with it.

If she were being truthful, she would have to admit that it wasn't even Kris' fault. There was no way he could compete with the person at the center of her life, the man whose every move went straight to her heart. He was unavailable to her and would stay that way. Okay, so every now and then, they would give in to their deepest desires, and they would satisfy each other as no one else seemed able to do. Immediately afterward, remorse would follow. And sadness. And danger. The last time had almost killed them both. Literally. It could not happen again. They were wrong together, and so she would keep her feelings buried in the deepest recesses of her soul.

Anya lit her second cigarette in ten minutes, berating herself. The acrid smoke filled her nose. The smell was awful, and she couldn't escape the connection to that horrid man near Nyborg, Russia. She shuddered at the painful memories, falling into them as if it had happened yesterday.

They had taken the train from Moscow to St. Petersburg, as if for a short two-day visit. Thank God the air was chilly; it meant they could carry more luggage and sweaters and coats, all filled with precious items if they were lucky enough not to be stopped. Anya's mother had chosen the cheapest seats, which meant they were sitting up for eight hours without a break. It didn't matter for Anya; only twelve years old, she could eat or sleep anywhere. Natasha was barely five feet tall, with very slender legs and ankles. When not pregnant, she joked that she looked like a stork. Now her huge belly filled with twins made it difficult for her to get comfortable anywhere, let alone a noisy Russian train crowded with children and people who forgot to bathe. And soldiers. Soldiers who took their turn through the aisles, watching carefully for anyone to step out of line.

"Eat, *Bubeleh*. Eat. You'll need your strength."

"You eat first, Mama. You're the one who needs to feed your belly." Anya intended to be funny, but her worry made her sound anxious instead. But she was right. Natasha Pashkov needed sustenance. She was under too much stress.

Anya made it a point to smile sweetly at one of the ramrod straight-backed young men in uniform, looking very, very serious to cover his nerves. He couldn't help but smile back at the radiant, beautiful child-woman, her curves to come already visible.

Her mother gave her a sharp look. Anya shrugged, whispering, "It's better not to pretend we don't see them, Mama. We're pretending enough." Natasha looked shocked by her daughter's innate survival instincts.

It may have been 1996, and it may not have been the Soviet Union anymore, only Russia, and Yeltsin may not have been Khrushchev or Stalin, but this was still a country searching for itself after the dissolution of its empire, a financial crisis, and it was preparing for another imminent war with Chechnya. Everyone was nervous and on alert. There were soldiers everywhere, and all those people who would do anything to escape. Natasha and Anya were the wife and daughter of a prized academic who had taken asylum in the American Embassy in Bern. That did not go over well with officials who cared about important state scientists who held important secrets.

Aleksander Pashkov had been planning his family's defection for over a year. He understood that while the creation of Russia under Yeltsin might look like progress to the outside world, it was the same oppression as always. Aleks was a computer virtuoso, a rare commodity, and that gift had kept him safe through the repressive regimes and then Glasnost. He was worth a great deal to the Russians, who thus overlooked his family's Jewish heritage – unless it suited their purpose to rub his nose in it. He was valuable, not only to the government, but to the military. Charming and affable, he had contacts everywhere.

Aleks was also methodical and had planned to leave when everything was precisely in place. His twelve-year-old daughter had been assigned to the prestigious Moscow Science Academy, which kept her protected. Then Natasha, his wife, who'd always had difficulty conceiving, unexpectedly became pregnant again and they discovered it was twins.

Anya and Natasha were supposed to have been with Aleks in Switzerland, but the authorities wouldn't let them join him for his conference. He feared his defection plan had leaked and he was forced to get them out another way. Even though his family was under constant surveillance, they improvised while he was in Switzerland. They had to time it exactly so the mother and daughter disappeared while Aleks was safe inside the United States Embassy in Geneva.

The new, hastily devised plan was for Natasha and Anya to take the train to Vyborg, Finland, but at the last minute their contact insisted they get off in St. Petersburg. He was worried this escape plan had been compromised as well, and wanted to take no additional chances with his own life or theirs. He told them he'd have a car waiting for them, and they could drive the rest of the way – it was only a couple of hours on the M10, and a two-lane highway was less conspicuous than the direct route. So far he'd been right.

When they disembarked they found the car exactly where he'd promised, in the back of the parking lot, under a snow-filled birch tree. The key was where it was supposed to be, under the right front fender. But it was a junker. Natasha looked at Anya with dismay. Anya knew her mother wasn't much of a driver – Aleks mostly drove. She watched her mother gingerly approach the car. Anya shared her worry that it wouldn't start, or if it did, they'd get stuck somewhere along the way. But there was no choice, so Natasha slid into the seat, barely managing to fit behind the wheel.

The car sputtered but started, and Anya took the map to read. All went well until they were two miles southeast of Vyborg; the car simply died. Because the city was in the boundary zone between the Russian and the Finnish worlds, the military presence was strong, and the two naval air bases nearby made Natasha and Anya feel even more vulnerable to discovery.

Anya proved to be very good at reading the map, but she didn't know if her very pregnant mother could walk the two miles to the train station. They weren't sure their papers were clean enough to get through the border checkpoint, but they couldn't turn back now. Natasha walked as if their lives depended on it. They decided to approach the station by going around an HVDC back-to-back facility for electricity exchange between the Russian and Finnish power grids. Vyborg had changed hands between Russian and Finland so many times during the last several centuries, it was hard to say who had influenced what, but it was beginning to be a thriving town. More important, it was a border town, which meant it was impossible to know who belonged to what faction.

Mother and daughter held hands as they navigated through freight yards on the way to the station, north of the City Center. If they were lucky, freedom was near.

They weren't lucky. Believing the train station almost in reach, they were hurrying, and didn't see the two men. They were grabbed as they went around an empty freight car. The men looked like they could be gypsies or homeless or transients. They were both bearded, dirty, wearing clothes and coats that obviously had belonged to someone else. One was in his forties, with eyes that seemed to go in every direction at once, and a grip of steel. He held onto Natasha as the younger one with the dead stare had Anya in a vise.

"No! Leave us alone! Leave my daughter alone! I will pay you!"

The older one ignored Natasha as he grabbed her. "You'll pay us anyway." He looked at the younger man. "You can have the girl." Natasha screamed at him, but he covered her mouth with his filthy hand. "Don't worry. When he's finished with her he'll sell her to a good farm."

The younger bum's only reaction was to drag a fighting Anya toward an empty train car. Anya kicked him and he hit her, hard, then pulled her around the corner, and inside.

Inside the train car, the man with dead eyes dragged Anya toward the back. When she went to gouge his eyes, he slapped her again. She collapsed on the floor, terrified, looking around frantically for something, anything, to hit him. She heard two loud pops outside and wailed: "Mama!"

The ugly man briefly turned at the noise, then shrugged. He had his prize. He didn't see Natasha lift herself onto the train car as he pawed at Anya. She was crying and kicking and fighting, but he was much stronger and meaner. He hit Anya again, hard, and she went down. He never saw Natasha coming. She shouted: "Stay down, Anya!"

The man turned around, surprised. Natasha lifted a Makarov and fired it. She was a very good shot – Aleks had taught her well. The first into the throat, and another into the heart to make sure. She ran to her daughter, who was bleeding from a cut on her forehead, near her hairline.

"Mama." She clutched Natasha, trying not to sob.

"It's okay, *bubelah*. But we must hurry. No one can see us here."

"The other one?"

"Dead."

Determined not to falter, Anya held onto her mother, picked up her small suitcase, and never looked back.

They managed to get on the train, the last one of the day to Vainikkala. Natasha had cleaned Anya's cut in the restroom, and pulled her hair over so it wouldn't be noticeable. Apparently calm, they were likely in shock, but alert enough to be grateful that the rest of the trip was uneventful. After all their fears, their papers were barely examined. As soon as the train arrived in Finland, the contact was there to greet them. The three of them said not one word until he dropped them off at the American Embassy in Helsinki. Aleks' contacts in Switzerland had made all the arrangements.

That night Anya's brothers were born on American soil, in Helsinki. Peter and Boris were U.S. citizens long before the rest of the family.

After the U.S. Military had sneaked them out of Finland and Switzerland, Aleks and his family were settled at the Presidio in San Francisco. When that closed, he worked with military contractors in the Silicon Valley. When Aleks had repaid the American government with his service, he went into the private sector. He moved his family once again, to Seattle, for the rapidly expanding opportunities there. Now he was a well-off man, part of an American family living the American dream, but they would never be extravagant. Old habits die hard.

Besides, Natasha would say, why move again to a bigger house? They had everything they wanted right where they were, including Emanuel Congregation, an Orthodox temple within walking distance. The family knew that on the long miserable exodus out of Russia, Natasha, never a practicing Jew, had promised God she would become devout if He would get all of them safely away. God delivered, and Natasha faithfully and happily kept her end of the bargain.

There was a sudden noise of a car down the street starting, and Anya forced herself out of the involuntary trek into the ugly past. She vowed to shake it off, as she did every time it happened. Anya would never have her mother's faith, but she figured if she could live through that, everything that came after would be a piece of pie. Or, as Jake would correct her, a piece of cake.

Anya picked up her phone and turned it back on. She'd had it off while she was dressing for dinner and kept it that way on the drive here. The uninterrupted solitude was rare, her little rebellion against the world she lived in daily. If she'd known she'd go into a funk about the past, she would have left the phone on, along with blaring music. She sighed, then read Jake's texts about the case in Vancouver. Good instincts on his part, of course, and maybe some progress. God knows, they could use it. Anya could not get herself into the celebratory mood the evening deserved. Her uneasy feeling was not going away. She wasn't responsible for the Chinese immigrants, she knew that, but she felt guilty nonetheless. She and her mother had been so lucky. They had escaped to a new life, while these people, experiencing similar horrors, had no way out.

It was time to move, she realized, even if she had to bring her melancholy with her. She locked the car, and trudged up the brick walkway, hoping things would get better and fearing they wouldn't.

## CHAPTER SIXTEEN

The flicker from the television was the only light in the darkened living room. Garth was curled up in the oversized leather chair, watching his favorite show, *Kung Fu*. He'd seen this episode at least five times, the one where Kwai Chang Caine was trying to escape from the Emperor's henchmen in China, and fell in love with an exquisite young Chinese girl on his way out of the country. Garth loved to watch David Carradine move as Caine. He didn't know the show was almost sixty years old, and he wouldn't have cared. He also didn't know that his father could do many of the things the Shaolin Priest Caine could do. On the other hand, his father didn't know Garth loved to watch *Kung Fu.*

"Garth, chow's ready."

The boy was intent. This was his favorite part, the one where the girl didn't betray Caine to the Emperor's thugs.

"Son, where are you?" Tony Fortune called again.

"In here, Grandpa. The show's almost finished, okay?" The bad guys were catching up. Garth knew Caine would get out of trouble, he always did, but he wanted to make sure.

Grandpa Tony stood in the doorway. "It's stew. Your dad called, he was working and he's going to be late. We're eating without him." Garth glanced over to him and caught his breath. Oh, no, not again.

*A shadow descended on Tony, surrounding him. Violence. Pain. Blood. Men in uniforms, beating Tony. Tony fought back. Garth was running, running, running, caught. Grandpa Tony was lying on the ground, bleeding, still. An ugly, scary man grabbed Garth. "Gotcha."*

He quickly turned off the TV. The Shaolin Priest Caine would be okay, but Garth wasn't sure about his Grandpa. Tony put his hand on the boy's shoulder and guided him toward the dining room. "Stew's your favorite, right?"

"Next to Hershey Bar sandwiches."

"God only knows what they'll think of next."

Garth kept his eye on his grandfather for more signs as they sat down. Tony took the boy's hand in his own, then bowed his head. Garth did the same.

"Thank you, Lord, for what we are about to receive. Amen." Tony crossed himself automatically. He had often told Garth that he wasn't much of a Catholic anymore, but he had faith in something bigger than himself. Garth understood that, but right now he stared at his Grandpa as Tony began to eat. "Pretty damn good, if I do say so. Aren't you hungry, Gar?"

He took a bite. The stew was delicious. "It's great, Grandpa. Really."

"Okay, what'd I do wrong? Too many carrots?"

"Nothing, really. Nothing. I was wondering, you know, Grandpa, what was it like when you were in prison?"

"It wasn't exactly prison, Gar. It was a prison camp." Tony kept on eating, dipping a slab of French bread into the stew gravy until it soaked brown.

"What's the difference?"

Tony didn't have to think at all. "You get treated better in prison." He took another bite as Garth looked startled.

"No, honestly. There are supposed to be rules of war, but there aren't, not really. Having absolute power over people seems to do something to men. Now to women too, but I haven't personally experienced that. It's like any connection they feel to other human beings shuts down. It's always the same."

"They hurt you, didn't they?"

Tony didn't hesitate. Like Jake, he always told his grandson the truth. "When they felt like it. But physical pain isn't the worst thing in life. I got through it. So did a lot of others."

"Then what is the worst thing in life?"

Tony had spent five long years pondering that question. He answered instantly. "Losing faith. In God, in yourself, in the people you love. Giving up hope. I think that's the worst thing that can happen to anyone. What's with all the questions, Garth?"

"Promise you won't laugh?"

"No promises. But I'll do my best."

"When you were standing in the doorway, I saw you in the prison again. It scared me."

"That would scare me, too. You have a wonderful imagination and I hope you never lose it. But that's all it is."

"No, you don't understand. When I see these things, it means something bad is going to happen. We should leave the house now. Please. Let's go find dad."

"You don't have to worry," Tony reassured him. "Everything bad that's going to happen has already happened. Of course you're upset. It's a reaction to Mrs. Dooley's heart attack. That's all, believe me."

Garth could barely stand it. He shoved down his stew, trying not to choke. Also trying not to cry. Why wouldn't they listen to him? "Can I please be excused?"

"I must be losing my touch."

"I'm sleepy, Grandpa. You're right. I miss Mrs. D. No offense meant."

"No offense taken, son. It's early, but go on, get ready for bed. Then you can watch TV."

Garth ran out of the dining room, up the stairs. For twenty anxious minutes he sat in his room. He knew if he stayed there long enough,

Grandpa would be in front of the TV, fast asleep. Garth had to get out of there, away from Tony, or Tony would be hurt. He *knew* it.

# CHAPTER SEVENTEEN

ANYA OPENED THE front door quietly. She loved her family, but their extroversion exhausted her. And each time she came, she imagined her parents' disappointment that she was not married, had no children. It was irritating that the boys, 23 years old now, weren't under this kind of pressure. She understood how young they were, that they had no memories of discrimination, and, of course, they were male and expectations were different. But her resentment at the ease of their lives erupted in some small way every time she walked into the house.

The wonderful smells emanating from her mother's cooking helped her prickliness to dissipate. In her mother's kitchen, kosher was king. Aleks and the children weren't very religious, certainly not kosher, but they'd never cross Natasha on her own turf. At home, they respected and honored her, knowing it would break her heart if she saw the steak and shrimp they devoured at the Sizzler.

Natasha had very high standards of behavior. Again Anya sighed, wondering what her mother would say if she knew Anya was having an affair with a married goy for the past three years. Had been having an affair, she reminded herself. It was over.

She stepped into the kitchen and came up behind her mother, who was stirring a pot with the same precision she did everything in her life. Anya put her arms around Natasha and kissed the top of her head, careful not to move the *sheitel* secured on the top of her natural hair.

"Hello, darling. I hope you're hungry."

"For your cooking, Mama, always."

Natasha turned around and looked into her daughter's clear eyes. "What's the matter, *Anyachek*?" She spoke in Russian, which she and Anya and Aleks used for conversations they didn't want the twins to understand.

Anya replied in English, a signal she didn't want her mother to delve any further. "Nothing, Mama. Everything's as fine as it could be. Where are Papa and the boys?"

Her mother backed off, not intruding on her private child's private thoughts. "They're cleaning up. They'll be down in a minute. Would you like some wine? I have the good Baron Herzog Cabernet."

It was the only kosher wine Anya tolerated and her mother always had it for her. "I'd love some. I'll pour you a glass."

Her father burst into the kitchen. "Aha! I thought I heard my sweet *tochter*. Are you hiding from me?" He gave her a huge hug.

"In plain sight, Papa. Would you like some wine?"

"Of course."

Natasha smiled at her husband. "Sasha, darling, please hand me that potholder."

He gave her the potholder, but not without surrounding her with his big arms and kissing her neck. She blushed, always did, even after all their time together. She was the only one who called him by his Russian nickname. Everyone else called him Aleks.

He was a huge man, with enormous, gentle hands and a beard that was still brown, with only a few flecks of gray intruding. Anya suspected he didn't mind so much wearing the yarmulke around the house because it covered his balding spot perfectly. She knew it was one of the few things he was vain about, along with his piercing intelligence.

Anya poured him a glass of wine and she and her parents toasted.

"*L'Chaim.*" As they sipped, Boris and Peter tromped into the room, bickering as usual. Their faces lit up when they saw Anya, not that they would ever tell her how much they worshipped her. The twins were fraternal, not identical, thank God, and it was their sacred duty in life to give Anya a hard time.

Boris squeezed her shoulder. He was the taller and heavier of the two, methodical, near-sighted, across the border of brilliant. Peter was a runner, built like a gazelle; he had a shorter attention span and a much bigger gift for laughter. Both were capable of great intensity, but Boris was destined for academia, while all Peter wanted to do was compete in international marathons and become a jet-setting playboy. Peter aimed a fake punch at Anya's solar plexus. Careful not to spill her wine, she misdirected his fist and twisted his wrist, taking him down to his knees.

"Say uncle."

"I'll die first."

She looked at Boris, who lifted his hands in surrender and backed out of her way, leaving his brother on his own. Anya put a little more pressure on Peter's arm. "Ow!" She immediately let go. Peter made a big show of rubbing his wrist. Anya smiled. "I'll count that as 'Uncle.' Exactly the way I like it, a quick, easy death." He grumbled and took a sip of her wine.

"All right, *kinder*, enough play. It's time for prayers." Like the obedient children they were under this roof, they followed their mother into the dining room. Natasha gathered her family around her and stood in front of the Challah twist she had baked fresh.

"*Baruch Atah Hashem Eloheinu Melech Ha'olam Hamotzi Lechem Min Ha'aretz. Baruch Atah Hashem Eloheinu Melech Ha'olam Asher Kid'shanu B'mitzvotav V'tzivanu Leishev Basukkah.*"

Anya sneaked a look at her father, who beamed at his wife with love. Watching her parents together often brought tears to her eyes. And this time was no different. Damn, she loved her family.

# CHAPTER EIGHTEEN

GARTH SNEAKED DOWNSTAIRS, dressed in his Seattle Mariners' hooded sweatshirt. His dad had given it to him for his last birthday, after the best day ever at T-Mobile Park. In one of the pockets, as always, were the lucky coins Grandpa Tony had given him. He slipped past the old man, who was snoring rhythmically on the big leather chair. A pen and pad lay on the table in front of him, and the television screen was still on, a recording of an earlier soap opera rolling along. Garth made sure Tony was sound asleep, as he tiptoed past him to the kitchen, through the side door to the garage. He pulled out his old-fashioned bike, his dad's from thirty years ago. It was exactly what Garth had wanted.

Pedaling furiously down the block, he did not notice the car parked a hundred feet toward the corner, in front of a neighbor's house.

The two men in the car didn't see him, either. Their eyes were focused on Garth's front door. But when the boy turned the corner, something caught Victor's attention. He wasn't sure what, but he never doubted his instincts. He jabbed Tom. "Check it out."

"Check what? I didn't see nuthin'."

"I don't care what you think you didn't see. Something moved. Check it out. And try to look like you're out for an evening walk." Tom lumbered out of the car.

Several blocks away, Garth realized he'd forgotten his cell phone. He was mad at himself and frustrated. For a moment he thought he should go back, then he changed his mind. Instead, he turned, pedaling toward the Mobil station on Lake Washington and Montlake, which he knew had one of the few pay phones left. He was on a mission and relieved that no one else was around. He kicked the stand and leaned the bike against the well-lit pay phone booth, close to the Safeway. He waved to Dave, the station's owner, who was helping a customer across the lot. Dave waved back, as Garth deposited two quarters and pushed Anya's home number. He could hear her beautiful, no-nonsense voice. "It's Anya. You know the drill." Then a long beep.

Garth hung up on her answering machine, even more frustrated. Luckily he had another fifty cents in his pocket and dialed another number, her cell. He got the same message. As it was playing, he had to raise up on his tiptoes to reach the number of the pay phone, and left that in his message. "911, Anya. 911!"

He hung up, pacing next to the phone, waiting.

# CHAPTER NINETEEN

Anya wiped the brisket juice from her chin as her brothers polished off the roasted potatoes. They laughed at her sloppiness, teasing her, making general fools of themselves. It was their job. Tonight she tolerated it. Right now they were yelling about politics. As her father pounded the table for emphasis, Anya's cell phone beeped, indicating a voice message. It startled them all.

"Aleks, what have you done now?" Natasha accused her husband.

"It's only my phone, Mama. A message. Papa had nothing to do with it."

Peter, the baby by seven minutes, glared at his sister. "They don't even leave you alone at dinner. You're a workaholic."

"What would you know about a job? All you do is run and go to school!" She fumbled in her pocket for the phone. A worry line deepened across her forehead as she listened to Garth's message.

Boris egged on his brother. "She's got you there, Pete."

"What do you think you do, Boring? Study, study, study is not working for a living."

"Boys, quiet," Natasha said. "Anya is calling the station."

"It's not the station. I don't recognize the number, but Garth left a message saying '911.' That's his signal for an emergency." On the other end, Garth grabbed the ringing phone. He sounded relieved. "Anya, you have to come over!"

"What is it, Garth? Where are you? Why aren't you home?"

"I had to leave. I'm at Dave's Mobile gas station, near the Safeway. Something's going to happen to Grandpa Tony. I know it. Dad's not home. I had to leave the house so Grandpa'd be ok."

"What do you have to do with it?" She was trying not to make a big deal out of it, for Garth's sake. Besides, her entire family had stopped eating and talking in order to listen in on her conversation.

"I don't know why, but I do. I didn't call Dad because... because he doesn't believe me."

"Stay where you are, Garth. I'm coming to get you."

"Hurry, please." He hung up before she could turn and face her family.

"Sorry, Mama. Gotta go." She grabbed her purse and checked her weapon. Her father watched carefully. "To visit the boy, you take your weapon?"

Anya hesitated. "He has a bad feeling." She was defiant when she said it, defending Garth ahead of time. Aleks ignored Boris' and Peter's catcalls.

Her father followed her as she headed for the door. "You trust those feelings?"

"I don't know what to believe. He's been right before."

"He's undoubtedly a natural. Children are much more open."

Anya was surprised. "You've seen this before?"

"I've seen more than you can imagine, *Anyachek*. Take Boris and Peter with you, please."

"I'm a cop. If I need help, I'll call for back-up."

Anya blew a kiss to her worried mother, and slammed the door. Aleks waited briefly, then nodded to his sons. All play between them stopped. The boys got up and followed her out.

# CHAPTER TWENTY

GARTH SLUMPED DOWN in front of the pay phone, holding his breath.
His head started pounding again. Rather than fight it this time, he let
the images come.

*Two men hurting Tony. Punching and kicking him. Tony lying on the floor,
clutching his chest. Bleeding, bleeding, bleeding. One of the bad men turns
around, looking for something, shouting at Tony, "Where is he, old man?
Where's the kid?" Hits him again.*

Garth snapped out of his reverie and jumped up. He raised the kick-
stand on the old bike and pedaled as fast as he could down the block,
toward home. The rain started falling and Garth pulled his sweatshirt
hood over his head. *Gotta get there, gotta help him.* The mantra kept
rolling over in his head to the rhythm of his bike wheels.

· · · ·

ANYA REACHED OUTSIDE the Volvo window and slammed the red
light on the roof as she raced through Ravenna's slick hills toward
Montlake Bridge. She was thankful that her parents lived only ten
minutes from Garth. If she'd been in her condo on Queen Anne Hill...

she stopped herself as her phone buzzed with a call from Alex. She hesitated, then answered. He was brief. "Take the 520 to Montlake. There's a game at UDub."

She hung up, forcing herself to focus on making the bridge before it was raised. She checked her watch – five to the hour, and the bridge went up on the hour and the half-hour for a few minutes. Minutes she knew she couldn't afford to waste. She pushed the speedometer to ninety, cursing the salesman who talked her out of a six-cylinder. She glanced in her rearview mirror, at her brothers still on her tail, speeding up when she did. Something else to deal with later. She hoped they didn't kill themselves along the way.

· · · ·

GARTH SLID THE bike next to the garage and ran toward the house. The front door was ajar and he heard the sounds of a fight coming from inside. He didn't even think about not going in. He pushed the door open all the way, and saw Tony, bloodied but still fighting. A tall man wearing a ski mask grabbed Tony from behind as another masked thug pummeled him in the head with the back of his fist, over and over again.

"Where is he, old man? Where's the kid?" Back and forth, he hit him, asking the question, over and over again.

Garth screamed. "Stop it, stop hurting him! I'm the one you want! Stop it!"

Victor's eyes lit up as he let Tony collapse down to the floor. "Just in time, kid." He turned to Tom. "Take care of gramps."

"No! Leave him alone, or you'll never get me!" Garth ran out the front door.

"Leave him. We can come back. It's the kid we want." Victor and Tom sprinted out of the house, running after Garth, at full speed.

The boy was already on his bike, racing down the street, Victor and Tom running behind him. Garth slowed down intentionally, almost letting them catch him, then pedaled furiously, leading them on a chase through the neighborhood he knew and they didn't. Victor pointed, shouting an order at Tom. "Get the car." He ran after Garth as Tom pulled open the car door and turned over the engine.

. . . .

STILL SEVERAL BLOCKS away, Anya's car slid through the waterlogged intersections approaching the bridge. She was going, no matter what. She slammed through the warning rail as it was coming down, her brothers following her. They flew across the bridge, barely making it. When she screeched up to the phone booth, Garth was nowhere in sight. She sped away in the direction of his house.

. . . .

GARTH SLIPPED BEHIND a large trash container at the end of the block, throwing his bike behind it. He gasped for air, terrified and out of breath from pumping so hard.

Two huge hands swooped down and grabbed him. Garth had miscalculated. He pounded his small fists on Victor, who smacked him across the face. Garth was stunned. He'd never been hit before. "Cut it out, brat, or I'll go back and finish Gramps."

The threat made Garth stop struggling. Victor threw Garth over his shoulder like a sack of dirty laundry, and sauntered toward the waiting car.

Anya was speeding around the corner. She screeched to a stop in front of Jake's house and ran up the stairs. Tony limped outside toward her, holding his side. Blood dripped down his cheek from a cut over his eye. "They're after Garth. Two of them."

"Use my radio, Call for back-up." She whirled as Boris and Peter slammed to stop behind her car. "Keep the fuck out of my way, you ignorant little creeps." Her Smith and Wesson appeared in her hand as she rushed around the corner. Her brothers ignored her and loped close behind. She stopped as she spotted Victor carrying Garth toward a sedan. "Freeze. Police!"

Victor laughed, holding the terrified boy in front of him as a shield.

Anya ran across the street toward the waiting car, not able to get a clean shot. Tom leaned out of the driver's side and fired at her. Anya dove out of the way, then jumped up as she saw Victor slide into the car with Garth.

She pulled herself up and fired at the driver, hitting him. The car swerved, then Tom turned the car around and aimed it right at her. She kept firing at him as the car kept coming at her.

Peter ran toward her, diving in and pushing her out of harm's way. They both watched as the car sped off into the wet darkness. "What's the matter with you! You coulda been killed!"

Anya pushed Peter as he tried to help her up, then slugged him hard in the arm. "Idiot!"

"You're the idiot. That guy wasn't going to stop even if you were shooting at him. Wait until I tell Papa."

Anya ignored him. "Did I hit him?"

"Yeah, I think so."

Boris ran up. "I couldn't see the plates. They're covered in mud. I'm sorry."

"Shit. Shit, shit, shit. I lost Garth. Shit."

# CHAPTER TWENTY-ONE

JAKE WAS ALMOST home, humming along with the Big R Radio oldies' station. When he saw the strobe-light reflections of flashing reds, he pressed his foot heavily on the Explorer's accelerator, speeding toward the house, the calm release of his sparring session with Max giving way to the dread he'd been feeling all day.

He assessed the situation as he drove: two patrols, an ambulance, Anya's Volvo and her parents' RAV. The slam of his car door was barely noticeable in the din of two-way radios and the loud chatter of the neighbors.

Anya huddled on the curb, head down, furiously sucking in cigarette smoke as if her life depended on it. Her brothers flanked her, refusing to leave her side. Tony was leaning on the edge of the ambulance's tailgate, waving off the ministrations of two paramedics. Jake looked around; only one person was missing.

"Jake!" Anya cried out. She had spotted him instantly, dreading this moment. He strode toward her. Her hand shook as she lit yet another cigarette.

"Garth? What happened?"

"He's gone. They took him. Two of them. I tried, but… I was too late."

"Who?"

She shook her head, her eyes wet. "I don't know. I notified Dispatch and put out an APB on the car, but the plates weren't visible. Thackery's waiting for us. I'm so sorry."

Jake, stoic, nodded and moved toward the ambulance. Anya turned to her brothers. "Please. Go. You're in the way now." She hesitated, then: "But thank you."

They looked at each other without speaking, kissed her, and left. She turned and watched as Jake stood by his father.

There was a lump the size of a golf ball on the side of Tony's head. One of the paramedics was dabbing antiseptic on the blood that poured from a nasty cut above his eye and several on his scalp.

Jake suspected there were more, unseen injuries. "You okay, Tony?"

"I'm fine. Tell these two nervous Nellies to go someplace they're needed and let me alone. We have to find Garth."

Jake made a supreme effort to control himself. "What happened?"

Tony pushed the two paramedics away. "Enough!"

The younger, braver of the pair, a woman wearing a name tag of 'Blair,' insisted. "You gotta let us take you in, Mr. Fortune. You could have severe internal injuries and not know about it until it's too late."

"I've had more internal injuries in my life than you can imagine, young lady. I'm fine. Now, go away and let me talk to my son." They moved only a few feet, refusing to give up their territory. Tony started to get up, but Jake put a hand on his shoulder, keeping him seated. He exhaled a deep puff of air, then the military man took over and he ran down the sequence of events for Jake.

"They were after Garth specifically. I don't know why. Pros. Two of them, wearing ski masks. I was on the chair, working." He looked up at Jake. "I fell asleep. I woke up with these two assholes pounding on me, wanting to know where Garth was. Well, I sure as hell wasn't going to tell them. I got a few punches in but I'm not as young as I used to be. I told 'em Garth was at a friend's. I didn't know I wasn't lying. He must've sneaked out while I was napping." Tony shook his head. "It was my fault. I was supposed to be watching him."

Anya scrambled closer. "I'm as much to blame." She retained her composure, looking Jake in the eye. "Garth called me from the phone near the Safeway. He'd had a vision, and he was scared to death. He saw his grandfather in danger, and thought it was his fault. He begged me to hurry up. I told him to wait for me, but he was gone by the time I got there. It only took me a few minutes, but it wasn't soon enough." She hesitated, wishing the image in her head could be obliterated. "A tall guy was carrying Garth across the street, using him as a shield. I got off a couple of shots, but I couldn't take the chance I'd hit Garth."

"Almost got herself killed, that's what she did. Stood in front of that car until her damn fool brother pushed her out of the way."

She ignored Tony and went on. "I couldn't see much, but he wasn't wearing a ski mask, Tony."

Tony stopped her. "I ripped it off and I got a good look at him. Get me to an artist, Jake."

Jake knew they were in shock, and as much as he tried to control it, so was he. He felt as if he were underwater, like everything they said was coming through some kind of filter, muffling the reasons behind it all. "Why Garth?"

"Maybe he saw something he shouldn't have..." Anya trailed off.

"No. He would've told us that. He told you he had another one of those visions. He was worried something was going to happen."

"I thought I talked him out of it. I should've listened." Tony's sense of guilt was plain on his face.

"And I should have been here," Jake said. "I wasn't. My guess is this is personal, it's the only thing that makes sense. Taking Garth is a message to me. So if you want to lay blame, lay it on me. But that's not going to get him back."

Tony looked up at his son. "He came back to protect me, you know. You'd have been so proud of him. He marched into that living room, bold as anything, and demanded they stop hurting me. He yelled that he was the one they wanted, and then ran away so they'd chase him.

He sacrificed himself to save me. I've seen grown men run from easier situations." Tony did not look at all uncomfortable with the tears that streamed down his face.

Jake's eyes flickered, unreadable, as he shoved his pain down so deep that an interior door might have slammed shut. He spoke quietly to his father. "Go on, get yourself looked at. You won't be any good to anyone in the condition you're in." He lifted his hand to fend off Tony's protests. "I'm going down to the station. I'll put in a call for the artist. You can come over after you're treated." He turned back toward his car.

"Do what he says, Tony." Anya squeezed his arm.

"You go with him. He thinks he can handle this like a cop. He can't."

"I know. Neither of us can. I'll be right behind him."

Tony watched them walk away. Anya was limping. She'd bruised her hip when Peter had tackled her and pushed her away from the oncoming car. Sighing, Tony lifted himself up into the ambulance, the two hovering paramedics right behind him. Most times, he knew he could deal with anything, but this was different. Garth was his hope for the future. He found himself praying his grandson could buy them enough time to find him. When they did, he was going to kill the scum who took the boy, simple as that.

# CHAPTER TWENTY-TWO

GARTH WAS STILL curled up in the stern of the motorboat, The tape the Man had slapped over his mouth was itchy, and Garth was desperate to scratch it, but he knew to be as still as possible. He was sure the Bad Man, the one the Driver had called Victor, would kill him in an instant if he didn't do exactly what he was told.

Victor made that clear at the first place they took him, an old warehouse in the International District. That's where they tried to fix the Driver. It didn't work, so Victor had dumped the Driver into the Sound. That was only a few minutes ago. Blood had been gushing from his shoulder, where Anya had shot him. Garth was sorry she'd missed Victor. He might've had a chance with the Driver, but not this one. Garth's eyes had widened as Victor had hit the Driver with his gun, knocked him out, and dumped him overboard. Victor had grinned when he looked at Garth.

"Leaving a witness is a bad mistake. If you don't do exactly what I tell you, that's what I'm going to do to you. Got it?"

Garth had no doubt he could be thrown overboard any second, especially after he yelled at Victor. He wished he could fight back like the Priest Caine could when he was threatened and held prisoner. He wanted to be strong like Grandpa Tony was in the prison camp, act like he did when the guards beat him up, but he didn't know how. He figured the best thing he could do was close his eyes and pretend to be asleep. Soon he wasn't pretending. He drifted in the place between fear and sleep, lulled by the rolling of the boat. The air smelled familiar to him, and that helped a little.

He was wakened when Victor ripped off the silver tape covering his mouth. Garth suspected Victor had done it as he was falling asleep simply to terrorize him. It worked. His heart started to pound faster than he could count and he could barely breathe.

"Better, little boy? Here, drink this." He put a bottle up to Garth's lips. He eyed it with suspicion.

"It's water. Drink it." Garth took a sip. He hadn't realized how dry his throat was. "Good. We wouldn't want my boss to think I'd mistreated his little prize. Spoils of war is what he called you." Garth didn't know what Victor was talking about. He gulped down the rest of the water.

"That's enough." Victor pulled the bottle away, scraping Garth's chin. "I don't want you puking all over the boat."

"I don't get seasick."

"That's the least of your problems."

Garth thought if he wasn't dead yet, the guy wasn't supposed to kill him for some reason. He felt safe enough then to venture a question. "Why'd you take me?"

"Don't get talky, kid. If it was up to me, I would have dumped you with ol' Tom. But it's not up to me. Not yet."

Garth shuddered again, but this time not from the cold. *No, not now, please. Please.* But there was no choice. He closed his eyes, and let it happen. Garth flashed on a *round Chinese man whose eyes were cold as a snake. Black marbles of death. He was pouring tea.*

Victor jolted Garth back to reality. His hand was on Garth's shoulders, shaking him like a rag doll. "I thought you didn't get seasick."

"I don't. It doesn't matter." He looked up at Victor's face. Not the right one, not the one he'd just seen. It was a face that scared him even more than the kidnapper's. Garth could tell Victor was crazy, but the Chinese man was worse. Victor's hand still clutched Garth's shoulder like a vise. It would leave a nasty bruise. Garth stared into his eyes. "The Chinese man won't like it if you hurt me."

Victor's hand instantly released the boy's shoulder. Victor stared down at Garth, a shocked look on his face. Garth slumped back against the deck and closed his eyes again. There was nothing else he could do.

# CHAPTER TWENTY-THREE

THE SMALL FIGURE slid through the darkness on Feng's island. She was able to fit through the shallow dirt trench dug out beneath the stretched-out chainlink fence. The rain had muddied the path even more than usual, so her senses were vigilant as she trod through the soaked brush. She slipped several times, but continued with purpose.

Her jaw clenched as a slight sound captured her attention. She ducked behind a small boulder, holding her breath. Her senses were alerted by soft footfalls of steps in front of her. A flame flickered as a guard stopped to cup his lighter in one hand. She was close enough to sniff the acrid aroma of a strong Asian cigarette.

Fear choked her so tightly she thought her lungs would burst from lack of air. She knew she ought to go back. This was the first time a guard had come this far to patrol the perimeter of the compound. She couldn't chance being caught. The penalty was unthinkable. Yet, as soon as he left, she shook off her fear and forged ahead.

She almost cried out in despair when the light in the front of the convent flickered and died. Too late. The rain had slowed her down. It was time to turn back. She'd have to figure out another way of getting through. Soon. Events were way beyond her control now. God knows she had tried tonight. She agonized that maybe if she had left earlier… she stopped herself. No, she'd had no choice.

She sighed and turned back toward the compound. It was always easier getting in than getting out, which made her determined not to let down her guard, not to get caught.

Tomorrow night would be too soon to try again. She knew she'd have to wait until the next night. And hope the man would understand the messages and come to save them all before it was too late.

# CHAPTER TWENTY-FOUR

JAKE SAT STONE still in Captain Thackery's office. He glanced at Anya, who was shivering. Normally the squad room was stifling because the ventilation system never worked properly, having been installed by a contractor who was now in prison for graft. But tonight she'd thrown on two sweatshirts and a turtleneck, and apparently the layering didn't help. He could barely imagine what she was feeling.

At this hour there was usually only a skeleton shift, but tonight every cop was here, sifting through the meager information, trolling their contacts, doing everything they could. Jake had spent a lot of late nights here, but now the room felt strange and empty even in the midst of so much activity. Through the Captain's glass partition Jake watched without seeing the detectives moving around the squad room, trying to use activity to push out the thoughts of how grateful they were this hadn't happened to their family. He kept thinking of his son, imagining him alive, afraid, cold at best. Jake tried to move his thoughts away from Garth, but it was like lifting heavy furniture from one end of the room to the other all by himself.

He forced himself to concentrate on what Captain Thackery was saying, barely noticing that Anya was even more shell-shocked than he.

Thackery leaned toward Anya. "Anya. Focus. Stay with me here. It wasn't your fault, not anybody's fault. The best thing we can do for Garth is figure out who took him and where, and go get him back."

She looked as if she understood, then finally met Jake's eyes. He appeared calm and certain. "Look, taking Garth is connected to the illegals. It's a personal act. The faxes were personal, to me. It's a warning. I know he's still alive."

Thackery was adamant. "Then you should go home, and wait for a call. You know they'll contact you."

"Not necessarily. They're not after money. It's to throw us off, I'm sure of it. And the first twenty-four hours after a grab are too important for me to sit at home and wait. Whoever they are, they know how to reach me if they want. Garth's alive now, but we don't know how long."

"I still want to bring in the Feds."

"Not a chance. They have their own priorities. My only agenda is getting my son back. That and making sure it never happens again." He said that in such a flat tone, it was clear he was in a state of shock.

Thackery continued. "I'll go along with you, but only for the first 24. After that, we'll pull in all the help we can get. If we don't, Homeland will have our asses."

Jake grimaced. "DHS couldn't find the hull of a ship if barnacles led the way."

The Captain shrugged. "Doesn't matter. They'll be worried about a smuggling route turning into a terrorist route, even if it's only starving Chinese labor now. And they could be right, so we'll inform them as a matter of routine. Later."

Before Jake could object, the door squeaked open and Soto stuck his head in. He looked at Jake. "We found the car in the International District. No sign of anyone, wiped clean. No blood except where Anya popped the driver. We're processing the blood for DNA now. No plates on the car. We're checking the VIN against the stolen car list, but my guess it was a souped-up junker from a chop shop."

Jake wasn't comforted. "We'll never trace them through the car."

"Never's a long time, buddy. CID, plus auto and robbery are alerted. They're ready to coordinate simultaneous busts on every chop shop in town, and deal for info. No one's gonna let this one slide." Soto pulled his head back like a tortoise who'd seen all of the world he wanted to, and left.

Jake turned to Anya and Thackery. "It'll take too long."

Anya's voice was shaky. "Everyone's put the word out to their snitches, Jake. Something will come back soon. You'll see."

There was a brisk knock on the door, then Sergeant Kirk Pelham came in without waiting to be asked. He looked at Jake with sympathy. "Sorry, Jake."

Thackery plunged ahead. "Kirk's the primary, Jake. He'll run the three teams."

Jake had known this was coming. Pelham was a good detective who had mentored Jake early in his career. A lifelong bachelor, some suspected the bulky detective was gay, but no one knew or cared. He was polite, smart, and kept to himself off-duty. Methodical to the point that people underestimated him as dense, he never let anything go uninvestigated. He'd made Sergeant before any of his peers because he was like a hound with a bone. None of that mattered to Jake. None of it.

Thackery put up a hand to abort Jake's protest. He gestured toward Pelham. "You know Kirk's good. If I had my way, I'd send you home. Whether or not you're aware of it, you're not operating on all cylinders. If you were a surgeon I wouldn't let you operate on your kid. The same thing applies here. If it's personal, and I think you're right about that, it's either a warning or payback."

"Or both."

"Either way, the purpose is to distract you, or pull you off the case altogether. We're not gonna accommodate them. We're gonna double down on our investigation."

Pelham watched Jake's face and interrupted Thackery. "Every piece I find, you'll get. That's a promise."

Thackery stared hard at Jake. "So either go home or focus on the

Snakehead case." That's what they had dubbed this morass after hearing Ling's story, focusing on the perps responsible for the smuggling. "Let everybody else focus on Garth."

"Fine. Pelham's the primary, I don't care what you call it. You follow up your leads, but the cases are obviously connected and I'm not stopping at some invisible line because it might relate to Garth. Nothing personal, Kirk. My kid is out there because of me, and I'm going to find him."

The threat was implicit. Thackery knew Jake would walk away from the department in an instant unless he handled him very carefully. "You heard Kirk. Every piece of information will be pooled no matter how insignificant it might seem. That goes for you, too. Got it? We're working in the dark here and who knows what'll break the case. Every piece, Jake. Or you're out now."

"Deal."

"You too, Anya."

Soto knocked and poked his head in again. "Your dad's here, Jake. Says he has an appointment with a police artist. I don't know why they released him, he looks pretty beat up."

Jake bolted out of his seat. "They didn't release him. He left."

. . . .

TONY LEANED AGAINST Jake's desk in the squad room, looking like hell. Six stitches had closed the cut over his eye, but the swelling and bruises on his face were already turning rainbow. And those were only the obvious injuries. He and Jake glared at each other. "Don't start, Jake."

Jake didn't. He knew better. His father was too stubborn to argue with.

"Where's the artist?"

"Waiting for you in Room 1. She has a partial description for you to look at before you start. We think it could be the same guy involved in a case I'm on."

Anya followed them to where Jeanie Kim waited, a laptop on the table in front of her. Pretty, slender, vaguely exotic looking, she was a struggling portrait artist, which was now out of fashion, so she supplemented her income by sketching for the cops. It paid the rent, and it was good practice for her.

"Mr. Fortune, I'm Jeanie. This may take a little time, so please have a seat. When we're done here, an officer will ask you to go through some mug shots as well."

Tony looked impatient, as if every minute not doing something was wasted. "I'm ready, let's get it done."

Jake and Anya hovered, as Jeanie was matter-of-fact. "Let's start with his general physique. How tall was he, sir?"

"About 6'2", 220, a lot of muscle. Long limbs, arms too long for his torso, moved well."

"Then let me begin with this partial description given by Anya and earlier witnesses..."

Tony peered at it. "Looks like him. But his nose is smaller, too small for his face."

"Are you sure, sir?"

Tony's smile was cold. "I always remember who hits me." Jeanie smiled at him, and began to shade the nose on the partial rendering. As Jake leaned in again, Tony turned around and snapped at him. "Go do something worthwhile. I need to concentrate."

Jake was ready to argue, but Anya put her hand on his arm. Her touch helped. "You're right, Tony, We'll be in the squad room. Let us know when you're done." She guided Jake into the corridor. "Coffee?"

"Yeah."

They headed to the small kitchen, while the rest of the squad buzzed around them, avoiding direct eye contact. Jake wondered if they thought Garth's kidnapping was a contagious disease. Anya poured and they drank in silence. She pulled out a fresh pack and lit another cigarette, not caring that it wasn't allowed. "You okay?"

Jake nodded yes, but he felt like he was watching someone else in his body. Disassociated, that was the word he was searching for. He wondered if this was what it felt like to be on uppers. "I'm okay. Don't think about Garth, Annie. Think about the perps. I'm gonna make some more calls." He'd already put out the word to over a dozen snitches. It was time to troll the bottom half of his network.

They walked back to their desks, focusing on their lifeline, the telephone. Jake watched Anya concentrate. He sat down across from her and pulled out his snitch list from a locked drawer. He knew all the numbers by heart, but he didn't trust himself anymore. It was a long time until first light, and he was afraid it might be too late already.

# CHAPTER TWENTY-FIVE

GARTH FIRST HEARD, then felt the motorboat engine slowing down. As the craft headed toward a small dock, he sniffed the air. He was sure they were in his beloved San Juans because he recognized the smells, but he didn't know which island. If he was right, then it was likely he'd been here before and could find his way around if he managed to escape. Victor hadn't bothered to blindfold him, for which Garth was very grateful. His eyes followed Victor's movements as he thought about how to get away. His wrists were chafing from being bound, but at least the tape had been removed from his mouth. He watched as Victor tied off the boat. Then he turned back to Garth, snapped off some duct tape from a roll and covered Garth's mouth again.

"Not done yet, little boy." Once more, Victor slung him over his shoulder. Garth was enveloped by fear, his heart pounding out of control. He tried to breathe, but panic was setting in and his small body involuntarily began to squirm.

Victor squeezed him more tightly. "Don't move, you little shit. I'm carrying enough crap as it is."

Garth willed himself to be still. His father, Grandpa, Anya — all of them would be terrified; he had to help them any way he could. Garth made his body go limp, as Victor trudged along a dirt path, but he kept his eyes open so he could find his way out. He was so focused on the sounds and smells of his surroundings that he was startled when Victor put him down. Garth could make out strange shapes in the dark; he gasped when he realized they were in a tiny ramshackle airfield. A small Cessna sat on the barely paved runway. Garth froze. He wanted to run. Anywhere. If he got on that plane, no matter how small it was, it could take him far away and he would never get home.

Victor half-dragged him to the plane, up the steps, and inside a utilitarian cabin with a couple of seats and a squat-looking man at the controls. The pilot looked at Victor. "Ready?"

"Go." Victor strapped Garth into a makeshift seat. He tried to look out the window, but Victor slammed the shade shut. He grinned at the boy. "Just in case, kid, though you're never gonna get back anyway."

Infuriated, Garth steeled himself. No matter how, no matter where he was headed, he vowed that he would find his way home. His anger carried him through the brief trip, close to half an hour. As the plane descended, Garth sighed in relief. It couldn't be that far away. The plane landed on a longer runway and pulled to a quick stop.

When Victor pulled him off the plane, Garth looked around at his surroundings. He was sure they were still in the islands, but this one seemed unfamiliar. He tried to memorize the terrain, but stopped short when Victor turned him around to walk toward an iron gate, bordered on one side by a guard shack. On either side of the gate stood two sentries, each armed with automatic weapons. A tear slid down his cheek, and Garth lowered his head. There was a good chance that he'd never see home again.

# CHAPTER TWENTY-SIX

THE SILENCE BETWEEN Tony and Jake was palpable as they approached the pitch-black house. Two cop cars had followed them and were stationed on either side of the street. The men ignored Jake when he gestured for them to leave. The senior officer shrugged. "No can do. Orders."

Jake slammed the door as he and Tony entered through the kitchen. Tony watched his son pace, then flipped on the overhead light, dimming it almost immediately. "They're doing their job. Leave them be."

Jake's response was cold. "We don't need babysitters. We need action."

Tony ignored him. "Will they call?"

Jake shook his head. "No. They'll play cat and mouse first."

"So, what can we do?"

"Nothing. They did a facial recognition search on every database we have and came up empty. Jeanie sent the sketch to all major departments in the state and on the West Coast. To Homeland and other agencies. On our end, every detective in every department will mine every CI they have. That's what will give us our first lead."

"So we wait."

"Yes." Jake moved to the living room, opened the liquor cabinet. Tony was right behind him as Jake pulled out a bottle of Glenfiddich and poured two shots. He handed one to Tony, and slugged one down for himself. Tony did the same and held out his glass for another. Jake poured them both a second shot.

"I know you're frustrated." There was pity on Tony's face.

"No point in talking about it."

Tony stared at his son a beat longer, sighed, and walked over to the TV. He saw Jake watching him, a stunned look in his eyes, as if he couldn't believe his father was actually going to turn on one of his shows. Jake spoke much too softly. "What are you doing?"

Tony was calm. "Making sure that Garth's shows are being taped."

Jake moved in behind him, checking out the screen. The recording list included *Kung Fu*, which had been Jake's favorite show in college. Jake looked at his dad, startled. "*Kung Fu*"?

"He loves it. He's seen every one from all the series, including the crap movies. He can quote them. And he does, all the time. One day, his favorite is Grasshopper, the next it's the Master, he alternates, but I think it's Caine he loves." Tony looked his son in the eye. "Caine reminds him of you." He shook his head as if he realized something for the first time. "Of course. Caine had instincts. Visions. Garth can relate to him."

Jake stood there, frozen with guilt. "I didn't know. I didn't know any of it." His stomach churned at the knowledge, yet again, of how little he knew his son.

His father was looking at him with compassion. "None of us is perfect, Jake. Not as a parent, or a human being. I can't count the number of regrets I have about us when you were younger. And still. You learn from it, and move on, hopefully to do better."

Jake's eyes met his dad's, and he nodded. "All well and good. I want that chance. But what if I don't get it?"

Saying those words out loud terrified him. He couldn't imagine what Garth was going through. He had to find his child, to punish, no, to *kill* the men responsible. He was determined to have a second chance to know Garth. And to give Garth the chance to know him. But the bad feeling in his bones was back and he was petrified what it meant.

# CHAPTER TWENTY-SEVEN

GARTH SHIVERED, NOT only from the cold. He was marched toward the big house behind the gates. The front door was elaborately carved wood with a stained glass rendering of ferocious dragons. He watched Victor carefully. He seemed distracted as he pushed open the door, which startled Garth with its loud squeal. Garth would find out that everything around here was well-oiled and the squeak was deliberate. Feng called it his "late-warning system", his attempt at humor.

Victor ushered Garth through the opulent corridor. With each step, Garth's heart beat faster. The unknown lurked at the end of this well-lit hallway and it was a terrifying unknown. Garth tried to rein in his imagination, but finally he sighed deeply and gave himself over to his fate. Victor knocked on the door, then pushed it open without waiting for a response.

Garth froze when he looked across the room. His eyes met Feng's and he recognized him as the Chinese man in his vision. But the real Feng was much more terrifying. Victor pushed Garth towards Feng and he tripped. Feng reached out to steady him, but it was not a comforting gesture. Garth knew he was in even worse trouble than he could have imagined as Feng stared down at his little prize. Feng was calm. "You belong to me. You must behave properly."

Garth nodded. He believed Feng to his core. Victor carefully watched the interchange, then dropped his bomb. "How did he know you?"

Feng, rarely startled, reacted as if his entire being went on red alert. "Explain."

Garth, already frozen in place, barely breathed.

"The kid described you when we were on the boat."

Feng turned to Garth. "Is this the truth?"

Garth shook his head no. Feng looked at Victor. "What did he say?"

Victor hesitated, having boxed himself in, then shrugged. "He said the Chinese man wouldn't like it if I hurt him."

Feng glared at Victor. "Did you? Hurt him."

Victor denied it. "Nope."

Garth remained quiet as Feng turned to him. "Who told you?"

Garth was truthful. "Nobody."

Feng made himself clear. "You will not win this battle. I will destroy everyone you love and then you will tell me the truth. You may as well save them and tell me now."

Garth swallowed, knowing the threats were real, so he told the truth. "I saw you in my head."

Feng stepped back and stared intently at Garth's face, then sat down in his comfortable chair and gestured for Garth to sit in front of him. Garth did as he was told.

Victor was frustrated. "You don't believe the little shit?"

Feng looked up at Victor and dismissed him. "Go get something from Cook. I'll call you when I need you."

Victor looked annoyed, but shrugged and did as he was told. As soon as he left Feng turned back to Garth. "Water?"

"Yes, please." Feng poured him a glass and handed it to him. Garth tried as hard as he could to steady his hand, but the tremor of fear did not go unnoticed.

Garth sipped from the glass, stalling. Feng let him drink, then demanded of him. "Tell me what you saw."

Garth remembered being terrified. "That bad man threw the other one into the Bay. I thought he was going to throw me over the side, too."

Feng waited for the boy to tell his story.

"He hurt my arm. Then I saw your face. And I knew he wasn't supposed to hurt me. So I told him you'd be mad."

Feng sat back in his chair. He'd been leaning forward, towards Garth. "This isn't the first time you've seen things in your head? How often?"

Garth shrugged. He'd stopped counting a long time ago.

"Every day?"

Garth thought quickly. "Sometimes."

"What do you usually see?"

Garth didn't understand. "I don't know. I see something and know it's going to happen."

"Give me an example."

Garth hesitated. He didn't want this man to know he saw what was going to happen when he was taken. He searched his memory quickly and settled on something. "Mrs. D."

Feng looked at him. "Who is that?"

"She takes care of me. I saw her sick, then she had a heart attack. She's in the hospital. But she's gonna be okay." Garth didn't realize that he had instinctively touched on the one thing that would make him incredibly valuable to his captor. He could tell healthy from sickly, which would give Feng an extreme advantage in the people trade.

Feng smiled. Garth didn't know if the man believed him, but he felt like he'd passed some test. Feng got up and patted Garth's shoulder, which was not reassuring to Garth at all. "Very good, little boy. Very good. Now you can get some sleep. We may do very well together." Feng's words chilled Garth to the seat of his soul.

# CHAPTER TWENTY-EIGHT

## First Day After

JAKE KEPT TELLING himself it was a dream, but his anxiety raged anyway. Exhausted, he slept restlessly on the big chair in the living room, in front of the TV, an infomercial playing without sound in the background. His face reflected the pain he wouldn't allow himself to feel in his waking life. Worse, he couldn't pull himself out of this nightmare.

*He and Garth were being chased by men in masks and hoods, multicolored and multilayered with small gashes for eye holes. They were running to get away, slipping on snakes, racing towards the water as the shore turned into mud, then quicksand. Jake knew that in the distance there was a safe place. He could hear the Church bells ringing and saw a ferocious looking nun beckoning him to safety, towards a walled sanctuary. The bells became louder and more insistent as Jake got closer and closer to the stone building. At the last minute they were caught by masked men wielding swords.*

The bells rang louder and jarred Jake awake. He sat up quickly, shivering, and realized it had been a nightmare. And the bells of the sanctuary translated into the insistent ringing of his cell phone. Jake grabbed for it, answered as if he'd been awake and ready for anything. "Fortune."

His hopes were dashed in an instant – it wasn't Garth or his colleagues. It was Sasquatch, a long-time confidential informant. "It's Sasq, Chief." Sasq was really Richard Agay, with a long rap sheet of petty crimes and an IQ of about 100. He was nicknamed in the fifth grade because he was short and had size 11 feet. He wasn't short anymore, and he was a reliable, if low-level snitch. And a junkie. "I got some 411 for you."

He said that the street was buzzing about the cop whose kid was snatched. Sasq gave Jake a half hour to meet him at their regular spot. "Bring cash, will ya?"

Tony had left to get a little sleep at home, so Jake didn't have to explain himself to anyone. He grabbed his gun, and cash from the kitchen pantry stash that he kept for emergencies, and was out the door in less than a minute. He wanted to be at the meet first, not because he didn't trust Sasq, but because he didn't trust anyone except his partner. Better to be early and prepared than on time and surprised. His car left the garage and was halfway down the block before the uniforms watching the house realized what happened. Jake didn't want anything or anyone scaring his snitch away.

. . . .

What Jake didn't know was that Anya had prearranged with the detail outside his house to call her if anything remotely suspicious happened. They did, waking her out of a restless sleep. "Yeah. Pashkov."

"Anya. Benjaminson here. Jake's on the move."

"Thanks, Chuck. Appreciate the heads-up." She threw on her clothes, grabbed her gun, and was on the road in under three minutes.

Jake also didn't know that before they left the station she'd sneaked an app that Aleks had designed onto his cell phone. It was based on the 'Find Friends' app, but much, much more sophisticated. She activated it with one hand as she sped off to keep an eye on Jake. She was only a few minutes behind him, and he had no idea.

. . . .

Jake normally loved Seattle this time of night. The city was hushed predawn, there was no traffic and no people. Only the hills and the water, mountains and quiet. It took him barely fifteen minutes to get to 3rd, between Pike and Pine. The area was empty, except for a random car passing by. He parked down the block, out of sight. Jake made sure there was no threat, then headed to their regular spot, the alley behind a fortune cookie factory. The locals called it 'stab alley' for obvious reasons.

Jake's internal radar screamed at him when he turned down the alley and saw Sasq waiting for him. This guy was never early. And he was shifting from foot to foot like he wanted to pee. Jake approached him from behind, wary and quiet, startling Sasq when Jake tapped his shoulder. He turned quickly.

"Yo. Chief."

Jake marched up to him. He hated the nickname but had tolerated it before. Nose to nose, he looked at Sasq's pupils. He wasn't high, which meant he was compromised. He could see that Sasq was anxious to give him the information, grab his cash, and be on his way, but Jake backed him into the trash bin and pinned him there. He watched Sasq's eyes flit side to side, unable to focus. Jake kept his voice soft. "What do you have for me?"

"The Snakeheads."

Jake's didn't react. "What about them?"

"Word is your kid was grabbed as a warning."

Jake played along. "What kind of warning?"

"To lay off them."

"Uh huh."

Sasq squirmed and hurried on. "Your kid is okay. But they shipped him to Vermont or Maine or someplace far like that."

Jake frowned. "Tiny area of the country to look for my kid, doncha think? All of New England."

Sasq was starting to look desperate. "Maybe if I had a little more money," he said, "I could, you know, narrow the area down some."

"Good thinking. Except you're giving me a load of bullshit. And I don't think you're smart enough to come up with it. So that means someone paid you off." Jake slapped him across the face twice, hard. Sasq looked into Jake's eyes, clearly shocked. "So how about you tell me who fed you this crap."

Sasq didn't deny it. "I dunno." Jake slapped him again, harder. "I dunno. Honest!"

"There's nothing honest about you, Sasq."

Sasq freaked, as if this were a Jake he'd never seen before. "I never saw the guy! Word was out for any snitch of yours! It was all by burner, I swear. He paid off my dealer and gave me the info to pass on to you. I didn't know it was a lie!"

Jake glared at him. "There's so much you don't know. It scares me how someone so fucking stupid could still be alive. So ignorant that I am afraid where we're all headed. There should be a penalty for that, don't you think?"

Sasq looked frantic, but was unable to move away from the trash bin. "Swear I'll find out. For nuthin', swear."

Without warning, Jake punched him in the gut. "Too late. Too late for everything." Jake's pent-up rage exploded, and he longed to direct it at Sasq. But something in his core screamed this was a bad thing. It took every ounce of restraint to contain his white-hot anger, but he did. When he heard a car screech to a stop behind him, he did not even turn around, simply backed away.

Sasq sank onto the gravel, holding his gut. "Goddamn." Jake turned to see Anya leap out of her car. She glared at him. "Asshole."

Shaking with the effort to control himself, he agreed. "Okay, I'm an asshole. But the little sonovabitch lied to me about Garth."

Anya helped Sasq up and looked him over. Nothing terrible.

"Jake may be an asshole, Sasq, but you should know better than to poke a tiger."

Jake sighed, back to reality. "It's a bear, Anya."

"Bear, tiger, I don't give a damn. Let's take this piece of shit back to the station and book him. I'm sure he's done something." Jake gave her a brusque laugh.

As they walked back to the car, Jake turned to Anya. "Thanks, partner."

"That's what I am. Don't you forget it."

# CHAPTER TWENTY-NINE

GARTH HAD FALLEN asleep an hour earlier. He needed to make a plan, but there was no way to fight his exhaustion. He was dreaming that *Jake and he were running from bad men in masks, slipping through the mud. He could hear Church bells in the distance, and the hair on the back of his neck bristled as he looked back but saw no one following him.* The feeling was so intense he shook himself awake, his heart pounding. He was in a strange bed in a strange house, and turned to see someone next to the bed, staring at him.

He stared back at a small Chinese girl, who was maybe eleven. With immense calm she put her fingers to her lips, and shook her head. He instantly obeyed, sitting up and regarding her with curiosity. She sat down. "You don't belong here," she whispered in a sweet, singsong voice.

"I know. I should be home. With my dad."

"I am Li Li." She sounded tense, but went on talking. "Feng Wah is my father."

There was compassion in Garth's eyes. "It doesn't matter. You're not like him."

"Thank you," Li Li said, looking relieved. "My mother says I must honor him and be grateful to him for giving me life, but I do not have to like him or what he does."

Garth smiled at her. He liked this girl. Li Li smiled back, then whispered once again. "We don't have much time and you must be very careful. Tell no one about me. Feng Wah is very smart. Give him whatever he wants and you will be safe. My mother and I will try to help you."

"You're afraid of him, too."

"Of course. Though more for my mother than me. I am the only one he has any feeling for. But that could end." She snapped her fingers. "Like that."

"What will you do?" Garth asked, frightened for both of them.

"You don't need to know. Pretend that we have not met. Be ready. And understand that we will do our best." She left the room, closing the door quietly behind her. Garth heard the outside lock click into place. Closing his eyes, he sighed. He felt better than he had in what seemed like an eternity. He was no longer alone.

# CHAPTER THIRTY

JAKE KNEW HE could be facing suspension for his actions with Sasq. He was damn lucky that the cops watching his house had notified Anya and that she'd tracked him down. He refused to make excuses, though he had controlled himself in time and Sasq's injuries were minimal. He knew what he deserved for going off the reservation.

Captain Thackery had given him an hour to cool off, then called him into his office. Jake had the grace to be apologetic, but Thackery stopped him. "I understand. I don't approve. I'm not happy. But I understand."

"Thanks, Cap."

"This isn't the end of it, you know. I'm pulling you off the street for the next couple of days. Desk only." Thackery put up his hand to stop any dissent from Jake. "You just proved that you're not yourself. And I get it. Now go to work. Solve the damned Snakeheads case. If it happens to lead to something about Garth, so be it."

Jake kept his mouth shut and got out of there as quickly as possible, slumping down into his desk chair. He felt relieved and guilty at the same time; glad he hadn't completely lost control, guilty that he'd taken out his angst on Sasq, who was only a pawn. A stupid pawn, at that.

Soto was hovering over Jake, skittish but determined, a large mailing envelope in his hand.

"What'd you find on the rendering my dad did with Jeanie?" Jake asked.

"That's why I'm here. Well, one of the reasons. We ran it through every data base we have access to, and some we don't. And we got nada."

"Nothing?"

"Nothing."

Jake sighed. "I'm surprised. Most skells like him aren't smart enough to stay under the radar that long. He's either very good or very lucky."

"Or both."

"Yeah. Or both. What's the other thing?"

"Huh?"

"The other reason."

Soto did not look comfortable but he plunged ahead. "Whatever you need, Jake. Whatever. Legal, not legal, doesn't matter."

Jake stared at him. He knew this was hard for the kid. "Thanks, Soto. Much appreciated. I'll try not to get you into too much hot water."

Soto looked relieved. "Thanks." He handed the package to Jake. "This came for you first thing." He marched off, his burden lifted.

Jake looked at the return address on the envelope. It was from Vancouver BC PD. He ripped it open and pulled out a copy of a thick file, and a note from Sharrone.

> *Figured sooner rather than later. I'll buy my wife something pretty and she won't be too pissed. Good luck.*

Jake smiled. Nice of the guy to go out of his way. He started to open the thick file when he saw Anya marching across the room towards him. He put the file down. It could wait. "Sasq booked?"

"Yeah. Not too bright. That balloon of heroin in his back pocket nailed him."

"Damn. He swore he'd stay clean. And then he does this, tries to play me. Guess I expected too much."

"No kidding. Now it's time to talk." Anya guided him out of the squad room.

. . . .

Outside, morning traffic was picking up. The fog clung to them like the hazy fear they felt as they walked the few blocks down the hill to Gallagher's in silence.

Megan pointed to a booth in the back. "Coffee's fresh." They slid into the back booth.

"Why didn't you call me?" Anya sounded fierce.

"I didn't want you involved."

"Bullshit. You went off bulldozing people as usual."

Jake was quiet as Megan brought them two cups of steaming coffee and a plate of homemade muffins. "Breakfast?"

Jake shook his head, but Anya smiled. "Sure. No time this morning. Can I have the usual?"

Megan left to grab Anya's bagel, cream cheese and bacon. Anya turned back to Jake, the smile gone. "Your temper tantrum cost you hours you could've spent finding Garth."

Jake didn't flinch. "You're right. I fucked up. It won't happen again."

"Eat some breakfast, then. We'll start fresh. And we will find him."

"I know." But Jake wasn't sure anymore. He looked up, startled to see his father striding towards them, his face multicolored and swollen. Tony plopped down next to Anya and kissed her cheek.

"Want breakfast?"

"No thanks, Anya. Not very hungry." Tony Fortune had faced great adversity in his life, but never the possibility of losing his young child. He turned to Jake, his voice soft. "How are you?"

"Still standing."

"So, what are you planning on doing?"

"We're figuring that out."

"I want to help."

Jake didn't know what to make of this. Of course Tony wanted to help, but Jake couldn't imagine how. He was at a loss.

Anya interjected, breaking the tension. "Of course, Tony. But we have to get a handle on it first. Jake got something he thinks might be related to our original case, and we're going to check that out."

"Okay. Let me know. Don't forget, I know a lot of people. Not civilians. All branches. And every single one of them will want to help, and will have the ability to get something done."

Jake stared at his father for a moment, realizing how deep the man's suffering was. He softened his tone. "Will do, Dad. Promise."

"Good. While you're checking out your case, I'm heading to the hospital to break the news to Kate Dooley. I don't want her finding out by accident."

Jake couldn't believe he'd forgotten about Mrs. D. "I'm glad one of us doesn't have his head totally up his ass. Thank you."

"You're welcome, son. Now go do what you do best. And when I get back, give me an order and I'll follow it. I'm a good soldier." He grabbed two of the muffins off the untouched plate. "She'll like these. That woman has the damndest sweet tooth." Tony got up, kissed Anya again, and hurried out.

Jake put his head back against the booth, and closed his eyes. Inside his head, he was beating himself up. "I can't believe how much he knows about the people in my life that I don't know."

"Never too late to learn, partner. Now eat something, because it's early and it's already been a long day that's going to get even longer."

Jake listened to her. Anya was right. Anya was always right. So he ate, but he couldn't stop imagining what Garth must be going through. And it chilled his soul.

# CHAPTER THIRTY-ONE

ONE OF FENG'S servants unlocked Garth's door. Garth was dressed and ready in clothes that had been laid out for him earlier. The servant was silent, so Garth said nothing as he was led through the house to the dining room. He acted surprised when he saw Li Li with Feng and Feng's wife. Light streamed in the leaded glass windows behind the sumptuous breakfast that was set out on a priceless buffet.

Feng was expansive and introduced Garth to Pearl and Li Li as if it were a normal celebratory occasion. Pearl was gracious and Li Li looked bored. Feng chastised Li Li for not being a good host. Li Li looked at her father and apologized.

"I am sorry, Father." She turned to Garth. "Please follow me and I will show you what Cook prepared for breakfast." Garth got up and followed Li Li.

"Much better, child. Our young guest will be with us for a while. I know you'll make sure he is taken care of."

"Yes, Father." Li Li served Garth some bacon and eggs off the sideboard, and then sat next to him, as she was told. Garth sneaked a glance at her. She looked okay, but he could feel the energy vibrating off her. He carelessly dropped a piece of toast to break the tension, then he made a fuss and bent to pick it up. "Oh! I'm sorry. Sometimes I'm really klutzy in the morning."

Feng waved him off. "Do not worry. The servants will deal with it." He signaled the server to pour him some orange juice, then probed Garth with a veneer of consideration. "Our little friend here is young, but he may be very gifted. A little like your mother, Pearl, only he doesn't read faces, he reads people and future events. Isn't that right?"

Garth deliberately finished chewing before he answered. "I don't know how it works. Sometimes I see things, but I can't make it happen." He politely turned to Pearl. "What's face reading?"

Feng put up his hand to stop him cold. "It doesn't matter. What matters is helping me in my business. And if I can help you harness your natural ability by allowing you to practice." He jabbed at Garth deliberately. "I'm sure your father taught you that practice makes perfect."

Garth was afraid to commit to anything, and knew he was being manipulated. He nodded in agreement. Feng shrugged off Garth's reluctance and gave a rare smile. "Soon I'll give you a chance to show me if you really can do what you say. I have a large number of personnel arriving shortly."

Pearl kept eating, with only a furtive glance at her daughter. Li Li watched Feng carefully. She knew he prized her above all else, but she also knew what he was capable of.

"You will be able to look at them and inform me who is healthy and who will become sick. Those who are not capable of work will be sent back."

Garth eyes widened, knowing in his heart what "sent back" meant.

"In the meantime, you can rest, relax and let your energy flow through you."

Garth gathered his courage. "Being near the water helps."

"Very well then. My wife and daughter will act as your companions. Li Li will show you around the compound. The air will be good for you."

Garth answered simply. "Thank you." But he knew it wasn't a genuine offer, that there was a catch. That was confirmed when Feng

Wah continued.

"You can breathe the sea air, walk around the compound and enjoy your freedom. As far as it extends."

Garth looked down at his plate, his shoulders slumped, trapped. After a silent, uncomfortable fifteen minutes had passed, Li Li took charge. "May we be excused, Father? I think we should start while the weather is still pleasant."

"Of course. I know you will be a thorough guide." She bowed her head to him and led Garth outside.

Pearl turned to her husband, aware that he trusted her face reading skills. She asked quietly. "You believe the boy is gifted?"

"Perhaps. He showed some promise, but it could be a ploy. Information he received from his father. That would be unfortunate."

"He has an expanded Third Eye. And an enlarged curve on his upper forehead in the Palace of Inheritance. He has clearly inherited some strong talents. It is possible."

Feng nodded. "I will watch and will know if he is truthful.

Pearl looked downward. The conversation was over.

· · · ·

Outside Garth followed Li Li, happy to be outdoors and imagine he was free. Having her with him was a bonus. They seemed to calm each other, even though they'd met only a few hours ago. He could see the water, but it seemed so far away. "How far away are we from the beach?"

Li Li shrugged, matter-of-fact. "It doesn't matter. You're on an island and there's nothing close to us." She brushed his hand, pointing surreptitiously: a camera was lodged in the branches of the tree they were under. She touched her lip as if to wipe something off of it, but he knew she was saying that whatever they said could be heard.

"I'll show you the rest of this trail." As they wound up a hill, she tripped slightly. Garth instinctively steadied her, and she squeezed his hand and looked down. Another camera.

She pulled away quickly. He nodded that he saw what she wanted him to see. A fence blocked any access further up the trail. There was barbed wire on top of it. Li Li murmured. "There's nowhere to go that my father won't see you." She turned to face him. "Let's take the long way to the beach. It's pretty."

They turned right into one of the guards, a tall, biracial man, Tighe. He refused to budge. "You're not allowed here, Missy."

Li Li glared at him. "And you're not allowed to tell me what to do or where to go. I go wherever I choose. Move, or I will report you to my father."

Tighe stood immobile.

"Now." Li Li looked at him as if he were lower than low, then shrugged. "I warned you. You deserve the price you will pay." She turned to go back the way they came. Garth held his breath. He'd never seen anyone her age confront an adult that way.

Tighe shrugged and stepped aside. "As you choose, Missy."

She grabbed Garth's hand and they moved quickly across the trail, zigzagging towards the beach. Garth waited until he was sure they were alone, then whispered to her. "I woulda been so scared to talk to him like that!"

"I have to talk to them that way. It's the only thing they understand." She looked sad, then Li Li smiled at him. "Besides, I'm scared all the time."

She turned away so he couldn't see the pain in her eyes. Garth whispered, "Can they hear us?"

Li Li shook her head. "Not in this spot."

Garth whispered again. "Why do you and your mom stay here?"

Li Li looked at him as if he were nuts. "How would we get away? Where would we go? He has eyes everywhere."

"My dad could protect you."

She got a funny smile on her face. "He can't. We tried. Look what happened. It's our fault you're here."

Garth was firm. "No. It was Feng Wah's fault."

She shrugged. "Perhaps. But it is what it is, as my mother says. We're as much prisoners as you are. And I have seen what he does to prisoners."

Garth looked at her with compassion. "You think he would hurt you?"

"I know he would. I was five when I saw him shoot someone who disobeyed him."

Garth gasped, as she continued matter-of-fact. "He didn't care that I saw. He knew I could do nothing." She shook off the memory. "We need to keep moving or they will notice. We'll go this way." She took his hand and moved down the trail, past two more cameras she pointed out quietly.

Garth whispered. "Can I say something?" Li Li shook her head no. He realized there were few safe places on the island, something that Feng Wah wanted him to understand. His hope diminished as he followed her inside the perimeter of the compound.

It took them an hour of zigzagging to reach the beach, and they had run into two more armed guards. Tighe had reported their progress and they were being watched. They stood clear of Li Li and she ignored them. Garth realized there were eyes everywhere. The guards they'd run into, and the ones they hadn't, who were watching too. The cameras and microphones.

Li Li stopped suddenly, putting her hand across his chest to make sure he didn't go further. He followed her gaze to a trip wire he'd almost run into. He looked terrified. "What is that?"

"A warning system. Alarm bells will go off everywhere. Pay attention where you're walking."

Garth nodded, intimidated. He jumped, startled, when he heard bells pealing in the distance. He recognized them as the bells from his dream the night before. He looked at Li Li, quizzical. "What are those?"

She shrugged carelessly but her face said otherwise. "There's a convent on the other side of the island. They're quiet neighbors. We have nothing to do with them."

Garth instinctively knew this wasn't true. "Why are they allowed to be here?"

"The Church had a 99-year-lease on the island with the last owners. Feng Wah thought it was wiser to let it run out in a few years than to fight. There are fewer nuns all the time."

Garth filed away the information. He knew somehow it would be important to him. He was startled when they came to a secluded clearing, surrounded by trees, and found a small picnic table and chairs. Pearl was bustling around the table, laying out a picnic. Li Li squeezed her mother's hand affectionately. "My mother wants us to have a nice time today."

Pearl smiled. "It's a beautiful clear day. It would be a shame not to enjoy the weather." She indicated he should sit on a polished bench. He slid in, next to Li Li, opposite Pearl.

"Tell me about your family, Garth." She saw tears well up in Garth's eyes. "Talking will help."

Garth nodded. "I live with my dad. He's a cop. My grandpa comes by to be with me sometimes, when Mrs. D. needs a break."

"Mrs. D.?"

"My sitter. She got sick and went to the hospital. But she'll be better soon. And then she'll come home."

Pearl smiled and said nothing about their mutual situation. Garth knew what she was doing but was so relieved to have a moment that felt like freedom, even though he knew it was a lie. Pearl was kind and gentle and Li Li let her take the lead. "Sandwich?"

Garth nodded. He had eaten very little at breakfast, and he realized he was famished. When they finished devouring their sandwiches, Pearl shooed them away. "Go finish your walk. I'll clean up."

Garth protested butLi Li took his arm. "It's okay. She likes to do it."

Pearl nodded. "I'm happy to tidy up. It gives me something real to do." She smiled at Li Li, and nodded. "Go ahead, Li Li."

Li Li took Garth's hand. "There's one more thing you must see."

They hiked down from the secluded picnic area, towards the water. Garth breathed in the air, grateful for the clean scent and crisp coolness. They came to a clearing, close to the dock, beyond the airstrip where Garth's plane had landed. Li Li watched Garth carefully as they neared several large wooden shacks. These kind of shacks had no running water or heat. There was camouflage on the roofs so they couldn't be spotted from the air.

Garth gasped when he saw them. Li Li kept her voice low. "This is where he keeps them before he sends them to their buyers. He said that next time there will be more than a hundred."

Garth's chest constricted and his eyes blurred. If he weren't only nine, he would have thought he was having a heart attack. A vision descended on him, a terrifying one, worse than he'd ever experienced before.

Li Li watched Garth carefully as he shut his eyes and his body stiffened. She didn't disturb him as he went further into himself, almost holding his breath.

*Garth saw the flames all around him. The heat became increasingly more intense with every breath. He could hear screams of people being burned and watched over a hundred people, Chinese workers, as they tried to escape. But there was no exit and he could only watch in horror as they died painfully. He started to shake with distress right before the images stopped.*

His eyes snapped open and his knees gave way. Li Li reached out and steadied him, kept her hands on him until the shaking stopped. Garth's eyes filled with tears. He spoke in a whisper. "That was the worst ever."

"I was afraid for you."

Garth tried to laugh but it came out almost a sob. "Me, too."

She prodded him gently: "What did you see?"

"It was my fault. People were dying in a fire. All Chinese people."

She was sharp with him. "Don't let Feng Wah do that to you! Whatever happens, it is his fault, not yours."

"I don't know what to do."

"Nothing. It's another bit of information. We will put it aside and the pieces will come together when we need them. That is how it works."

Garth was grateful for her comfort, but wasn't sure she was right. "How do you know so much?"

"I have to. It's how we survive." She reached out and squeezed his hand. "Have faith. We will find a way. But we need to remain strong."

Garth was grateful not to feel so alone. But scared, because he had no idea how he could remain strong or how he could prevent the events he'd just witnessed.

# CHAPTER THIRTY-TWO

JAKE HAD SPOKEN to every one of his snitches. Again. It took him five hours. They'd heard about Sasq, of course, as their drumbeats worked better than a viral tweet. Jake experienced various reactions, but the only constant was that no one knew anything more than Sasq had told him.

This was puzzling in itself. Jake realized that whoever had Garth, he was smarter and had more layers of insulation than they'd realized. He knew Anya had done the same thing with her CIs from the desk next to his. Soto reported they'd received no response yet from any international agency on the sketch Tony made. And they'd been unable to triangulate the point of origin of the ferry based on Ming's information. Jake hung up on the last call, ready to start over again, when he realized he hadn't looked at the file the Vancouver detective had sent him. He slapped himself internally for being so off his game, but he realized he wasn't himself.

He heard Anya's voice talking to her snitches, listening with half his attention, and it soothed him as he started reading the reports on the missing and dead prostitutes. His interest grew as he read through and he started to get excited. Anya noticed his intensity as he turned the pages faster. "Something?"

"Could be. According to the report, the pimp who was convicted originally told the detectives that the girls were part of a group 'imported from China'. He wouldn't give details, but from their investigation it feels like it could be related to our case. Traveled by boat. And for all we know, they culled the young attractive girls out of our group first and are operating with them here as well."

Anya agreed. "We could be asking our snitches the wrong questions."

"Yeah."

"You want to talk face to face with the cop in Vancouver, right?"

"I do."

"And the pimp."

"Yep."

She looked at her watch. "Driving's the best option. We can do it in two and a half hours."

"I like your style. Most people take three hours."

"Don't tell anyone I said so, but that's why we have a bubble."

Jake actually smiled. "Except that Max and I have an appointment and it's too late to do both this afternoon."

"Tomorrow, then. I'll start again on my CIs from this perspective."

Thackery approached Jake and Anya. "Pelham and all the other guys have trolled their resources. Only thing they got was vague rumors of a big-time operation. That was obvious before we started. But no one has pinpointed the organization or where it's from."

"I figured you'd have let me know if you had any solid info."

Thackery hesitated, then reluctantly pushed ahead. "We're gonna bring in the Feds to run this, Jake. We'll wait another twenty-four hours to see what we can do, but the last thing you want is the trail to go cold. Everyone's doing the most they can."

Jake was shaken. "I understand, Cap. If I weren't personally involved, I'd be doing the same thing. I'm hoping it won't be necessary."

"You got something?"

"Strong hunch there's a case in Vancouver from two years ago that's connected to the Snakeheads. Not directly to Garth. To the illegals."

Thackery was cautious. "And."

Jake pointed to the file. "I've been reading the case file and it's worth a trip to Vancouver to talk to the detective and the perp."

"Anya?"

"Absolutely agree. It's the closest thing to a lead we have."

Thackery appeared relieved. "Okay. Go meet with him, then."

They were interrupted when Max Woo sauntered in. "Ready?"

"Ready."

Thackery voice was stern. "What're you ready for now?"

"I think the Old Woman knows more than she's saying. Now that the detainees are more comfortable, and we have Ling's information, I want to talk to her again. There's nothing to lose."

"Makes sense. Take a shrink to talk to someone who hasn't said a word to anyone about anything. Go with God."

Anya ushered them out. "I'll stay and start to contact my guys again. I have plenty to take care of here and we don't want her to feel like we're ganging up on her."

Jake nodded and left quickly with Max. They had work to do. The clock was ticking and time wasn't on their side.

# CHAPTER THIRTY-THREE

THE WINDSHIELD WIPERS barely kept up with the drops as the rain
pelted Max's Jag. The rhythm of it was almost comforting to Jake,
slouched in the passenger seat, eyes half-closed. He trusted Max to find
the way to the Center on Bremerton where some of the illegals were still
being held. Jake sighed deeply as he fought going to sleep.

"Let it go, Jakey. I'm driving and it's okay." Max's calm voice soothed
Jake and he allowed himself twenty minutes of relaxation. He jumped,
startled, when Max parked his car and turned off the engine in front
of the detention center. He looked around, on alert. "It's all good. Your
body needed to replenish. Every twenty minutes adds up. You might
want to remember that."

Jake shook off his exhaustion and followed Max inside. As a consultant shrink to Seattle PD, Max had connections everywhere. He'd had
been able to sidestep the Federal restrictions covering the detainees.
Jake knew enough to keep his mouth shut as a guard led them to a
locked room and opened the door.

The Old Woman sat in a chair, spine erect, looking out her rain-
fogged window to the green lawn in the distance. She appeared almost
content when she glanced at Jake and Max, then turned back to her

window vigil. Jake knew she recognized him.

Jake told him what to say and Max translated, speaking in soothing Cantonese. He emphasized the urgency of the information he hoped she could give them. His young son's life was at stake. She finally looked up into Jake's eyes as Max continued to translate. Max questioned her about the starting point of their long journey, asking if she knew how long they were at sea and what it was like on the freighter, where they landed, and how long they spent on the smaller boat.

The Old Woman listened intently, then nodded once. It was clear she had made her decision. She looked out the window again, staring into the distance. When she began to talk, her memory was clear and cogent. She knew precisely how long it took on the freighter from the Zhejiang coast in China to their first destination. The crew complained that they had to slow down the knots because they were off the main lanes and had run into rough seas. "Not really as bad for them as for us," she told them drily.

It was fourteen days to the first stop, a small island. They stayed there only half a day before they were loaded onto a smaller boat. She thought they sailed slowly at night to avoid being seen, and that took another day. That poor girl had her baby with her, and if they had gone faster, maybe he would have survived. She wished she could tell them more, but she was never allowed onto the deck except when they changed vessels and when they landed.

Jake looked at her with appreciation. "What is your name?" He watched the indecision on her face as she decided to trust him. She smiled. "Chu Wen."

Jake smiled back at her. "Thank you for helping my son, Chu Wen. I am obligated to you."

Max began to translate, but Chu Wen put up her hand to stop him, and said haltingly in English. "You welcome. Ugly people. They killed poor Yao Gen. All he wanted was to be happy. Him and little Xian. Too much death."

Jake nodded to Max to translate again. "I will do my best to see that you get immunity and sanctuary."

Max objected. "You can't promise her that."

"It's not a promise. It's a hope." Max sighed, then told her. Her eyes filled with tears. She turned away so they wouldn't see, then: "Thank you. I wish to stay in your country." She hesitated, then added: "My daughter Jia is here with my grandchild. She has papers. I wanted to see them."

Jake patted her shoulder. "We'll do our best." They started to leave when Chu Wen called them back. She looked at Max shyly, and explained she left one thing out. She was an artist, and she saw the man in charge when they docked on the small island. "He was cruel. Would that help?"

Jake was stunned, as Max translated for him. "It could help a lot. I would be very grateful."

She agreed, through Max, to create a picture of him, but she needed pen, ink and paper. Max promised she would have what she needed as soon as possible. When she was finished, someone from his office would pick up the drawing. Chu Wen nodded and thanked them for the supplies. "I am pleased if I help."

Max and Jake were silent until they got back to Max's car. Jake called Soto and gave him the information about the immigrants' timetable at sea. He didn't tell him a picture might be coming. Soto said he thought it could help them to know how far the last stop was before the illegals landed in Seattle. Jake told him the source indicated it was about two days. But they went very slowly to avoid being seen, so it was hard to estimate.

"Okay, Jake. I'll get back to you ASAP."

"I know you're not supposed to share information with me on Garth's case, no matter what they told me."

"And that sucks. But we're not. What do the lawyers call it? The Chinese wall? Appropriate. I told you, you're one of us and we'll keep you in the loop as much as possible." Jake appreciated his support and told him so.

Max took off back to Seattle. "Now you promised you'd take some-thing to help you sleep."

"I promised. And I will. Happy now?"

Max pulled onto the street. "No. But it will do in a pinch. I won't be happy until Garth is home safe."

# CHAPTER THIRTY-FOUR

MAX'S PILL KNOCKED out Jake for two hours. It was dusk when he wakened groggy, but a scalding shower and double espresso got him going. Tony had left him a note that after seeing Kate Dooley he'd be with his buddies, strategizing, and didn't expect to see him tonight. Jake had no idea what strategizing meant, but decided not to give it another thought. He answered the phone on the first ring. It was Soto. "I wish I had more for you."

Jake tried to swallow his disappointment. "Nothing?"

"My gut. We're 75% sure that the illegals docked on one of the San Juan Islands."

"But you have no idea which one."

"That is correct. But what we do think is that it would be remote. Which means that there are at least a hundred of the islands that can be discounted."

"And at least fifty or more left."

"Yeah. The farthest out or the smallest or the ones that are uninhabited to our knowledge... or... or. Sorry I don't really have shit, big guy."

"It sounded like a real longshot." Jake slumped in the chair.

Soto had delivered the bad news, and now tried to buoy Jake's spirits. "It's a start, Jake. We contacted the Coast Guard and the San Juan County Sheriff's office. You know they have jurisdiction over the islands. Lucky for us, the Sheriffs are run by Frank Ortiz. He used to be a Loo here. Frank put out an immediate alert. He's on our side."

"I appreciate that, Soto. But with the terrain, and nobody to search, it could take longer than we have."

"Go ahead and give him a call anyway, Jake. I texted you his number. He won't burn you. None of us will."

"Thanks. For everything." As soon as he hung up, Jake found Soto's text with Ortiz's number and called him. Ortiz picked up right away. He was a pro, telling no lies and making no promises.

"I've put out a county-wide alert. Tell me what else you want me to do."

Jake immediately suggested a flyover.

"Considered and discarded. The fog is so thick out here, it would be useless and dangerous. Anyway, the best way to search the islands is by chopper. Seaplane doesn't give you enough visibility. The concern is that too much air activity could easily spook the douchebags. Then they'd move your son and you'd have less than you have now."

Jake appreciated his candor and professionalism. "It's your backyard. What do you suggest?"

"I have someone monitoring all radio traffic and my techs are tracking IPs to see if there's any unusual chatter. Your techs gave us the computer information on the informant and we're gonna try to trace them, too. After the fog lifts, I'll do some high fly-bys with radar."

"It sounds like you've got it covered."

"It's never enough, and you know that. Too many islands, too few people, and too easy to hide. If you have any juice with the Feds, ask them to redirect a satellite. I don't know if they will or not, or if it will show anything, but it's worth a shot."

"Thanks, Sheriff. Can you keep me informed if you grab anything unusual?"

"Will do. Absolutely. We're all with you on this."

"I know. It's much appreciated." Jake hung up quickly. He felt his chest tighten, a rising panic, and utter helplessness. He could always manage, always do something, but right now he was afraid. And the fear became overwhelming, as if he couldn't move his body or breathe. He'd only experienced something like this twice before – when his mom was in her hospital bed and there was nothing he could do to save her; and when Peggy left, abandoning him and Garth, and he had to face a future of being alone, totally responsible for his kid. The same sense of failure permeated his being now. What if he couldn't save his son, a child who was depending on him?

He shook his head as if to clear that horrible image and make the terror disappear. He had to put it away, someplace deep, or he would fall apart, and then neither of them would be okay. Jake was jarred out of his misery when the phone rang again. It was Kirk Pelham. "We might have something. Might being the operative word."

"Tell me."

"A couple of tips came in from reliable CIs. Not mine, but two different detectives from the West Precinct."

"Good enough for me."

"They reported a possible sighting of Garth in an old warehouse near the waterfront, on Marion Street. Late on the night he was taken. It's been closed because of the new bridge project."

"I'll meet you there."

"You can meet us, Jake, but you're non-operational. Deal?"

"Deal." Pelham gave him the address, and Jake was out of the house quickly. He waved at the detail stationed in front to stay there.

Traffic was worse near the harbor than he expected, but he still made it right after Pelham's crew arrived. Three detectives, including Pelham, and four uniforms. Pelham nodded to the two detectives from the West Precinct, shook their hands, and introduced Jake. "Assessment."

Jake didn't know either of them. The younger one with a bushy moustache, Matt Schimmel, let his older, more experienced partner, Art Eisen, do the talking. "It looks deserted. The electrical's off at the main breaker. We've heard no sounds coming from inside, and a quick look around shows no cars or foot traffic in or out."

Schimmel chimed in. "I've been in this building since it closed operations. There was nothing left inside except some old scrap machinery and some broken furniture."

Jake asked. "Are there any operational security cameras?"

Pelham shook his head no. "We've gotten an under-the-door tactical camera set up to go. As soon as it does a sweep, we'll head in. I don't want to bust into the unknown. It could be booby-trapped for anyone entering. Or exiting." He signaled to one of the uniforms in front to operate the camera. It took twenty minutes to determine there was no one waiting inside to set off a trap. No trip wires, no armed men visible.

Jake tried to contain his anxiety, but he was ready to bust down the door. "Kirk, I know you said non-operational, but it's my kid we're looking for. Let me go in first. If anything's gonna go sideways, it'll go sideways on me."

"Not a chance. We go by the book." Pelham radioed to two uniforms who were already positioned in the back of the barren site that the team was about to go in, and indicated to the two in front to get ready to use the Halligan bar.

"If Garth is there, he could be locked in something. A crate, a room…"

"…I understand. We're not going in shooting. Follow behind us."

Jake's phone buzzed. He saw it was Anya and turned it off. Not the right time.

Pelham waited two minutes, until Schimmel and Eisen were in position in the rear. He clicked his com twice, and the two uniforms in front pushed through and breached the front door. Pelham and Jake went in right behind them. They crouched down near the door inside the huge, empty, dark room. The concrete floors echoed their footsteps inside the massive warehouse, as their Nightfighter flashlights illuminated the area quickly.

Jake knew instantly there was no one there. No one alive, anyway. They did a complete tour of the facility and confirmed that it was empty. Jake thought he should be relieved, but he wasn't. Especially when something caught his eye as the light flickered over a tangle of trashed office chairs. He moved towards them, and Pelham noticed. "See something?"

"Don't know yet." Jake hurried to the stacked chairs in a corner. There, in the middle of one of them, was Garth's Mariners' sweatshirt, folded neatly, like Garth always did. Jake felt his heart stop and he held his breath. He put gloves on and carefully lifted the shirt from its resting place. Jake was certain it was Garth's. He reached inside the pocket with his gloved hand and felt Garth's lucky coins.

Jake looked at Pelham, weary. "He was here."

"You sure?"

"Yes. It's his jacket. I can feel the lucky coins Tony gave him."

"I'm sorry, Jake."

"Yeah. Me, too. But at least he was okay enough to send me a message."

Pelham hesitated. "How do you know he did that?"

"Because he always folds his shirt exactly the same way. And he kept the coins in his right pocket."

Jake handed Pelham Garth's sweatshirt. He knew they'd want to process it. "Thank the guys for me."

"Will do."

Jake turned and walked away, elated and defeated. As soon as he got home, Jake headed straight to the liquor, and pulled out a bottle of tequila. He took a slug. And then a second one. Then he closed his eyes, depleted. The phone rang and he made no move to answer it. The answering machine picked up and he could hear the concern in Anya's voice as she berated him for not contacting her, and for not answering her seven messages. He took another slug of tequila and then became alert when he heard a car stop in front of the house. The door slammed and he knew who was walking up to the front door. He would recognize Anya's stride anywhere. She used her key to enter, slammed the door. "Why didn't you notify me?"

"No time. We found... nothing, really. Except Garth's Mariners sweatshirt."

"He left it for you to find?"

"Yes. He folded it the way Tony taught him. And his coins were in the right pocket. He left me a message."

"So you know he was okay there."

"Yes."

"I would've been there."

"I know."

"You are a complete asshole."

"Yep. No question about it." He wasn't quite slurring his words, but on the edge. What he really wanted to do was dive into oblivion but even he couldn't allow himself the luxury of such irresponsibility. "And I am powerless."

"You are powerless because you want to be Superman and you're not. You're only a man. A terrified father. Admit it, accept it, and move on."

Jake slumped into the chair. "I'm not as strong as I thought. And certainly not as strong as you."

"I'm strong because I *know* Garth is still okay. But if we let the fear take over, we're doomed. And so is he."

Jake looked at Anya, his face as vulnerable as his own child's. "Tell me what I can do, Annie. I don't remember being this scared since I was a kid and Tony was missing. It's like the same thing all over again and I can't change it."

They were both shocked when Jake's eyes filled with tears. He couldn't stop them from flowing down his cheeks. Anya knelt beside him and gently wiped his face. He buried himself in her arms and wept.

# CHAPTER THIRTY-FIVE

KATE DOOLEY CAREFULLY shifted her position without dislodging any of the equipment she was attached to. She sighed, gave up, adjusting herself as best she could to ease the pressure on her back. It helped, and she was grateful for every moment without discomfort. She wasn't an optimist, hardly, but she could take happiness wherever she found it. A gift of some kind, for sure.

Her son, Matthew, had arrived from yesterday, bursting to take his ma "home". She understood his need to have her near, but Ennis, County Clare, hadn't been her home for many years. They'd lived so close to Shannon International Airport her whole life, but she'd never been outside the UK. She'd worked as a physical therapist since her twenties, and after her husband died, she was happy to find a job with a very wealthy man, Fred Harrigan. Harrigan was a tech genius who traveled the world, but he suffered from painful sciatica and needed constant help. She deliberately chose to leave behind everything she'd known and see the world. Harrigan paid her to travel with him all over the United States for two years, until he settled in Seattle for his business.

She loved being here. The weather reminded her of Ennis, but this city was so much bigger and more exciting in every way. When her client improved, she realized she wanted to stay. Harrigan helped her get a green card, and she never looked back, especially once she met Garth. She knew then she'd see her own family only for visits. Her children had their own lives and that's as it should be. No matter how hard they pushed, she knew she'd win. It was hard to move a firmly planted tree.

And she hadn't, of course, counted on meeting Tony, not at this stage of her life. That was a bonus. A definite, unexpected surprise that no one knew about except the two of them. Or so she thought, and she knew he felt the same way.

Down the corridor, Tony was hesitating, then shook off his trepidation and moved towards Kate's room. He had postponed this visit all day, hoping he'd have better news, any news, but he still had nothing and he'd stalled as long as he could. Tony had run into a handsome young man in the hospital corridor; Matthew Dooley had his mother's kind eyes, but his face was haggard with jet lag and deep concern. Yet he agreed with Tony.

"You go ahead and tell her, Tony. Ma doesn't let an obstacle get in her way. Never has. With her faith, she'll be fine."

"It won't hurt to have her light a candle for us, Matthew."

Matthew briefly smiled. "More than that, if you don't tell her, we'll all be in hellfire and brimstone for the rest of our lives."

"Go on and get some food, son. I'll wait with her until you're back."

"Thank you. I have to call home with an update, too." He moved down the corridor, exhausted. Determined.

Tony hesitated, took a deep breath, then pushed open the door. He saw the tubes were down to half, her color was back and she looked on the road to well.

Mrs. D. lit up when she saw Tony, but she couldn't miss his battered face and his anxiety. She lit into him, anyway. "Where have you been, old man? Did you see my Matthew? He looks like hell and needs some food and rest. Somebody's got to look out for him."

"Kate, he's a grown man. And he looks like crap because he was worried about you. Like we all were. But you're looking fine, now. Better than fine." He strained trying to keep his tone light, figuring out how to break it to her about Garth.

"Well, you don't look so hot, that's for sure. You look like you were run over by a Mack truck. And I expected you this morning, so what's wrong, then?"

Tony was calm, which helped her stay calm. "It will be all right, I promise."

She went pale. "Garth."

"Yes. He was kidnapped in retaliation against Jake. But we're certain he's okay."

Mrs. D seemed to fade into the bed. "How can you be certain?"

"Because it's a warning. And they know that every cop and Fed would be in a massive manhunt against them."

"They should be anyway."

"They are, Kate. Everyone is on it. I swear."

"Don't swear. Promise." She closed her eyes and took a deep breath. Tony stood helpless, worried about her.

"Should I go find your doctor?"

She opened her eyes, firm. "No, you idiot. Go find Garth. Don't waste another minute here."

Tony leaned in and kissed her cheek. "Will do, Katie. Will do."

# CHAPTER THIRTY-SIX

THERE WAS A chill in Jake's room. It was dark, and plain, about as individual as a Motel 6. A bed, a dresser, lamp, bedside table. No pictures or mementos or trophies.

Anya thought he was asleep as she pulled a quilt over him. It was the one personal touch and Anya was surprised he still used it. The one his mom had finished for him during her final illness, when she was trying to keep busy. Anya turned to go as his hand reached out and circled her wrist. His eyes opened. He looked spent and vulnerable. "I'm sorry."

"You have nothing to apologize for, Jake. I keep telling you that. You're human. I hope you just proved it to yourself."

"I've always known that, Annie. No escaping it. Foibles, failures and all."

"You left successes out of that equation. And so much more."

He gently pulled her a little closer and she sat down on the bed next to him. He turned on his elbow to face her. "Thank you. You don't know how much I appreciate you."

Jake was still a little drunk. She teased him. "I'm glad you finally figured that out." Her voice got softer and more serious. "And I'm glad you let yourself feel the stress you're under. Now you can move ahead and function. And we can get up in a few hours and start again."

He looked at her, hesitated, then plunged ahead. "Will you stay?"

"Sure. Go to sleep. I'll be downstairs if you need anything."

He took her hand. "I didn't mean downstairs." The words, now said aloud, hung in the air.

"I can't. You know I can't."

He pushed her. "Annie. You can. You have."

"Stop, Jake. You know what happened. We made love. A lot. It was incredible." She looked at him, unflinching. "And then... then it all turned to shit." Neither of them had forgotten. It had been this unspoken chasm between them for over a year.

The memories flooded Anya. It was a year and two months ago, very early morning, the first big rain of the Fall. They were in bed together at her place, the embers glowing in the fireplace. Jake was spooning her, his arms surrounding her, kissing her neck, her ear, and she shuddered with pleasure at his touch, knowing they were going to make love again. And again. She was wet in anticipation, kissing him passionately, when they heard gun shots that sounded very near. They jumped up immediately.

"Where?"

Anya was pulling on her clothes. "Close. Down the block maybe."

They were dressed and armed in two minutes, rushing out of her Craftsman on Warren Avenue after calling for backup. The street she lived on in the Queen Anne District was filled with lovingly restored older homes. One of her next door neighbors, Bill Davis, was outside his house with Milly, his mini-dachshund, both terrified.

"Did you hear that, Anya?!"

"Yes. Where'd it come from, Bill?"

"I think it was the Burtofts."

Anya nodded at the house for Jake.

"Milly and I just walked by there." He was trembling. "There was a big SUV in front I didn't recognize."

"Go inside your house and stay there. The cops are on their way. We'll deal with it."

Jake was already moving fast down the street, his gun drawn. Lights were being turned on inside houses, but nobody else came out. Anya followed Jake, catching up quickly. "The yellow Victorian on the left. I'll take the back. I don't know if we can wait."

They could hear sirens in the distance, but it could be minutes before backup arrived, and they didn't know if they had minutes. When they heard a piercing scream from inside the house, they split up. The Victorian had no outside lights on. They approached cautiously, Jake moving in the front, using hedges and roses as cover. As he maneuvered next to the wall on the porch, he saw the front door was open. He inched his way towards it, when someone in a ski mask dashed out. Jake instinctively tackled him, turned him over and cuffed him deftly. "How many in there?"

The guy shook his head, opening his mouth to scream. "Make a sound and I promise you'll never make it to the jail." Jake tightened the cuffs so they hurt.

"Ow! One. One guy." Jake heard the sirens getting closer as he dragged the perp into the bushes. "Keep your mouth shut, asshole. Or else."

Jake moved towards the back when he saw Anya come around the side of the house. She wasn't alone. Another masked burglar had her in a chokehold with one hand and the other held a gun to her head. She tried to slow down his progress but he tightened his chokehold, as Jake's gun aimed at the perp's head.

"She's dead meat unless you get my partner into the car and outta our way."

"Can't do that."

"Get rid of the gun, motherfucker, or I'll kill this bitch. No bullshit."

Anya called out as best she could. "Shoot him in the head, Jake."

"Yeah, Jake. Shoot." He laughed.

"Take the shot!" Anya was furious at Jake and at herself for letting the bastard get the jump on her. She watched Jake look for a way out.

"Okay, guy. I'm putting the gun down."

Anya was horrified when she saw Jake begin to lower his gun, even though she was certain he had a back-up. She waited until she could feel the perp instinctively release his arm around her neck and start to lower his gun hand to aim at Jake. She stomped her heel on his foot, chopped his gun arm down and elbowed him in the gut with her other arm. All of this took two seconds. She knew for certain that Jake would have raised his arm and taken aim at the robber as she took him down to the ground. Anya grabbed his gun, cuffed him, then kicked the guy hard, in his midsection. "Asshole."

"Fuck you, bitch." He groaned as she kicked him again, harder, but Jake pulled her back.

"Enough."

Anya turned on Jake, livid, her eyes blazing. "I told you to shoot, goddamnit!"

He stepped back from her fury. "I didn't have a shot."

Anya didn't hesitate, slapped Jake across his face, hard. "You had a shot. You were protecting me. And you know why. I don't need protection. I need back-up, partner. And it's never going to happen again." She walked away from him as the patrol cars screeched up to the house. He tried to follow her, but she waved him away. "I'm checking on my neighbors. You book 'em."

She could feel Jake's eyes on her back, knowing he'd fucked up everything. Her neighbors recovered from the trauma, but she and Jake never did.

Anya shivered and shook off the unwanted memory. She seemed to be having a lot of those since Garth was taken. She looked at Jake, knowing he knew exactly where she'd gone in her head. "Annie. That was then. Stay. Please." She didn't move away. Jake whispered. "Hold me."

She was torn, but then he said the words she knew were the most difficult for him to ever admit.

"I need you."

She didn't trust herself to speak. She understood he was spiraling into his own personal hell, and she couldn't let that happen. She also knew she was giving herself an excuse, because she wanted him, desperately. She always wanted him but never allowed herself to be with him. She nodded and lay down next to him, whispering: "I'll stay. Turn over. Go to sleep."

He turned away from her as she spooned him, her arms surrounding him. He sighed deeply and closed his eyes. She lay behind him, finally letting herself feel him in her arms. Her breath was soft on his neck as she couldn't help but nuzzle him. His scent drove her wild, no cologne there, only a clean masculine aura that made her crazy every time she got close to him. It made her want to rub against him, but she held back. Her arm circled his chest and he took her hand and lifted it to his mouth, kissing her fingers gently, moving to her palm.

She couldn't help herself, and rubbed her cheek against his neck, then her soft lips touched his skin. She stayed curled around him, as she began to nibble on his ear. She moved her hands, stroking his muscular, strong chest. She always thought it was perfect, exactly enough hair to know he was a man.

"I..."

"Shhh, Jake. No talking." Her fingers stroked his skin, which was like the finest satin, so sensuous to the touch as her hands caressed him slowly. She couldn't believe how such a man could have skin that excited her senses so much she felt like she was falling into an abyss.

Jake groaned as she touched him, then she carefully unzipped his jeans. She pulled them down his body slowly, teasing him, torturing him. "Turn over."

Jake turned on his back to face her, as she straddled him. Their eyes burned into each other as she whispered. "Hold on, baby. You have no idea what I'm going to do to you."

He let out a small groan as her lips moved up and down the insides of his strong legs. His body was as beautiful as she remembered, as she dreamed about. She never stopped feeling him, as her kisses moved up his thighs towards his groin. Anya teased him, avoiding the one thing he was desperate for her to touch. "Soon enough, baby."

Her fingers and her mouth explored his body, caressed it, kissed it. He was growing bigger and harder, ready to pounce as soon as she let him out of his glorious purgatory.

She finally began to fondle him where he wanted, needed it the most. She put her beautiful mouth over him, teasing with her tongue. He groaned as she moved all around, pulling, licking, her fingers dancing on him.

Anya pulled away only long enough to strip her jeans off. She stood in front of him, beautiful, knowing he was longing for her, showing him everything he wanted to see and touch every day of his life.

She pulled her top over her head, then shook out her hair, a sight that made Jake gasp. He reached up to run his hands through her hair and pull her down on top of him. She pulled away slightly and he held his breath as Anya unsnapped her bra and dropped it to the floor. She smiled at him, knowing what she was doing to him. Of course he'd seen her naked before, and she felt him watching her all the time, knowing that he imagined her that way almost every time he'd looked at her. She flaunted her upturned breasts, deliberately making him writhe.

She moved her hands over her own body, so he could watch her touching what he couldn't have. She stroked herself, slowly and lovingly, circling her nipples gently. Even half drunk, Jake moved to lunge across the bed and pull her down. And then she slipped off her thong, some kind of silk that had wrapped her perfect bottom in blue lace, straining to caress her narrow hips. She stood in front of him, stroking herself. "I'm wet." She was torturing him.

"Let me..."

"Not yet." She finally lay down on top of him, rubbing against him, slowly, gently holding his arms above his head. He could've broken free anytime and rolled her over and entered her and she understood he desperately wanted to, but she pulled him to her, sliding up and down his body until he groaned again.

She rolled him on top of her, reaching between his legs, holding him where it mattered, moving her hand up and down until she was certain he couldn't bear not being inside of her. He stroked between her legs, using his fingers to gently open her even more before he plunged inside of her.

The power had shifted. He had her under him, his thumb rubbing her almost unbearably slowly, to the point of hysteria.

Finally, finally, in a moment so intense and poignant because they didn't know how they got there and they didn't know if they would ever get there again, they couldn't get enough of each other, moving in perfect unison. Not a movie, but a dream, a ballet where everything fit.

The rolling waves hit them at the same time, with an overwhelming intensity they couldn't control and thought they'd never feel again.

Until the next time. And the next. Two hours later, they were spent. And rested. And grateful. They slept.

When Jake woke up at five, Anya was gone. She'd slipped away a few minutes ago, but there was a note next to him.

*It broke my heart to leave you last time. Partners or lovers. You have to choose. I can't do it again."*

Jake was more than sober now, and the emptiness in the house overwhelmed him. He would have broken down and wept again if he thought it would make him feel better, but instead he threw on his sweats, and slipped out through the back door. The only thing he knew to do was to outrun the misery and get ready to start again.

# CHAPTER THIRTY-SEVEN

GARTH AWAKENED WITH a start and sat up instantly. He'd fallen asleep so quickly he wondered if someone had done something to his food to put him out.

The big house was quiet, except for the low hum of the generators outside. He didn't know what had brought him out of such a deep, dreamless sleep. That he didn't dream was unusual, too. He rubbed his eyes and found they were wet. He must've been crying in his sleep.

He reached over to the glass of water next to the bed when he started to shake. This was going to be bad, he knew. And it was what woke him up out of a sleep that was supposed to go on much longer.

*Fists flying, hurting, kicking to the ribs.*

Garth grabbed his own ribs, his breath coming with difficulty, feeling the pain he was seeing inflicted on someone else.

*Hitting back, hard but not hard enough to get him to stop. Screaming. A woman. Oh, no, no, no. Anya. Anya's hurt. Anya is lying on the ground, gone. Gone. Gone. Victor smiling.*

Garth snapped out of his vision because someone was screaming, wretched, wailing screams. He realized it was his own voice, coming from a dark, ugly place. He couldn't move, frozen in his wails, even though he heard running down the corridor, and the door unlocked and flung open.

"Stop it, little boy!" It was Feng Wah, and he was incensed. Garth couldn't stop sobbing, even though he saw Li Li and one of the security guards hovering in the hall.

"I said stop!" He raised his hand as if to slap Garth.

Garth tried to get his breath, and tried to remember how to do that. He reminded himself to inhale slowly and then exhale. He did it for about thirty seconds, until his heart had stopped pounding out of his chest and his sobs had muted into a whimper.

"What was that all about?"

Garth could barely get it out. "Anya. My godmother."

Feng was now impatient. "A nightmare? That's why you scream this house down and waken me out of my sleep?"

Garth shook his head. "It wasn't a nightmare. It was real. I saw it. He hurt her. The Bad Man hurt her."

Feng became more curious than angry. "Explain."

"She was on the ground. I don't know if she's dead." He glared at Feng Wah. "He hurt her."

"Victor." Garth nodded. "We'll see about this, then. Now go to sleep. No more racket."

Garth stared at him. "I have to go home. I have to be with her."

"If what you say is true, there is no reason to be there. She'll be dead. If it isn't true, you'll have to deal with me here."

Feng Wah left and Garth heard the door lock clicking behind him. The sense of menace he felt was pervasive and all he could do was shudder and pray.

# CHAPTER THIRTY-EIGHT

*Second Day After*

THE DAWN WAS covered by heavy overcast as Anya drove way too fast, distracted, confused and pissed at herself. She'd left Jake to make a decision she didn't have the guts to make, and she didn't know how to handle her reaction. She had peeled away from the front of the house as if demons were chasing her. She didn't acknowledge the patrol cops outside, but more important, she missed seeing the dark SUV parked across the street and down the block, which was now following her at a smart distance.

Luckily for her there was no traffic when she plowed through a red light on Roosevelt. She was shaken, realizing she was in no condition to drive, so she pulled over. That forced the car following her to drive by, pull ahead and wait in the shadows the next block over, near 10th Avenue.

Victor figured he'd gotten lucky. When he parked near the cop's house for surveillance, he didn't expect he'd get a twofer. Of course he should have realized the two were banging – who wouldn't hit that piece of ass? He knew he could outwait her and continue the tail. She needed to be punished. She'd caused him to off one of his better men. This'd be payback, and the Frog, which is what he privately called Feng Wah, had told him to handle her in whatever way he thought best.

Anya was shaken by her own irresponsibility, on every level. She sat in the car and deep breathed. She chanted, under her breath, as she focused. Once her heart stopped racing, she reached for a cigarette. She knew it was stupid, but then so many of her choices last night were wrong, what the hell difference did another one make? She finished two cigarettes in quick succession, numbing herself in the process. Finally composed enough to drive with some competence, she pulled out into the light traffic and headed home.

Still distracted, she didn't see Victor fall in behind her, staying two cars back. Anya reached for another smoke, annoyed that all she found was an empty crumpled pack. She was disgusted with herself. But that wasn't going to stop her from buying more.

. . . .

JAKE WAS RUNNING, faster and faster, down the street, through Prospect Park, completely sober now. Jake had known the only way he was going to get his head clear and his focus back — about everything — was to outrun his thoughts. It had always worked before, putting him into an altered state that kept his endless doubts and frustrations at bay.

Jake had almost reached the state of mindlessness he sought when a stabbing pain attacked his gut. It didn't feel like a knife or a punch. Jake recognized it from a time long past and more recently when Garth was taken. It was an overwhelming feeling of dread in the pit of his stomach. His heart raced and he could taste his own fear and he intuitively knew it was about Anya, not Garth. Without a moment's hesitation to second-guess himself, he grabbed his cell to call her.

. . . .

ANYA PULLED INTO the 7–11 on 50th near the I-5. She didn't hear her phone vibrate as she turned off the engine. She had tossed it in the glove box when she'd run out of Jake's. She slammed the car door as Victor pulled into the small lot and turned off his engine and lights. The place was empty except for the East Indian clerk behind the register. Taj was a smart young college student who frequently used this quiet time to study. He looked irritable as Anya put on the best smile she could and asked for her favorite, hard-to-find brand.

"Benson and Hedges Menthol, please. If you have it."

"Most people don't smoke Benson & Hedges Menthol anymore. I'll have to check in the back." It sounded almost like an accusation.

"Sorry to be a bother. I'll take anything similar. Really doesn't matter."

He smiled at her and sighed. "Sorry. Didn't mean to be rude. It's been a long shift and I have classes in a few hours." He closed his physics book. "It's okay. I'll check."

She looked down at his book. "U-Dub?"

"Nah. Community. If I ace this physics class, then U-Dub next year."

She smiled at him as he headed to the storeroom. When he was gone, her impatience reappeared and she mindlessly drummed her fingers against the counter. She stopped as soon as he came out, triumphant. "You're in luck." He looked pleased with himself. "Well, if you consider cigarettes lucky."

Anya laughed, amused, glanced at his nametag. "Thanks, Taj. I appreciate the extra effort. And if you need a tutor, one of my little brothers is a physics genius. Let me know if you're interested." She handed him her card.

Taj smiled broadly as he stared at her. "Wow. I didn't think cops were that pretty."

She laughed again, a momentary relief allowing her to breathe. She glanced up and flashed on the magnifying mirror near the door. Someone else was out really early this morning. Her cop sense immediately heightened as she saw a man strolling casually past the front door.

She immediately recognized Victor from Jeanie's rendering and her brief exposure to him. She realized three things instantly: she was being stalked, she had no phone, and she had no back-up. Anya casually slipped her gun out of her purse into her jacket pocket. Then she pretended to fumble for the right change as she leaned into Taj.

"Don't react, Taj. Keep smiling and nodding and do exactly as I say. Go into the back, lock the door behind you, and call 911. Tell them an officer needs back-up, that Detective Anya Pashkov has spotted a suspect in a kidnapping."

Taj froze and started to protest, but Anya stopped him. "Now, Taj. And don't come out of there until you hear the cops banging on your door, no matter what. Swear."

Taj attempted a smile for her. "Swear." He did as he was told and moved to the back as Anya headed towards the parking lot.

· · · ·

JAKE DROVE HIS Explorer towards Anya's house, racing with the portable bubble on top, siren blazing, down the route he assumed she'd take home. He was freaked out, knowing beyond any doubt that Anya was in great danger. His police revolver was on the seat next to him, as his cop's eyes scanned the streets.

Anya's hand never left her gun as she walked towards her car. She could smell the danger, the pheromones of the predator as he stalked her. She whirled a beat too late as Victor tackled her, slamming her to the ground. Her gun was still in her hand, but Victor dislodged it as he punched her. Anya twisted away, her fighting instincts taking over as she landed a kick to his knee. She fought with every ounce of knowledge and strength she had, but Victor had four inches and fifty pounds on her.

She could hear the crunch of his nose breaking, but the pain only enraged him more. He dragged her towards the rear of the convenience store, her foot crossing in front of his, tripping him. He went down hard as she landed two more blows, gouging at his face, aiming for his eyes.

Victor pummeled her, slamming his fist into her midsection, as he whispered lies to her that he'd been watching her, waiting to teach her a lesson, like they taught the kid. Between breaths he taunted her that Garth was tortured, sold, killed. Victor heard sirens approaching in the distance. He wiped the blood off his nose.

Anya slipped into unconsciousness as Victor kicked her torso one last time. He headed back to his car and took off.

· · · ·

Jake spotted Anya's car in front of the 7–11 as Victor's car tore out of the parking lot. Jake noted the license plate automatically, especially as it was covered in mud and indecipherable.

He had to choose whether to follow the car or look for Anya. He knew, he *knew* that the car peeling out of the parking lot had something to do with Garth, and when he heard the two patrols blaring sirens turn into the lot, he made an instant decision to follow the speeding car.

Victor, more bloodied than he thought, saw Jake's truck following him, gaining on him. "Shit."

He pushed the pedal down and flew past Tashkent Park. He knew there was an on-ramp to the I-5 a few blocks away, and figured he could disappear if he made it onto the highway.

Jake suspected that's what the car ahead was doing. He pushed the accelerator as far as it could go, but his truck wasn't as fast as the small SUV. He knew a shortcut near Harrison and had to instantly decide whether to lose sight of the car in front of him. He couldn't call it in because reporting a speeding black SUV with dirty plates wouldn't help.

When the car made a sudden left onto Summit, Jake thought he'd be heading for Olive Way instead of the I-5. "Smart move." He gunned the truck, urging it to catch up with the sonovabitch in front of him.

Victor smiled, then groaned from the pain of it. He knew his nose was broken. "Bitch." But he'd fooled the asshole cop behind him. As soon as he got close to Olive, he veered off and headed for the on-ramp to the highway.

When Jake got to the corner, he saw the SUV's tail lights in the distance. He'd lost him. "Goddamnit. Damn it. Fuck."

He put the truck in reverse and raced back to the 7–11, furious he couldn't catch the bastard, worried he'd made the wrong choice. When he drove into the parking lot, there were three patrol cars, red bubbles turning, along with a Harborview ambulance. The cops were searching the lot, guns drawn. Jake had the door open as soon as his truck stopped rolling. He saw a body on a gurney next to the ambulance, and a young Indian man watching the paramedics working on Anya. He ran over.

"Stay back, sir." The two paramedics, a young woman and an older man, stopped Jake. Jake showed his badge and edged closer, his worst fears coming true. Anya looked way too still, like a crumpled throwaway doll. He moved next to her.

"It'll be okay, baby. Focus on yourself. You'll be fine, I swear. I'll take care of everything, I promise."

The older paramedic moved Jake back. "What you'll do, sir, is get the fuck out of our way."

Jake grabbed the guy by his arm. "Tell me."

He hesitated, but the woman answered without looking up. "Touch and go. Get out of our way so we can make it go."

Jake could only watch as they loaded Anya into the ambulance and headed for Harborview Trauma Center. He ran to his car and followed, sirens blaring. There was no way he could let Anya go through this alone. And then he'd take care of the perp who did this to her. This was not going unanswered.

. . . .

ON THE OTHER side of Seattle, Victor had gotten off the freeway and made his way to the Port. He'd pulled onto a dark side street to check his injuries. He was bleeding and in pain, he knew for sure his nose was broken and he hoped he'd killed her. He'd been hurt worse, but never by a bitch.

His burner rang, and there was only one person it could be. The Frog. He thought seriously about not answering, but knew he'd have to talk to him sooner or later. "Yes."

Feng Wah was in his study, now fully dressed, steaming coffee in front of him. "Where are you, Victor?"

"Seattle. Keeping an eye on the cop." He wasn't going to give him any more information until he knew what the Boss wanted.

"Where is the female cop?"

*Jesus. How the fuck did he know? Was he being followed? Only one way to find out.* "How did you know?"

"Tell me."

"She spotted me outside the cop's house. You said I could do what I wanted with her, so I figured this was as good a time as any. She's out of the picture."

"Were you seen?"

"I was followed. I lost him, and I'm wiping and ditching the car. No biggie."

"Very much a biggie, Victor. We took a cop's child, and then you took out a cop. They'll be looking even harder now. Although that may be to our advantage... Take care to hide your tracks, then get back here. The long way."

Victor was very annoyed, but didn't let it show. "Okay." He hesitated, then asked again. "How did you know?"

"I didn't. The boy did. He had a vision. He's the real thing. And he will be an asset."

The phone clicked off. Victor sat there, figuring out his next move.

The little boy, always the little boy. He may have to arrange an accident for that little shit, despite what the Frog wanted. The kid was too dangerous to keep around.

# CHAPTER THIRTY-NINE

HARBORVIEW'S ER WAS like a ghost town this early. Jake paced alone in the family waiting room. All they'd tell him was that they didn't know anything yet. Jake had called both Anya's family and Tony, and they were on their way.

He talked to Captain Thackery, and shared the info that Taj, the 7–11 clerk, had given the cops at the scene. Taj immediately gave the detectives interviewing him access to the security tapes of the parking lot and store front. Victor had kept his face hidden at the front entrance, but missed the hidden camera on the lip of the roof. It was grainy but he was recognizable as the same guy in the sketch – the one who attacked Tony and took Garth. Taj repeated what he told the 911 operator, that the lady cop said the guy was involved in a kidnapping.

Taj told Jake that he felt terrible he didn't help her. She was so nice, even offered to have her brother tutor him in physics. But she insisted he'd get in her way and should do what she said. If he'd known this was going to happen he wouldn't have locked himself in the back.

Jake, although not calm himself, told the stricken kid he did exactly the right thing. Pros should handle pros, and if he'd been hurt Anya wouldn't have been doing her job. Taj thanked Jake, but his words didn't make him feel any better.

Jake's reverie was interrupted when Anya's family burst into the waiting room. Aleks led the way, Boris right behind him. Peter followed, his arm around his mother, who looked stricken. Aleks stopped short of pushing Jake into a corner. "How is she?"

"She's being treated now. They haven't come out with a report and they wouldn't let me stay with her."

Peter yelled at him. "Then you didn't try hard enough!"

Aleks glanced over at Peter, knowing he was heading to push through the locked ER door. He lifted his finger and Peter stopped. "What happened?"

Jake certainly wasn't about to tell Anya's father they'd slept together, then she'd left, but he didn't want to lie either. "She was worried about me because of Garth. She stayed until she was sure I was okay. The guy must've been watching the house and followed her. I know she inflicted damage on him."

Boris fumed. "Who?"

"We don't know yet, but we have his photo and we hope it won't take long to ID him."

Peter and Boris, as if one person, teamed up on Jake. "You didn't protect her!" Boris accused him. They wanted to throttle him and Jake understood their instinct. He refused to defend himself. The tension was broken by Natasha.

"Stop it. Now. Recriminations help no one, least of all Anya." They all turned to look at this quiet, fierce woman. "Use all of that anger and energy and find who did this. The doctors will take care of her."

The boys backed off and Aleks held himself in check as the door opened. They all held their breath as the surgeon came in, his attitude all business and his eyes filled with kindness. "Pashkov family?"

Aleks stood up, unable to speak the question he was terrified to ask.

"I'm Dr. Joel Cinader, your daughter's surgeon."

Natasha didn't hesitate. "I'm her mother. How is she?"

"She's alive, Mrs. Pashkov. But she was badly beaten. We pulled her back but her heart stopped twice on the table."

Jake put his hand on the wall as if that could keep him upright.

"She's tough and strong but I don't want to pretend it's okay. She's in a coma, which I know sounds awful, but in her case, it's a blessing. As always, the first twenty-four hours are the most dangerous. She has multiple broken bones, a collapsed lung, and a bruised spleen which we may still have to remove. But her condition is too precarious for any more surgery right now. That said, her hands are bruised and I'm willing to bet she inflicted a lot of damage on her attacker while defending herself. She saved her own life. She's obviously a fighter, and that's a good thing." He stopped abruptly, as if he couldn't bring himself to interact any longer.

Boris and Peter looked and felt deflated. Aleks was more stoic, as Natasha took a deep breath. "Thank you, Dr. Cinader. My daughter *is* a fighter and she will win this battle, too. I'd like to sit with her please." It wasn't a question.

"Talk to her, Mrs. Pashkov. I believe it helps."

"I will talk and I will pray, Doctor. That will help Anya and it will help me." Natasha turned to her sons. "You two stay out of this. I do not want one more child in the line of fire." She then faced her husband and Jake. "And you. Go find this man. Show him no mercy."

Jake watched as she followed the doctor inside to will her daughter to live.

Aleks sent the boys home – he was adamant he didn't want them involved in any of this. They protested vigorously, but, as usual, their father won. As soon as he was sure they were gone, he turned to Jake. "Natasha was right. We have no time for recriminations or sentimentality."

"Agreed. It will paralyze us. And it's been difficult enough."

"This is what *I* will do. My old friends in the computer business, call them what you will, they keep in touch, and they are scattered everywhere. They scour the Web, the one you see and the one you don't, and they know more about what's happening in the world than most.

I will go to them for help to find Garth, and thus the people who did this to Anya."

Jake was puzzled. "I thought you were a tech guy, not someone who has black hat contacts."

"No man is only one thing, Jake."

Jake looked at Aleks with new respect. "Okay. I got it."

"No, you probably do not. My friends will expect help in return sometime in the future, legal or not, and I will willingly acquiesce. I will do this on one condition."

"Which is?"

"The man who hurt Anya is mine. His fate will rest in my hands and my sons' hands."

"I have no problem with that."

"You have my number." He turned to leave, as Tony hurried down the corridor.

"How is she, Aleks?"

"Holding on."

"I think I can help."

Jake sighed. Tony spoke before Jake could stop him. "We've spent too much time blaming each other, Jake, for whatever. It's time to stop and move on."

Jake waited what seemed like an eternity. Then he nodded. "What do you have in mind?"

"I still have buddies all over the world, out of the military and in the military. And because of my job, I'm in internet contact with all of them. They've got eyes and ears everywhere."

Aleks and Jake looked at each other and smiled for the first time that morning. Aleks patted Tony on the shoulder. "What is that saying, Tony? Great minds think alike?"

Tony looked at the two of them and instantly understood. "Let's go then, Aleks. Two old farts like us may be able to do more than any bureaucracy."

"Indeed, Tony."

Tony was calm. "Stay in touch, Jake. Coordinate. We don't want any intel falling through the cracks."

For almost the first time in his adult life, Jake wanted to hug his father. He restrained his impulse. "Thank you."

The two men headed down the corridor and out the automatic doors. Jake felt something behind him, and turned to see Mrs. D staring daggers at his back. Jake sighed.

"I've come to sit with Anya. I assume her mother is with her?"

"Yes, Mrs... D." This was the first time he had ever used Garth's nickname for her.

"She'll need some company, then."

"I don't want to put any more of a burden on you."

"I'm a big girl, Jake. And right now you need all the support you can get. Take it and be glad that people love you and Garth enough to care."

Jake could barely talk. Something about Mrs. Dooley's kindness and common sense got to him like no one else's words. "Thank you. You can't imagine how much I appreciate you." He choked. "And how much Garth loves you."

She was no-nonsense. "Well, it's mutual, then." She looked at him, thoughtfully. "Don't you forget, Jacob. Garth has the sight. I know it and you know it. He got his abilities from somewhere. So listen to yourself, Jake. Stop doubting and pay attention to what you know down deep."

Jake was jolted. Too much had happened and he hadn't processed that he sensed Anya was in danger before he knew anything. Mrs. Dooley realized she hit a nerve.

"No matter what, you and Garth are connected on a deep level. Follow that and you won't go wrong."

Jake, his vulnerability stripped bare, finally acknowledged aloud what Mrs. D. already knew. "You know, I remember my mom telling me that her mom knew things she couldn't know. I loved her but she was so sick so much of her life, it was hard to focus on the things she said. So there was no way for me to understand that. And I needed to bury it, like..."

"...Like you buried your grief when she died too soon."

"Yes."

"Well, now you can let that doubt go."

"Mrs. D., I have this feeling I know something but I can't remember what. I can't get hold of it."

"Leave it be, then. It will come." She started to turn her chair around and Jake moved to help her. "I can get there on my own. I know how to use this chair. Now you go help the old men find your son."

She pushed his hands away and Jake watched her wheel herself down the hall, towards the ICU nurse. He shook his head: that nurse stood no chance against the force that was Mrs. Dooley. And whoever had Garth had no chance against him.

# CHAPTER FORTY

GARTH STOOD IN front of Feng Wah's desk, intimidated, sure that was exactly what Feng Wah had intended. Garth fought against his fear, as he struggled with the burden of making life and death choices for people he didn't know.

"Tell me your process."

Garth was confused. "I don't understand."

"I need you to look at people and tell me about them. Their families, their needs, their health…"

Garth's instincts screamed at him. He suspected that their health was Feng Wah's only interest, no matter what he said. Garth understood at his deepest level that being useful was his best option to survive. "I can't make myself see things. They happen."

"Do not lie to me, little boy."

"I'm not a liar!"

"Everyone is a liar if they need to be. Show me how it's done."

Garth realized he would have to go along, even if he had to pretend to see something. He sighed. "Okay. I'll try. I promise."

Garth closed his eyes and pretended to breathe himself into a trance. He remembered how it felt to be there but didn't know how to get to that place. So he followed his breath and emptied his mind intuitively. He was faking it, saw nothing, but thought if he kept his eyes closed long enough he could make something up and tell Feng Wah a pretend story. He kept his eyes closed and focused on his breathing like he remembered Kwai Chang Caine doing on *Kung Fu.* As he felt the breath fill his little lungs, a familiar sense swept over him and his fake vision became real. Unfortunately it was as terrifying as the one last night and he gasped in anguish.

*Anya was lying in a hospital bed, unconscious. She was covered in bandages, with needles in her arms, connected to machines. She was in a deep, dark place and Garth didn't know if she'd ever wake up.*

Garth came out of the vision with a jolt but kept his eyes shut. His survival instinct kept him riveted to the spot, knowing that Feng was watching him. He knew he'd have to tell the truth and lie at the same time. He hoped the Universe would help him. And forgive him. Garth opened his eyes slowly, and looked deeply into Feng's eyes.

"I know you went away. What did you see?"

Garth looked guileless as he lied to Feng Wah. "You need to see a doctor, very, very soon."

Feng Wah was taken aback. "For what, young man? I am very fit."

Garth knew he'd scared him, and surprised himself with how easily the lies came out of his mouth. "I don't think so."

"Tell me what you saw!"

Garth intermingled his lies with the truth. "I saw you in the hospital. You weren't awake and there were needles and machines everywhere. You looked asleep, but it was more than that. It was like you might never wake up."

"Did I live in this dream?" Feng Wah was shocked.

Garth shrugged. "I don't know."

Feng stared at him, as if he was daring him to take back his vision. Garth held his gaze and didn't back down. "Then I will make a doctor's appointment, as you suggested. It's clearly a good thing I have kept you healthy here. Go back to your room until someone comes to get you."

Garth turned around and walked out. He felt a pang of guilt. He'd used his ability to intimidate someone, but that person was horrible and mean and hurting people, so there was a bit of triumph in his walk. He'd lied and it worked. He'd learned a lesson, maybe not a good one, of how to manipulate. But it was for a good cause. His sense of power dissipated when he remembered what he'd actually seen earlier this morning and now. He had to find Li Li and figure out a way to get off the island, to Anya. She needed him. And when Feng Wah found out Garth lied to him, he had no doubt there would be a terrible punishment.

# CHAPTER FORTY-ONE

M**AX'S SLEEK JAG** sped along the I-5 north to Vancouver at about 95 MPH. Traffic wasn't bad, and the red bubble light moved the slower traffic to the right and out of their way. Jake figured the normal three-hour drive would probably take a little over two if they kept up this pace. He'd already arranged that they'd get through Peace Arch Border Crossing easily, even without a Nexus Pass.

He was in a hurry, knowing the more time that went by, the worse it would be for all of them. He'd learned to trust his sense of urgency, and especially now, he planned to follow his inner radar without questioning it.

Max loved driving fast, but Jake knew he wasn't enjoying this trip. "I gotta say I was surprised you called."

"I know I'm in no shape to drive, Max. You're got a fast car, and a way with people. I may need that."

"She's gonna be okay, Jake. She's as tough as they come."

"I believe you're right. But the best way I can help her is to find the fucker who did this and get Garth back safely. Anya'd be even more pissed at me if I only sat and stared at her, willing her to get better and wake up."

They made it in what Max said was a personal record of two hours and ten minutes. He was familiar with the city, so he had no problem finding where they'd arranged to meet with Howard Sharrone on this typically overcast day. Sharrone wanted to keep their investigation quiet for the moment. He said he'd explain when he saw them.

Max pulled into a parking spot right in front of the Broken Rice Vietnamese restaurant, maybe five minutes away from the Graveley Street Police headquarters. It was a little early for lunch, so the normally crowded cafe was unusually quiet. It was a cut above the typical Asian storefront restaurant, with comfortable tables, mahogany and oak décor, and original paintings hanging on the walls. Large teapots were on display on top of the well-kept Buddhist shrine.

Jake noticed none of this. He zeroed in on Sharrone, at a four-top in the very back. He was a nice-looking ginger-haired guy in his early thirties who looked in his early twenties, wearing a neat but inexpensive suit he could afford on his detective's salary. But Jake recognized he was deceptively tough, aware of his surroundings, his eyes always looking for potential trouble.

As they approached, Sharrone stood up to shake their hands. Jake introduced Max, and they sat down quickly. "You made it fast."

Max preened. "I think we set a record."

Sharrone turned to Jake. "You've had a couple of tough days. First your kid. Now your partner. Sorry."

Jake was surprised. "You heard."

"Oh, yeah. Cops gossip more than my grandmother." He was completely honest. "You'd think it was the cop code, but it's mostly because we're all terrified it could happen to us. Now, let's order, then we can exchange info."

He'd barely lifted his hand when a pretty, young Vietnamese girl, Betty, hurried over. Second generation in Vancouver, she spoke perfect English. "The usual, detective?"

"Yes, thanks, Betty."

"Then how may I help you gentlemen?"

Max was ready. "I'll have the mango salad, spring rolls, and duck sliders to start. Then, of course, the Pho Tai." Max smiled at her, and she was able not to giggle as both Jake and Sharrone stared at Max. "What?! It was a long drive."

Jake rolled his eyes. He'd barely glanced at the menu. "Chicken Pho. Thanks." He waited until Betty had glided out of sight. "Why all the secrecy?"

Sharrone sighed. "My bosses wouldn't be too happy to know that I'm probing around a slam dunk closed murder case with the perp already in prison. Not that they'd object to my helping you, but... "

"...Done is done."

"Exactly."

Max shook his head. "But done is not done for you."

"Nope. I had a bad feeling about this from the get go. It was too fucking easy. Guy gave himself up, confessed, made a deal with the prosecutor, so no trial. All very fast and very nice and very neat. Much too neat. No case ever goes that way."

They stopped talking as the first of Max's appetizers arrived. He dug into the spring rolls, not worrying as some of the filling slipped onto the plate. "Damn, this is good."

As the rest of the food was served, Sharrone watched Max in awe as he devoured the savory delicacies. "You look like a man who enjoys his grub. No offense."

"None taken."

Jake barely looked at his soup as the other two ate.

He held off until no waitstaff was around, then pulled out the rendering that the Old Woman had drawn of Feng Wah. They had no idea if it was accurate, but it was so well done it could have been a photograph. They'd put it on the wire and tried a match, but the guy was a ghost.

Sharrone looked at it carefully, then shook his head no. "Not familiar. Who is he?"

"We don't have his name or base of operations, but we think he's running a massive ring importing workers. One of the illegals fingered him as the man in charge."

"You got someone to talk? Impressive."

"But so far it's led us nowhere."

"You think taking your son and beating down your partner came from this guy?"

"Fear tactic. And it's working."

"Not really. Or you wouldn't be here." Sharrone quickly finished his lunch and pushed his plate away. "It jibes with my gut about this call girl murder. It's way bigger than it appeared. I know it. And I know it because the guy who confessed made it easy to bury it. We've heard rumors of a major ring of upscale escorts for the high and mighty. Too convenient that there was no need to investigate further."

"Think we'll be able to talk to your perp?"

"His name is Yang Dai and he's been inside Kent for the last year. He barely survived a stabbing at the beginning of his sentence. Someone doesn't want him around. He's been out of the general population since then... Yes, it's all arranged for you."

Jake sighed. "Thanks for your help. My gut is telling me this is all interconnected."

Max spoke up. "Your gut is talking to you because you haven't touched your pho. Eat it now and then we'll head to the prison."

"Yes, mom." He did as he was told, quickly, wanting to get going. Jake thanked Sharrone for his help.

"No worries. I'm going to do some digging on my own. You'll share if you get anything. So will I."

"Absolutely."

"Good luck, then. It's about an hour and a half from here to Kent. They're expecting you. But he's not."

Jake laughed. Sharrone was a man made from the same cloth as he was.

"We'll stay in touch. This is gonna move fucking fast or not at all."

Jake restrained his instinctive wince. He refused to let fear drive him anymore. He was on a mission and he wasn't going to waste a moment.

# CHAPTER FORTY-TWO

ANYA WAS SLOGGING *through the grasslands of the Great Steppe, listening to the howling of the pack of wild dogs hunting her. She tried to pick up the pace, but her feet kept sinking deeper and deeper, slowing her down. She could feel their breath on the back of her neck, sending chills through her spine. She cried out for help, but knew it was too late. She was battered and bloody. The man had assaulted her and she was helpless to fix it. Then she saw the man go down in a heap, a gunshot wound to his head. Blood dripped onto the grass as her mother wiped her hands on a rag and picked her up. They had to keep moving.*

Anya's cry for help came out a small moan in the reality of her hospital room. Natasha took her hand, and leaned her cheek on it, murmuring to her daughter. "I am here, my love. No one can hurt you. I will protect you." She had been silently praying by her bedside throughout the morning, and wouldn't leave until Anya was out of danger.

In her deep delirium, Anya shuddered, sighed and relaxed a millimeter. Natasha, deeply connected to her daughter, took that as a good sign. Her voice was soft, but a bit hoarse from her hours of comforting. She cajoled her daughter, spoke of her love, berated her for putting herself in danger.

"God only knows why you became the police, my darling girl. You didn't learn that growing up in the old country, not with those bullies. Maybe you wanted so badly to be an American... like that bald man we watched on our little TV. Kojak? That must be why you did it." Her voice caught.

"And because you have such a big heart. You have to make sure everyone is protected so no one suffers as we did. But *genig,* my love. It's enough. You proved you can do it. It's time for you to live your life for you, not for anyone else."

Natasha knew her daughter would survive and heal. But she was anguished that she couldn't keep her out of harm's way. This time she would recover. But next? "You will come back to me, *Anyachek.* Wherever you are, I know you hear my voice and my words. It is time you woke up, my darling."

Anya sighed again, as Natasha's tears fell onto the sheets. She showed no sign of ever waking up.

# CHAPTER FORTY-THREE

GARTH PACED HIS room, trying to formulate a plan. But he was still so agitated by his vision of Anya, and by what Feng Wah wanted him to do, he couldn't focus. He had asked one of the maids where Li Li was. She said Li Li was having a riding lesson, and she'd be back in half an hour. She usually stopped for a snack afterwards. Garth watched the clock intensely, willing the minutes to pass.

His breathing became more anxious as he felt himself falling into his other world. He was afraid he was going to find out something else bad about Anya. He decided not to fight it, because it might bring him some information he needed. Not that he could fight it, anyway.

*Daddy was there. It was night and cloudy. His face was covered in mud and his eyes were dark and stern. He was swimming in the murky water, towards Garth. Garth knew his dad was going to save him. Save others on the big boat. Jake reached out to Garth, then disappeared into the water.*

Garth shook himself, grateful and anxious. His dad was coming to get him. At least that's what he thought. But he worried that he was wrong, and he was imagining it because he wanted so badly for it to be true.

He glanced at the clock and figured Li Li should be in the kitchen now. He took a deep breath and opened the door. Feng Wah had no one guarding him now because he knew that there was nowhere for Garth to go. Garth headed towards the kitchen. He'd already mapped out the house with Li Li's help, in case he had to get out quickly. He pushed open the swinging door into what Li Li had called "the butler's pantry". Garth guessed that it was only in houses that had butlers, like this one. It led into the kitchen, where Li Li sat having strawberries and vanilla ice cream. She was surprised that he'd ventured downstairs, and assumed he had a reason, but she cut him off, looking around. Garth was impressed how smart she was. And sad that she had to be.

"Want a cone?"

Garth knew he was supposed to agree with whatever she suggested. "Okay."

She turned to the Cook. "Please give him a cone with vanilla ice cream and sprinkles." The Cook gave her a sour look but knew better than to cross her. All the staff knew how much Feng Wah doted on his daughter. Li Li turned to Garth. "The sun came out. We can sit on the patio and eat."

The Cook gave Garth his cone. "Thank you." The Cook turned away, ignoring this child.

"Thank you for remembering my favorite, Li Li." She shrugged. "Sure. Follow me."

Garth followed her to the little patio area outside the kitchen, the one with table and chairs under an umbrella. They sat on the far side, watching the sun glancing on the water. Li Li kept her voice low and even. "I've checked. There aren't any mics on the patio. And the directional ones in the security room don't pick up voices out here. My father designed it that way. I heard him say that then there would be a pocket of privacy."

"You're really smart."

"I have to be. Why did you come looking for me?"

Garth kept it simple. "I have to leave. Victor hurt my godmother and she's in the hospital. I can't let her die. You have to help me get out."

He was startled when Pearl came outside with a bowl of local Cameo apples, sliced and covered in cinnamon and sugar. She offered a slice to Garth, who took one to be polite. "Good, aren't they? We grow them on the island." Garth smiled and agreed. He didn't know why she interrupted them and wanted her to leave. He still wasn't sure he could trust her, and he was uncomfortable around her.

Pearl leaned in, quietly. "Why are you out here? It is noticeable."

Li Li quickly and quietly explained. Garth was worried Pearl would try to stop him. Instead she listened. "It feels like it may be time for the both of you to go."

"Not without you, mama."

"Daughter, you must believe me. I think you need to leave soon. This young man can take you to his father for protection." She went on, drily. "Although he didn't protect his own son very well… "

Garth bristled. "My dad wasn't there. He didn't know what was going to happen. If he'd been home, I wouldn't be here now." Garth believed that down to his soul.

"Forgive me, Garth. Sometimes my sense of humor isn't very funny. None of this would have happened if I had left well enough alone."

Garth was surprised, as Li Li dismissed her mother's guilt. "I am not leaving without you."

"Yes, you will do as I say."

Garth didn't understand. "Your husband is the boss. Not you."

"Exactly. And had I not tried to help, we wouldn't be in this situation. I sent your father information through the nuns to try to save those people. And instead, I put my own child and you in grave danger. My husband is a very cruel man. But he would never suspect that I had anything to do with his downfall. He doesn't think I'm smart enough." Her tone was matter-of-fact, without rancor. "Li Li, I fear all of this may backfire and there will be no protection for you. It hurts my heart that you have seen Feng Wah's cruelty with your own eyes. Now things are escalating quickly. They expect more than a hundred new arrivals. They'll be loaded onto a private ferry this time and sent to the mainland.

Feng Wah will want Garth to cull through this group."

She turned, looking into Garth's eyes. "I know you do not want to do that, and if you are forced to, you will not be able to live with the consequences. So we must move quickly."

Garth felt sick in the pit of his stomach. He knew that Pearl was right. He couldn't fake it again and he knew that Feng Wah would catch on.

"We may have some luck on our side. My husband is flying to the mainland tomorrow night to see his doctor. I heard him make the arrangements."

A small smile flickered across Garth's face, and in that instant he looked exactly like his father. He had succeeded better than he had hoped.

"Li Li, we will use his absence, and the arrival of the prisoners to hide your disappearance long enough for you to make it to the mainland."

Li Li was distraught. "But mama… "

"…No. If I disappear, my husband's rage will be so intense it will doom the two of you. You will go to the convent. The supply boat that comes twice a week will be there. I will make sure they are paid well for your passage, and no one will be the wiser. It will give you the time to get to safety. There will be no more discussion."

Li Li looked defeated. Her mother opened her arms and reached out to her daughter. Li Li buried herself into Pearl's chest. Pearl gestured to Garth and he moved to her. The children clung to her as she held them in her calm embrace, but Garth knew that the most dangerous time was ahead of them.

# CHAPTER FORTY-FOUR

THE TRIP TO the Federal prison took Jake and Max barely over an hour. Kent Institution was a mild name for a maximum security penitentiary. Max sped down the BC-1, through bucolic countryside, small villages, and several separately governed Indian reserves. The land was mostly farming, "The Corn Capital of British Columbia", but in the past few years the residents decided it would be good business to draw tourists to Harrison Hot Springs. Those efforts couldn't hide the obvious: the prison was big business, and employed almost as many personnel as it had inmates. Fittingly, it was located on Cemetery Road.

The two buildings, Kent, and Mountain Institution for lesser felons, shared a courtyard. Max was directed to park his car closer to Kent. Clearly, Sharrone had called ahead to make arrangements like he said. Jake and Max were ushered into a standard, small room for prisoner visits. They were watched by one affable guard.

Yang Dai was brought in by another less than friendly guard, whose eyes never stopped being aware. The prisoner was slight and could have been mistaken for an accountant if not for the handcuffs, chains around his feet, his jumpsuit, and the bruises from another brutal beating he'd taken recently. Jake nodded to the guard that he could leave. "We're good, thanks."

The guard left reluctantly. He wasn't used to being told what to do. Jake eyed the small Chinese man in front of him. He didn't look much like a cold-blooded murderer, but then not many did. Yang Dai stared at Jake and Max. "Why am I here?"

Jake thought that this was an odd way to put it. He told the simple truth. "I'm Detective Jake Fortune from Seattle. This is Dr. Max Woo, consultant for the Seattle PD. We wanted to talk to you about the murder of the young woman who worked for you. And the disappearance of her associates."

"I have nothing to say I haven't already said." His voice came out muffled because his jaw had been so badly bruised.

"What happened to your face?"

"I slipped in the bathroom."

"Really? The guard who walked us here, Jimmy, said that since someone beat the shit out of you, again, you're now in isolation. Sounds to me like someone isn't too happy with you."

Dai looked down at the table in front of him and didn't respond.

Jake prodded, his voice subtly gentle. "Looks to me like you could use a little protection."

Dai couldn't help himself, he half-snorted, half-cried. "Yeah, that'll happen in here."

"You're a walking dead man, then." Dai was startled by Jake's candor. "So if you're a dead man already, what difference will it make to answer my questions?"

Dai kept his eyes down.

Max hadn't said a word, only sat back and watched Jake prod the prisoner. He interjected: "Where is your family? Here?"

Dai's head jerked up. They knew Max had hit a nerve. "No."

Jake pressured Dai further. "So your family's still in China, then. I'm sorry. You must be very worried about them."

Dai backed up as far as he could in his seat. "Leave my family alone. They've nothing to do with me. They disowned me!"

Jake stared at him. "Because you warned them they had to."

Dai looked like a wounded animal caught in a trap. "What is it you want from me? What? I confessed. I'm in prison. In solitary. What other penance is necessary for me? I want to go back to my cell now."

Jake looked at him intensely, then said with no inflection. "I think you're innocent."

Dai was shocked.

Max smiled at Jake. "Innocent may be taking it a bit far, Detective. Not a murderer is more likely."

"Okay, I'll go along with Dr. Woo. You're innocent of the crime you confessed to, although you're still a sleaze bag pimp. But no murderer."

Dai looked from one to the other, not knowing how to respond.

"So it makes sense that the only reason you confessed to a crime you didn't do is because the person who did do it held something over your head.

Max chimed in. "Like your family. In China."

"The one you said disowned you. I don't buy it. I think you disowned them. To protect them, because if you didn't, someone threatened to make them pay. Well, we're here to tell you that there is nothing – nothing – stopping the people responsible from harming them anyway. You're here and can't protect them. You can't even protect yourself inside. You've already done their bidding. So why should they keep their word?"

Dai was heated, and blurted out: "Because if they don't keep their word, everyone will know!"

"And? 'Everyone' will fight them?"

Dai collapsed back into the chair, defeated. "I don't know. I don't know what to do."

Max appeared sympathetic. "We can help you there."

"Dr. Woo is correct. If you tell us what you know, we can go after the people threatening your family. We can arrest them, or make sure they are incapable of hurting anyone again. So your best bet, Dai, is to help us help you. Tell us the truth."

"You can't help me. They're too powerful."

"Only because you hand them your power. One person can't take them down, but we can. We have an army behind us. One that's on your side."

They both waited. Dai's handcuffs clanged as he rubbed his eyes, over and over again, for several minutes. He finally looked up at Jake. He'd made a decision. "You are correct. I'm a dead man walking, but it will be sooner rather than later if they discover I've spoken to you today. Can you get me out of here?"

"We've talked to the VPD. You'll be placed in protective custody outside of Kent until this whole thing is resolved. You can check with your lawyer to make sure when a deal's in place."

Dai panicked. "Not my lawyer!"

"So he's their lawyer."

"He's not mine!"

"Got it. He's another avenue we'll explore, then. Now I want to hear your story. The truth. Dr. Woo here will be watching and he's an expert in knowing if people are telling the truth."

Max nodded at Dai. "I am an expert."

So he told them. He claimed he wasn't a bad guy. He'd been on a foreign exchange student program and wanted to stay, so he'd simply disappeared. "When I ran out of money and I couldn't get a legit job is when I got into it deep. I was hired by a guy named Victor."

Jake didn't react but was optimistic as Dai fell silent, remembering. Now it wasn't only a feeling and circumstantial evidence, but a direct hit. This group was connected to their case and this guy was his best shot to track them. Jake didn't want to lose the momentum. He prodded Dai to continue. "It's time to come clean."

"Victor isn't only a prick, he's terrifying."

"Did you ever meet the people above him?"

Dai shook his head no. "They kept me out of the loop. I was only responsible for the girls."

"How'd they recruit them?"

"Ha. They didn't recruit them. They imported them. The immigrants pay the Snakeheads to smuggle them from China into Canada and the U.S. They don't know they'll still owe money and be sent all over the country. They cull out the really pretty ones, the ones they think will make them a lot of money on the meat market. Others were stolen from their villages. They don't care how they get them."

He took a deep breath, trying not to shudder. Jake didn't interrupt him. "I ran twelve girls. Victor brought them to me, but they were escorted by a woman named Pearl. I met her only once. She treated them okay, insisted they be taken care of. I think she was probably forced like the rest of us. Victor treated her carefully, though, I don't know why. But when she was gone he did whatever he wanted."

"What happened?"

"Three of them decided they'd had enough of ugly old men abusing them. They ran. The one I... Bao... the one I took the blame for, Victor caught right away. I don't know what happened to the other two, but I can guess. Bao probably gave them up in the end. Nobody ever found them that I know of."

He seemed depleted, but Jake pushed him. "The other girls?"

"As far as I know, there are nine left. Victor had a backup handler for me. I have his information. You can probably trace the girls through him."

Jake was elated but didn't show it. This was the closest they'd been.

"It's high end, you know. Only rich guys are allowed near the merchandise. Victor was protecting the assets not only because they make a shitload of money off them, but they blackmail the customers into doing other business with them. It's big money and they didn't want anything ruining that, so they needed me to take the fall real fast."

"I get it. We'll tread carefully. They're toast. I promise you. Now give me that information and I'll do everything to make sure you're in the clear. And safe."

Dai hesitated, then: "I believe you. I don't know why, but I do." He seemed relieved, no matter what the outcome. He'd given up his burden.

Before Max and Jake headed back to Seattle, they confirmed with Sharrone that Dai would be safely moved, without notifying his attorney. Sharrone pounded his desk with glee when Jake told him his instincts had been dead on.

Jake swore to him he'd be back for the bust. He wanted in when the ring was taken down. He needed information from whoever had it, and nothing and no one was going to stop him from getting it.

# CHAPTER FORTY-FIVE

IT TOOK MAX even less time to get back to Seattle because traffic was so light at the Aldergrove/Lynden crossing. And he ignored the speed limit. On the way home, Jake wasted no time. He systematically checked with all his CI's again, as well as Anya's. There was nothing new, but now he added the name of "Victor" to spread among his snitches. He hoped that would shake something loose. He touched base with Cap to see if the coordinated efforts of local and Federal cops had anything, but they'd made virtually no progress. Thackery was elated with what Jake had accomplished in Vancouver, and he had no problem with him being the lead on the follow-up. He thanked Jake again for pursuing the Snakehead angle professionally and not crossing the line.

Max dropped Jake off at home. "Maxie…"

"…I know, Jake. It's all good, as Dylan said so brilliantly."

"You know that was an ironic lyric, Max."

"Yes, but it's true nonetheless. Go do what you have to. I'm here, day or night."

"I know. Thanks."

Jake knew Tony was in the house because the kitchen light was on. Tony glanced up from the pot he was stirring on the stove, and asked:

"How's Anya? I didn't want to call and bug them."

"I spoke to Natasha a few minutes ago. Nothing's changed."

Tony sighed. "That could be a good sign."

"Could be."

"You hungry?"

Jake realized he'd barely eaten all day. He actually was famished. Tony hadn't waited for an answer before he started ladling out his stew. He put down a steaming bowl next to a loaf of fresh baked bread. Jake appreciated his efforts. "Thanks. Smells really good."

Tony got food for himself and they ate together, silent, almost companionable. "Good day?"

"Progress." Jake hesitated, then: "I think I have to head back to Vancouver in the morning. Got a ride that's faster than Max's Jag?"

Tony smiled at his son. "Maybe. Let me make a call." He got up and Jake waved him down. "Finish eating first."

"Nah. I've been snacking on it all day. I wanted to keep you company."

Jake was touched by Tony's kindness. By the time he'd finished his dinner, Tony was back, satisfied. "Okay. Helo ride anytime 6 am on. It's an hour trip. Yours all day."

Jake looked up. "How'd you manage that?"

"Phil Herbert's an old Army pal. He's got a private fleet of choppers and seaplanes."

"Impressive."

"Yeah. He was our supply officer. He could always get anything we needed. Hasn't changed. Does sightseer tours of the San Juans and Vancouver and knows the area like the back of his hand." Tony had printed out the information. "The field's about twenty minutes out from here. Call him when you're leaving the house."

"Thanks, Tony. This'll help. We could be getting a big break tomorrow."

Unsaid was that if they didn't get a break, it would be almost impossible to know what to do next.

"Go get 'em, son." He patted Jake on the back and turned away, hiding the tears in his eyes. Jake saw, but would never let on that he knew.

"If you need me, Tony, I'll be at Aleks'. Maybe they've made progress with their computer geek friends."

"'Kay. See you later, then." He hesitated, then: "You're doing good."

. . . .

WHEN JAKE ARRIVED at the Pashkovs, he was grateful to see that the house had been transformed into a high-tech information center. Three computer nerds didn't look up when he walked in with coffees. Boris and Peter were doing something with tracking satellites that Jake didn't begin to understand. He figured if they knew what they were doing, it was enough for him. And if it was illegal, he didn't want to know, nor did he care.

Aleks looked up and acknowledged his presence. He saw the tray of Starbucks and sweets that Jake had brought. "In the kitchen would be fine."

Jake brought the coffee and food into the kitchen, where two young girls, closer to Boris and Peter's age, were sitting at the kitchen table in intense discussion. Jake didn't want to disturb them. Aleks followed him into the kitchen and grabbed a coffee. Jake gestured at the activity. "You've made progress."

"We've set up. We will make progress. We added two phone lines for data and two for calls."

Jake looked quizzical.

"Don't ask and I won't tell."

"I have no intention of asking. I'm grateful. How's Natasha?"

"Being strong."

"I'm on the way to the hospital and I'll relieve her."

"That would be a good thing. She trusts you."

"Can I do anything here first?"

"Keep us informed of anything you hear from your compatriots at the station. Tony is doing the same. Information in – good information

– then good information out. It was true before the internet and is true now."

Jake's cell phone rang. He could see that it was Kirk Pelham calling from his cell. Jake held up his phone before answering. "Timing is everything." He answered. "Fortune." Pelham asked how he was holding up.

"Hanging in. Told Thackery that we may have made some progress today, but I'll let you know when I know for sure. Do you have something?"

"Maybe. Dave Bell from INS checked out his contacts in Minneapolis."

"Where the last group of illegals were headed."

"Yes. We found the potential buyer. He clammed up until INS offered him something of a deal. All he could give them was a contact number, which we traced to Vancouver. They're still going at him and hope to get more."

"And?"

"And the number was paid for by a dummy umbrella corporation that Soto and the others are trying to decipher."

"What's the name of the dummy corp?"

Pelham hesitated.

"Kirk. It's my kid. And Anya. I'm not going to go Lone Ranger."

"Oyster Imports. So far it doesn't exist. So far."

"Thank you." He wrote down the information on a scratch pad for Aleks, who immediately disappeared into the living room.

"They'll have more in the next few hours. They've applied for a Federal warrant and as soon as it comes through they'll start tracing money through the banks. I'll text you all we have... Then delete it. Please."

"I will. Thanks, Kirk. This could be a good lead. I appreciate it."

"You'd do the same. Gotta go."

Jake moved into the living room and gave Aleks the rest of the information as Pelham's text came through. Aleks absorbed it and gave it to one of his techs. "We're not waiting for warrants. I don't know if this will lead anywhere, but we'll know long before they will."

"Thank you." Jake hesitated. "I've been saying that a lot lately... "

"There are people on your side, Jake. And not only because of Anya."

"I know."

"Do your best to make my wife get a little sleep."

Jake half-laughed at the idea of getting Natasha to do anything she didn't want. Aleks went back to supervise his people. For the first time since Garth was taken, Jake felt a glimmer of hope.

# CHAPTER FORTY-SIX

The hospital corridors were dimly lit, and the noise was down to a low drone this time of night. Jake acknowledged the guard outside of Anya's door. His demeanor dared the nurses to stop him, but they were too busy and too hassled to enforce the ICU rules. He steeled himself, then quietly walked in. Natasha had managed to have a small cot set up next to Anya's bed. Like a cat, she was immediately alert. When she saw it was Jake, she relaxed. He looked at her with compassion. "I'm supposed to make you leave to get some rest."

"Ha." She turned over and closed her eyes again.

He looked at the hospital bed. It was like he told Tony. Nothing had changed. Anya was still in a coma, her injuries still visible. Jake sat down next to her bed. He looked for the gentlest way to hold her hand in his. He didn't want to disturb Natasha, but he didn't care if she heard what he had to say. Jake kept his voice low, soothing, as he murmured close to Anya's ear. "I'm getting closer, Annie. I can feel it. That lead we found? I think it's going to pay off. And you'll be there to welcome him home." He hesitated a moment.

"You can't imagine how sorry I am. Not only for ignoring your fears, but for everything. Taking you for granted. Loving you and not admitting it to myself, let alone telling you. You and Garth are not only the best things in my life, you are my life. And I've been terrified that I lost you both. I know you will get better, Annie. I have faith in you. And I don't care how long it takes, we will see this through. And I'll choose, Annie. It's easy. I choose you." He gently squeezed her hand. He hoped that he didn't imagine that she slightly squeezed back.

Natasha spoke in a normal voice. She didn't give in to the situation and whisper. "She heard you, Jake. And she knows. We all know. And you are right, she will get better." Natasha half-smiled. "Or she will have me to deal with and she's too smart to want that."

She got off her cot and stretched. Jake came over and gave her a hug, holding onto her for her support and strength. "It's okay *boychik*. I've been praying. All will be well. Now leave me to my baby, and go find yours."

# CHAPTER FORTY-SEVEN

*Third Day After*

THE RAIN WAS pounding sideways against the new Eco-Star that Tony's friend, Phillip Herbert, was piloting. Phil pointed towards the landing site a few blocks to the north. Jake was grateful they had been able to take off at all, and that Tony's pal was a pro.

He wasn't very talkative, which suited Jake fine. They landed with great precision, as Phil set the bird down gently in the parking lot between the two buildings of the Vancouver PD's Graveley Street facility. He yelled over the rain. "You have my cell. I'm gonna go park her at the Vancouver/Burnaby Heliport and visit a friend. Give me half hour before you want to leave and I'll pick you up."

Jake shouted his thanks, and headed towards the high-rise. Sharrone was waiting for him at the entrance, wearing a dark brown slicker with a hood. "A rain hood? On a raid?" Jake ribbed him.

"No. For later when I actually want to stay dry. I've got four men for back-up. One of them did advance work, and is waiting for us at the target house. I'll bring you up to speed on the way."

Two unmarked SUVs took off, one with Jake and Sharrone, the other with two undercover officers. No red lights or sirens – they didn't want to spook the targets.

One of Sharrone's CIs had come through. He gave up that the nine girls left in Yang Dai's group had moved with another pimp. This one was hardcore — James Gai had a long record of felony assault, domestic abuse, and other charges that reflected his brutal nature. Whoever ran these girls figured they needed tougher supervision. So the VPD wasn't going in undermanned. They didn't want any trouble, and this was their way of preventing it. Jake was in complete agreement, and impressed by Sharrone and his colleagues.

Sharrone explained that the call girls had ended up in Spencer Court, West Vancouver, one of the most expensive areas in the city. The women lived together in a modern house set behind blooming shrubs, with a verdant lawn and large swimming pool. The girls went out on calls but also 'entertained at home'.

As soon as Sharrone's team got there, they drove past and spotted the two late-model Mercedes parked in the long driveway that the advance group had reported to them.

The team headed around the block, out of sight, and met with the two other detectives on stakeout. Both Jake and Sharrone were in civvies, raincoats, and could pass for businessmen. Sharrone stopped and handed Jake a Smith & Wesson. "How come?"

"It's my back-up. Registered to me. If you have to use it, it'll be my shoot. Less paperwork than if a Seattle cop shot a civilian on Canadian soil."

Jake stared at him a moment. "Got it. Thorough."

"My wife says I overthink. Sometimes that's a good thing."

"So what's your plan?"

"We ring the doorbell. We know someone's home."

"And we are who?"

"Realtors. Doing a door knock, is what I think they call it." He handed Jake a stack of papers.

"This is supposed to make me look legit?"

"You only have to look legit for fifteen seconds."

"I can handle that."

"Figured you'd be okay with it."

They waited until the other two teams had deployed under cover behind and alongside the large house. Then they ambled down the path between the well-kept hedges, talking casually with each other. Sharrone touched his ear bud. "Got it." He turned to Jake. "Teams are in position and there appears to be no activity inside or out." The two of them walked up together as if they had synchronized their movements for years, not minutes.

Jake rang the bell, and they could hear it reverberate inside. They waited thirty seconds, then rang again. Jake kept his voice low. "Do you hear someone moaning in there? I think there's someone down in the living room."

"I believe I do." Sharrone muttered into his mic. "Going in. Stay alert." Sharrone kicked the front door open so easily he could have done it a thousand times before. As if they'd choreographed it, Jake drew his weapon and went inside, to the right. Sharrone did the same to the left.

The house was dead quiet. Decorated modern, simple and clean, it was so neat it looked as if no one actually lived there. As they moved separately sweeping the rooms, they found nothing. Sharrone pointed upstairs. They did the same sweep of the seven bedrooms upstairs. At least those had a few items in the bathrooms and closets, but there was the same feeling of emptiness.

When they headed back to the first floor, Jake pointed down, and Sharrone nodded. They moved into the kitchen, where they'd noted a door that led to a basement. Jake reached over to the knob and slowly turned it. The door opened in and he pushed it quickly and quietly. It was well-oiled, but if anyone was hiding in the basement directly below them, he and Sharrone would be sitting ducks. But Sharrone had a trick up his sleeve. He clicked to the troops. "Basement. Cover all exits."

He pulled out a flash grenade and tossed it down the stairs. He and

Jake covered their ears. The blast was loud and the intense light would disable anyone who might be waiting at the bottom. Jake and Sharrone dashed down the stairs, to a basement that was still brightly lit and smoky from the grenade.

The basement was a revelation. It ran the entire length of the house, with separate cubicles and partitions. They could hear crying and whimpering in the distance.

A burly bodyguard stumbled out of the smoke towards Sharrone, whose gun was trained on him. Sharrone had him under control easily, but Jake could see out of the corner of his eye it wasn't the pimp they were expecting.

Jake turned, moving quickly through the smoke, when he saw James Gai emerge from a room behind Sharrone, with a gun in his hand, ready to shoot.

Sharrone turned in time to see Jake hit him with a flying sidekick, knocking the gun out of his hand. Jake took him down easily with a hammerfist. Sharrone nodded his thanks. "Pretty. Why didn't you shoot the fucker?"

"Still would've been too much paperwork. Besides, we need to know what he knows."

"Good move."

They cuffed and secured both prisoners, then did a quick sweep of the basement to make sure there were no more surprises. Sharrone radioed his men. "Team one, inside. Basement. Team two, secure perimeter."

They could hear whimpering farther down the corridor. The crying got louder as they approached a locked and reinforced door. Jake sighed, hoping not to find what he'd discovered behind the last locked door he and Anya had opened. He and Sharrone approached cautiously. Jake yelled at those inside. "Put your hands up and back away from the door!"

They opened the door with a key hanging from a lock next to it, and swung the door open hard, so no one could hide behind it. The crying got louder as they moved inside. Jake holstered his weapon as soon as he saw the women cowering in the corner of the freezing room. There were ten of them, in various states of dress. They were all young, pretty, and Chinese. Jake muttered to Sharrone. "Pay dirt."

Sharrone radioed his team to bring in blankets as Jake shushed the group, and spoke in a soothing tone. "It's okay. You'll be fine. Don't worry, we'll take care of you."

"You sound like you've done this before."

"Last week. Worse conditions."

Jake watched as three of Sharrone's team came in, with blankets and water. He looked over the group carefully as they were escorted outside. He wanted to see if he could spot the leader. He did, almost immediately. She carried herself regally, comforting the others as she translated what he said. Jake approached her. "What's your name?"

She sized him up carefully before she answered. In English. "Lan. Chin Lan."

"Please tell them we're going to get them someplace safe and warm. Food. Clothes."

She hesitated, then did as he asked. They started to chatter back at her, but she lifted her hand and they became docile. Then Lan followed them out.

Sharrone turned to Jake. "How'd you make the leader?"

"She didn't look afraid."

"Good eye. Okay, I'm gonna leave two men here in case anyone else shows up. Time to talk to these poor souls."

They transported the call girls to the relatively new Vancouver PD high rise on Graveley. Sharrone had managed to get several rooms set aside for the frightened group. Jake watched as Lan brought calm to the girls. The women were given tea and sandwiches, as well as jackets to keep out the cold. They still weren't talking to anyone, not the cops, nor the two translators Sharrone's CO had brought in.

James Gai and his sidekick hadn't said a word. Jake showed them the drawing of Feng Wah and they didn't react. Gai blinked quickly when he saw the rendering of Victor but both of them still kept their mouths shut.

Jake figured he'd return to them later. He still had his eye on Lan. He went through the three rooms with the interpreter, showing both pictures to the girls. They didn't recognize Feng Wah, but all of them recoiled at the picture of Victor. The interpreter asked each of them if they knew his name or where he was, but, like the last group Jake had rescued, they were terrified.

Until they got to the third room, where Lan sat calmly. Jake showed her Victor's picture. Her reaction was different than the others – it was disdain. When her eyes blinked rapidly as she saw Feng Wah's picture, he knew his intuition had been dead on. She knew him, of that Jake was certain. He turned to the interpreter and Sharrone. "These two young ladies can wait with their friends. Lan and I have things to talk about."

Sharrone told the guard to move the two girls. They were unhappy. Lan spoke to them in Chinese, calming them. She turned to Sharrone. "I told them they wouldn't be hurt. I hope I am correct."

"Yes. They will be treated well."

"And I?"

"Ma'am, I guarantee we won't lock you in a windowless freezing room in a basement like your employers did." Sharrone had made his point. "Now, you know something about these men. Probably about a lot of men. My partner here thought so from the beginning, I have to admit. So why not make it easy on yourself... and those others. Talk to us and we'll do our best..."

She cut him off abruptly. "...No promises. Please. I — we all — will take whatever punishment is necessary."

She was a woman who had seen and survived too many things. Jake interjected, keeping his tone soft. "You speak very good English".

Lan shrugged, but was pleased. "I studied in college."

Jake nodded. "You're obviously well-educated and the others look to you for guidance. To me that means you're smarter than they are."

"If I were, would I be sitting here with you, under arrest?"

"You're not under arrest. Not yet. As far as we know, you've done nothing wrong. But you do have information we need. To get justice for your three friends who were killed, if nothing else. And to find a young boy this man kidnapped."

He tried to keep his voice even, but she caught the break. "I'm sorry for your predicament. But I don't know anything that would help you."

"You know both these men."

She didn't answer.

"You have family in China that you're worried about. You all do."

She nodded slowly. "Yes. If we speak, they will be killed."

"How do you know it's not a threat to keep you in control?"

"They proved it. Several times. Bao..." Her voice broke, then she continued... "Bao died, as did Lihwa, I'm sure, and another I did not know well. Their families were punished. They showed us the pictures."

Jake took a deep breath. "Okay. I will be completely truthful with you. I can only promise we will do our best to keep your families safe. And the smartest way to do that is to destroy these men, and their organization."

"You cannot make that promise."

"What I can promise is that if we don't take them down, soon, they will know you and the others have been compromised. They can't be sure you won't give us information. What will they do then?"

Lan looked stricken, as Sharrone interjected. "It's a crapshoot. But I'd bet on us rather than them."

Jake agreed. "Your choice, Lan."

Lan hesitated, then agreed. "I will tell you as much as I know. In exchange, you will give me – all of us – our freedom."

"We will do our best and make sure the authorities know that you were instrumental in bringing down a major criminal. Here and in the U.S. But our governments have the last word. That's the only promise I can make."

Lan sighed. "I appreciate your candor."

"How did you get here?"

Lan stayed silent for a moment. Jake watched her mask of calm dissolve into acceptance. "I was twenty. Bao was sixteen. We lived in a village in the Northern Province of Shanxi because we were teaching at a small school. They took us from our beds in the middle of the night. Screaming didn't help. There was no one to hear us or care. Both of our families were a hundred kilometers away, but to ensure we remained compliant they invoked our parents' and siblings' names."

Jake saw the pain in her eyes as she tried to joke. "Clearly they had done their homework."

Jake nodded. "I'm sorry."

"So am I. We were taken through the streets at night to a small boat on the river." She continued, matter of fact. "The men were brutal. If you kill them, no one will mourn." She looked at Jake, carefully. "I have no choice but to trust your word that you will do your best to protect our families."

Jake was honest. "Yes. I promise that we will do our best."

She nodded, to herself, and to Jake. "We traveled by boat for a long time, with many, many people. Some had paid for passage. Others – like me and Bao – had been… taken. I was the adult. I was responsible for Bao. When we stopped at an island, we were split into groups, and we were separated from the rest. We knew too late we had been abducted because we were young and pretty. Saleable."

She pointed to the picture of Victor. "This man is Victor Kasan. I thought he was the boss, but I should have known better. He rules by brute force. We knew he was dangerous and did not contradict him in anything. Except for Bao… But there are many, many powerful men in this city who utilize our services. I should have known he was not the one they were dealing with." She barely touched the picture of Feng Wah. "This man is the leader. His name is Feng Wah."

Jake held his breath. Everything she said confirmed what he suspected. And now he had a name. "You met him."

She was matter of fact. "Yes. Twice. Once in the beginning, and once after we were taken to this house. Victor watched me for almost three years. Then he brought me again to this man, on an island, twelve days ago."

"Do you know which island?"

"No. But it was perhaps forty-five minutes or an hour from here on a seaplane."

"Tell us about the island."

She shrugged. "It was night when we landed. There was nothing to see but a large compound. I am not certain but I believe it may have been the same island where we were when they divided us into groups." Lan half-smiled. "The house was much nicer than the shacks."

"It must've been a small island."

She shrugged. "I could not tell. Big enough to house a Church."

Jake reacted, relieved. A way to whittle down the number of islands. "How do you know that?"

"We could hear its bells in the distance."

"Anything else you remember?"

"No. Now I want to forget it all."

"You've been an enormous help to us."

"Then please remember our families in China."

Sharrone interjected. "We promise. Now, if I showed you pictures of some of the rich and prominent men around here, do you think you could identify them?

"Of course. I wish I could forget them."

Sharrone told her in a soft voice. "In time, Lan. You will."

"Perhaps a list of the first names of those I dealt with might help?"

Sharrone looked stunned. "A very good starting place." He turned to Jake. "Do you have enough?"

"For now. Whatever info you get from the johns about Feng Wah or his organization…"

"…Will do."

Jake shook Lan's hand. "Thank you. For everything. We'll do our best to protect you and your families."

"I hope I was helpful in getting your loved one back."

Jake was startled. "That obvious?"

"Yes. Good luck. These men are not normal. They have no feelings."

Jake, shaken, left Sharrone with Lan to dig deeper. He headed home, this time with a plan, but he knew Garth's window of safety was narrowing by the minute. As soon as they found out about the raid on the house, Feng Wah and his cronies would strike back, even harder.

# CHAPTER FORTY-EIGHT

It was dusk on Feng Wah's island. Pearl, Garth and Li Li were settled on the patio, waiting for the sun to go down. They had watched Feng Wah's plane take off an hour earlier, but wanted to make certain he was really gone. They put nothing past him.

Almost as one, Li Li and her mother looked at each other. It was dark enough so that if anyone saw them, they would be dismissed as shadows. They got up from the garden table and gestured for Garth to do the same. They slipped away from the security camera and headed towards their hidden route to the convent. Pearl stopped at the edge of the path. They looked up when they heard the high-pitched screeching of two eagles flying overhead. Garth was in awe of their beauty.

"You see, it's a sign, my daughter. You are strong like the eagles. Fly away, free as they do." Li Li nodded, reluctantly. "You know I must stay here so no one will be suspicious."

Li Li didn't object this time. She silently embraced her mother, both of them keeping their tears at bay. Pearl gave Li Li one last, ferocious hug. "Stay safe."

Li Li didn't look back. Garth followed quickly and quietly. He didn't let the bird noises nor the rustling in the trees bother him, because he had put his trust in Li Li. The convent was on the other side of the island, and she had traveled this trail many times in complete silence. It took over an hour to avoid the cameras and security guards and get there without being seen.

Garth looked up at the bell tower, the one he had heard in his vision, and smiled. The walled structure wasn't in good shape, but Li Li had told him that the nuns kept it up as best they could without any real money or help from the Church. They knew that being moved from the only home they'd known in their adult lives was only a matter of time. For now they had their place and their silent prayers and each other.

Li Li quietly pulled a rope on the front gate. A bell tinkled in the distance. A few minutes later, the door to the courtyard opened. An ageless woman stood there, indomitable and implacable. Her face changed when she saw Li Li and she smiled. She ushered the two of them in.

"Thank you, Mother Mary Catherine."

"You are welcome, Li Li. Who is this young man?"

Garth was almost tongue-tied. This woman reminded him of every stern authority figure in his life, yet her eyes reflected nothing but kindness. "Garth. Ma'am."

"Welcome, Garth. Are you hungry?"

Li Li stopped him. "No, thank you. We're sorry to interrupt your prayer time, but we need..."

"...Shelter?"

Li Li nodded.

"Only the two of you?"

"Yes. We need to get to the mainland before my father returns in the morning."

"You are lucky and also unlucky, then, young lady. Unfortunately, our communications are not in service. We do not know why."

"My father, of course."

"Perhaps. But that means we cannot let anyone on the mainland know you are enroute. My guess is that leaving is more important than anyone knowing you are arriving."

"Yes, Mother Mary Catherine."

"Then we will be able to take care of you. Our regular supply boat leaves here at seven. But I'm assuming that you knew that, and that's why you've chosen tonight to leave."

"We thought so, but weren't sure. My mother... made payment."

"We can do this. But you must eat first, and then we'll find you some warmer clothing. It gets cold on the Sound."

Mother Mary Catherine brought the two of them into the warm, old-fashioned kitchen. Several other nuns were going about their business, but they remained silent as it wasn't their time of day to speak. Without being asked, Sister Angelica put two bowls of soup on the table, along with a homemade loaf of bread. Garth thanked her, then sat down. He hadn't realized how hungry he was, nor how his appetite had faded while he was held in the compound. Li Li said she wasn't hungry, but Mother Mary Catherine insisted she eat. "It's better to be prepared for anything, Li Li."

When they'd finished, Mother Mary Catherine gave them jackets and gloves and scarves for the journey. She pulled a knit hat over Garth's head that was so big, it covered half his face. She laughed, which made him more relaxed. She carefully folded it over so it didn't cover his eyes. "That should do, Garth."

"Thank you, Mother Mary Catherine. Can I call you that?"

"Well, it is my name... so yes, I think that would be fine."

He smiled at her, the first genuine feeling of calm surrounding him in days. He touched her hand and held it. She looked at him quizzically and waited. Garth relaxed. "You're not gonna die until you're really, really old."

Sister Angelica snorted, not able to help herself. Mother Mary Catherine looked grave.

Li Li stepped in. "He knows things like that. But he's not really weird."

"I'd say not, Li Li. Thank you for the information, young man. It will be God's will. Of course."

Garth didn't back down. "Well, I guess he doesn't want you to die soon."

"Let's pray that he protects you and Li Li as well. Understand, this will not be an easy journey. You must remain quiet and calm, no matter what happens. No matter if the sea is rough, or there are delays, or people are looking for you. It's probably going to be uncomfortable, but I have faith that you will be fine."

Li Li smiled. "We will. We have you on our side."

The Mother Superior smiled. "God, me, all of my sisters here, and most important, yourselves. Oh, and Captain Donny."

Garth looked at her, wary, hearing something in her voice. "Not to worry, Garth. He's a good man, but he's a drinker and perhaps not terribly reliable. But if he knows he has you in his charge, I've no doubt he'll rise to the occasion. Now, have some fresh cookies and warm milk. Then we'll go about seeing the best place for Captain Donny to transport you."

Garth and Li Li looked at each other, anxious. Freedom seemed just out of reach, and yet they had no choice but to plunge ahead. Li Li slipped her hand into Garth's, and, for this moment, they took comfort in each other.

# CHAPTER FORTY-NINE

NATASHA HAD LOST track of time. There didn't seem to be any day or night in the ICU. She was sitting by Anya's bedside, knitting. She didn't really enjoy it, but it kept her hands busy and her mind calm, and right about now, she needed both.

That nice surgeon, Dr. Cinader, had left a few minutes ago. He said Anya's vitals were stronger but they couldn't tell when she'd come out of her coma... or how long her recuperation might be. He took into account her youth, determination and overall good health. But he wouldn't lie – this was a crapshoot. There wasn't much else for anyone to do. Anya had to want to come back, and she had a lot of hard work ahead of her.

Natasha sighed, holding on to her faith in God, and her faith in her daughter. They'd come through so much to be here. She knew her daughter hadn't been really happy with her life, but she didn't feel comfortable meddling. Maybe when Anya started to get better, she'd reconsider that. Anya would hate her interfering in any way, but that would give her something to fight back against other than her body.

She heard Anya moan. There wasn't anything unusual about that, but every time she felt her daughter in pain, she cringed. Then she heard a murmur and looked at Anya more intently.

"*Anyachek*? Do you want to wake up now? I know it will be hard for you, but in the end we can make it better." She stroked her daughter's bruised hand, and could feel the bile rising in her, the desire to kill the man who did this. She had done it once before to protect her child and wouldn't hesitate again. Then she pushed down her anger because she knew it would serve no purpose right now, nor would it help Anya heal.

Anya's fingers curled around Natasha's hand, startling her. Natasha held her breath, willing Anya to open her eyes. "I'm here, darling. If you open your eyes, you can see me and know that you're alive and will be all right. I promise you with everything in me. You know I've never lied to you. Well, maybe once or twice, but only for your own good." She thought that would make Anya laugh if she could only hear her.

Natasha could tell Anya was agitated because the heart machine showed her pulse racing. "Ssh, baby girl. All is well. I'm here."

Anya's eyes opened halfway, slowly, dazed, out of focus.

"Good girl. Now open them all the way. Look at me so you'll know where you are. I'm real and I'm here."

Anya's eyes slowly focused on her mother. Natasha held her breath, and prayed louder in her head.

"Mama." The word came out in a whisper from Anya's parched throat.

Natasha beamed at her and sighed in relief. Now the work would begin. It would not be easy, but she knew her daughter would fight like hell.

# CHAPTER FIFTY

Tony was sitting intently in front of a computer in Aleks' living room. The rest of Aleks' team was still there, processing information when Tony yelled in excitement.

"Aleks! One of my guys in Hong Kong tells me the Chinese government has been tracking an underground Snakehead ring moving nationals to the US. He's going to check with his CIA contact there to see if they have any specific information."

"That sounds like a possible, Tony. Some of my web friends have similar information. We're honing in, but remind him of the time constraints..."

"...He knows. They all know." Tony turned back to his computer and was checking his website tip line when Jake quietly came in. Tony turned around, waved, and went back to his focus.

Aleks approached him. "Jake. I talked to Natasha. Anya woke up."

A wave of relief spread through Jake's body. "Thank God."

"And thank my wife... did you find anything?

"Yes." Tony got up from his computer and joined them. Jake pulled out the drawing he'd been carrying with him that they hadn't been able to identify. "His name is Feng Wah. He's behind, at the very least, the whole illegal worker operation, the murder of one young woman in Vancouver and disappearance of two, a call girl slave operation, and Anya's attack. I'm certain he's the one holding Garth."

Aleks smiled. "Yes."

Jake was surprised. "You found him."

"We found his name, but not him. It took my people a long time to do a background check, because he's managed to bury himself very deep."

Boris came into the room from the kitchen. "I heard you mention Feng Wah. I have a friend in Vancouver who is trying to unravel the thread, and his name came up. He's well-hidden, but we need one more connection before we know for sure."

Jake had more. "And we've narrowed down the island he's on to one with a Church, forty-five minutes to an hour from Vancouver via seaplane. And Aleks… the person who hurt Anya? His name is Victor Kasun. That's all I have."

Aleks look at his son. "Boris?"

"Done. I'll focus on him." He headed back to his computer, on a mission.

Jake gave Aleks a heads-up. "I'm going to let SPD know."

"Are you sure?"

"Yes. They won't interfere, and they could be helpful."

Jake called Pelham on his cell as Aleks clapped his hands for quiet. "People! Pay attention to the name Feng Wah. Find an island with a Church, forty-five to sixty minutes by seaplane from Vancouver, either the San Juans or Gulf Islands! Coordinate! Even if you think it's unimportant, throw it into the pot."

Jake got hold of Pelham right away. Pelham told him: "I was dialing you. We may have caught a break."

Jake listened intently as Pelham explained that the currents washed up a body along the shore of the Sound. They had suspected it might be the guy Anya shot, and ballistics confirmed the bullets matched Anya's revolver.

"We're making progress. I guarantee he's in the system. We should have him ID'd as soon as the M.E. can get prints off him. He was fairly degraded."

"The guy was a liability and they dumped him. More important, it means that Garth was taken by boat."

"We're pretty sure. The hunt is definitely focusing on the San Juans. Sheriff Ortiz has been alerted and is cooperating."

Jake hesitated, then revealed: "Focus on an island with a Church, forty-five to sixty minutes from Vancouver BC by seaplane. Could be the San Juans or it could be the Gulf Islands."

Pelham was surprised. "I'll pass that on to Soto. Off the top of my head, that'll get rid of eighty-five percent of the possibles. Good intel?"

"Yes. I got it when I was in Vancouver."

"You sure it's not gonna throw us off track?"

"Yes. The source was actually on the island. I believe her. She gave us other good info."

"Which you'll share, of course."

"Of course. Detective Sharrone's gonna bust a ring of Canadian fat cats ASAP, men who've been dealing with the big boss. His name is Feng Wah. That should give you something to start with, and I have my... CIs checking him out. Along with the asshole who did the beat-down on Anya. His name is Victor Kasun."

"Okay. We'll spread our search area to the Gulf Islands, one with a Church. Good work, Jake. Really good."

Jake thanked Pelham and made sure Aleks' people were on the same page. He retreated into the kitchen on the pretense of getting water, but more to give himself a quiet space to think.

Jake flashed on a fragment of his nightmare about Garth. Now that he had more information on where Garth was being held, he knew it had been an accurate intuition. He could sense he was getting closer to finding his son, which was his first priority. And he knew that the people responsible would pay, and pay big.

He was startled when he felt a hand on his shoulder. He turned to see Tony, smiling at him. "Faith, son. It's paying off. We'll have our boy back soon."

Jake was so touched by the gesture it was all he could do not to break down and cry. He looked directly into Tony's eyes, for the first time in much too long. And connected. Tony grabbed Jake into a bear hug, and Jake didn't fight him. He patted Tony on the back. "I know how much you love him, dad."

Tony pulled back, unshed tears in his eyes. "And you, son."

"Me, too. Me, too. Now let's keep on keeping on, dad."

Tony grinned. "You remembered!"

It was a phrase Tony had used all the time Jake was growing up. It had driven Jake crazy, but he finally realized the meaning. "I remember." He squeezed his dad's shoulder again and then turned to pour them some coffee.

"Jake, you've been going non-stop. Why don't you get a little shut-eye and let the computer geniuses work their magic?"

Jake hadn't acknowledged he'd been running on pure adrenalin. "Not a bad idea. Only a few minutes, though. We're getting close."

"I swear I'll wake you if anything pops. Anything."

Jake agreed, and grabbed a couch in Alek's small office. He fell asleep instantly. When he awoke two hours later, with a little more energy, he trudged back into the living room.

They had all been working around the clock for twenty-four hours, but the pace hadn't slowed a bit. Several people catnapped around Aleks' living room, there were pizza boxes strewn around, but the only empty bottles were water. No one had even had one beer as they were too intent on making progress. Tony was dozing in a corner chair. Jake adjusted one of Natasha's handmade quilts over him to counter the chill in the air.

Boris bounded into the room. "Got it!"

Tony shook himself awake and Jake and Aleks were alert as Boris explained. "My Vancouver guy hacked into..." He stopped and looked at Jake. Jake shrugged, and Boris continued. "...Never mind. Doesn't matter how or where. Feng Wah's bank accounts show spikes once a month with big sums. His companies are incorporated in Vancouver, but there are no signs he lives there, or even maintains anything but a monetary presence now. He moved there from Hong Kong , but left five years ago."

"Anything from the records of the Hong Kong or Chinese authorities?" Jake was certain Boris' friend hadn't stopped with the banks.

Peter answered for his brother. "*Our* contacts said the cops had a huge file on him, mostly blacked out. It seems he built interconnected criminal businesses, all with legitimate fronts, then took the money and ran. He paid off the right people, and those who could help charge him disappeared."

Aleks spoke calmly. "So he is a force with no morals. Not a surprise. Next step?"

Boris interjected, enthusiastic. "My – our – friends are still digging. We think he's in the San Juans, because there are more small islands. There will be records on him somewhere. And now that we know there's a Church, we've narrowed it down to a dozen."

Aleks told him and everyone in the room. "Focus on that. We have the names of his accounts and at least some of his companies. One of them will pay off."

Jake was grateful. "This answers a great deal. Except exactly where they are. But I have faith…" He glanced at Tony. "…I have faith we can discover that soon."

Tony smiled, knowing that Jake said that to acknowledge him.

Aleks agreed. "Let's go! We are close."

Jake's phone buzzed. It was Sharrone. "Howie. So, how'd you do?"

"How do you think I did?"

"I think you busted a lot of pissed off entitled assholes and had them arrested for something."

"Dead on, my friend."

"And you confirmed they dealt with Feng Wah through Oyster Co. for their high-end call girls."

"Did you plant a bug on me?"

"Didn't have to. I trusted you to confirm information I got elsewhere."

"Confirmed. Plus a couple of assholes had girls locked in their rooms as 'housekeepers'. I'm gonna make sure that gets in every tabloid in the country and that those mofos do jail time."

"Is the brass happy?"

"Well, so far we've nailed two fucking government ministers and a high mucky-muck in our Department in addition to the rich dudes. So I'm either gonna get promoted or fired. But maybe by the time they do the press conference, it will be glory time. I'll let you know."

"Thanks, Howard. Great job."

"You, too. Now go get that shithead. And don't get yourself killed."

"Do my best." Jake was pumped by Sharrone's information. He planned to wait a couple hours before passing along this new information on Feng Wah to Pelham and Soto, only because he wanted to let Boris and Peter's friends cover their deep web tracks. They'd put their asses on the line for people they didn't even know. That said a lot to him about a lot of things. And he trusted them to accomplish more without caring if it was legal. Tomorrow he'd have Feng Wah in his sights, and no one with or without a badge was going to get in his way.

# CHAPTER FIFTY-ONE

MOTHER MARY CATHERINE tucked Garth and Li Li into a hidden compartment on the supply boat, the *Belle Marie*, named after Captain Donny's mother. He looked on, helpless to object. Especially since he had been paid by Pearl, and the Mother Superior had given him extra cash, with the promise of more for a safe delivery.

"You stay quiet, no matter what you hear outside, understand?"

They both agreed, trying to be brave, as the reality of what they were doing finally hit home. Then Mother Superior turned to Captain Donny, whom she'd known since he was in her first grade class in Bellingham. "Keep them safe, Donny. Or you'll have me to answer to first, and then your Maker. And no more liquor. Give it up to me."

Donny was reluctant. "It gets cold out there at night, Mother."

She glared at him. He sighed and handed her a bottle of bourbon he had hidden away. "Coffee will work wonders. It will keep you warm and awake."

"Yes, ma'am. I'm not drunk. And I swear on my mother's soul I'll get these kids to the mainland."

She patted his cheek. "That's what I'm counting on." Mother Mary Catherine turned back to the kids. She was tender. "I'm going to close this cupboard door now. The trip shouldn't take very long, and I know you'll be fine. Be good."

She started to close the door, but Li Li stopped her. "Mother Mary Catherine! Please... watch out for my mother. Please."

"I will do my best, young lady. But she trusts you to take care of yourself and Garth, and that's what you need to concentrate on. All right?"

"Yes, we will."

The Mother Superior gently closed the door. It was pitch-black inside, and Garth had no nightlight to ease his fear. He knew, *knew*, that he was going to have visions on the trip. He whispered to Li Li. "Don't be scared. I might shake a little, or go away, but you shouldn't worry. I always come back."

He could feel her nod. And as the boat eased out of the dock and began to bob on the churning black water, he could feel himself heading into a terrifying place he didn't want to go. But he closed his eyes and shuddered, letting it happen.

When his horrible vision was over, he blocked everything he had seen until he could process it. But that exhausted him, and even in this dark scary space, he finally fell asleep, lulled by the movement of the supply boat, the darkness, and the comfort of Li Li next to him.

He couldn't tell how long he'd been out when he wakened with a start as the boat's engines shut down. He was grateful he had been able to sleep at all after the last visions. It was cold and damp and he and Li Li were shivering. Garth whispered to her. "Where are we?"

He could feel Li Li shrug as she whispered back. "I heard a buoy bell, so we're close to shore somewhere."

Garth sniffed the air, hard to do cooped up in a hiding place. "I'm pretty sure we're docked on the mainland. More garbage smell and less wind smell."

Li Li couldn't help but giggle, but she repressed it immediately. They were both startled when the door opened and Captain Donny kneeled next to them, grinning.

"Told ya I'd get ya here okay." He helped them out of the hiding place, and steadied them as the boat rocked gently. "Stay behind me, now. I'm gonna put you in the Master's shack, then get help. But you gotta promise me you'll stay there."

They nodded in unison. He gestured to them and they followed him like little ducklings, onto the dock. It was pitch black, with a few stars peeking through the cloud cover. That was good for them.

They made their way quietly up the dock to the Master's shack. It was locked, but Donny picked it within seconds. He ushered the kids inside and made them sit on the floor. "Stay here. I'm gonna unload my stuff from the boat, then get you to the cops, like Mother Mary Catherine told me. Don't say anything, don't move, don't let anyone see you. Got it?"

Li Li agreed. "Got it." They sat down on the floor, out of sight. As soon as they could hear Donny leave, Garth scooched over towards a table. "What are you doing?!"

"Calling my dad." Garth reached up and pulled the landline to the floor, next to him. He dialed Jake's number at Seattle PD.

Pelham picked up at Jake's desk. He stifled a gasp when he heard Garth at the other end of the phone. "This is Garth Fortune. I need to talk to my dad. I didn't call his cell because he doesn't like me to. Is he there?"

Pelham signaled wildly that this call should be traced immediately. "No Garth, but I can connect you. Where are you?"

"I'm not sure. A boatyard somewhere. On the mainland."

"Okay, son, we'll find you. Stay put while I get your dad."

Pelham transferred the call to Jake's cell. Jake had gone home to change, and picked up immediately. His heart almost stopped when he heard the urgency in Pelham's voice. "Garth's calling. I'm putting him through. We're tracing his location."

Jake held his breath until he heard his son's voice.

"Dad?"

Jake could barely stop his voice from breaking, his relief was so all-consuming. "Garth... are you okay?"

"Yes. But Li Li and I are scared. Can you come get us?"

"Yes, of course. Are you safe now?"

"I think so. But I don't know for sure where we are."

"Don't worry. My friends are tracing this call and they'll know exactly where to pick you up. Please stay with them until I get there."

Garth hesitated a moment. "Okay, dad."

Jake got a text from Pelham that they'd traced Garth's location, Squalicum Harbor, in Bellingham. At a boat yard about an hour up the Coast, and the local cops were on their way. "Good news, son. The police are on their way. You're about an hour north of me, so it'll take me a little while to get there."

"Okay. Dad... is Anya better?"

Jake was stunned, but knew better than to ask Garth how he knew about Anya. "I think so, Garth. She's awake now and her mom's with her."

Garth choked back a sob. "Then I think she'll be okay."

"Me, too. And Garth... I love you. I've missed you. Take care of yourself until I see you."

Garth was rocked by this. His dad rarely said mushy things like that. It made him more determined than ever. "I know. I love you too, dad."

Jake hesitated, then let go. "And Garth, I believe in you. If you 'see' anything, trust yourself. Follow your instincts."

Garth half-smiled. He didn't think his dad was going to be happy that he was planning to do exactly that. "I will. Promise." Garth hung up and muttered under his breath. "But please don't be mad at me."

He turned to Li Li who looked at him with a question in her eyes. "My dad said the police are on their way. They'll protect you."

"That should make you happy and it doesn't. How come?"

He didn't want to burden her. "Please stay here and wait for them, okay? I have to... do something."

She looked at him. "Where are you going? Feng Wah could be looking for us right now."

"I have to go back, Li Li. I have to get Captain Donny to take me back."

Li Li was shocked. "Are you crazy? Why? Why?"

He hesitated, then decided to tell her the truth. "I had a bad vision on the boat. I don't know why, but if I'm here, if I'm not on the island, my dad will die. Everyone will die. You understand, don't you?"

Li Li shook her head. She had dealt with a great deal in her life, but this was beyond her. "No. I don't."

"My dad said to follow my instincts. I have to protect him. I have to protect all those people. It was bad. I saw them screaming and crying on a boat and they were drowning and my dad was shot and fell into the water."

"And my mom?"

He told her the truth. "Yes. I think she was there, too. Go hide in one of the boats, Li Li. Don't stay in here. I'm worried that maybe Captain Donny lied and he isn't coming back. I have to find out. Wait until you hear the police sirens."

She followed him outside onto the dock. They instinctively kept in the shadows. "Be careful, Garth. Please."

Garth gave her a hug and slipped away, a determined, scared little boy. It took him five minutes to walk to the far end of the Marina, on his way back to Captain Donny's boat. He took his time because he knew the police were on the way – his dad told him so and he could hear the sirens as they got closer and closer. He quietly moved towards the harbor, until he spotted the supply boat. He planned to beg Captain Donny to take him back to the island, so he could save his father's life. He would offer him money, and swear he'd get it one way or another.

It was scary dark at this end of the Marina. He didn't remember it being like this when they arrived, but he'd been so rushed then that he hadn't paid enough attention. He had an uncanny sense of direction, so he knew he was going the right way. His dad joked that he could use Garth as radar and sonar if necessary. He'd almost reached the boat slip when a hand reached out and grabbed him. He looked up at a glaring Victor. Garth was momentarily glad to see that somebody had hit Victor in his face and it was all swollen and cut, his nose bruised and bent, and his voice sounded funny. "You're a lucky little shit, you know that? The boss won't let me hurt you. Not yet, anyway. But he is waiting for you, so you're gonna be a smart kid and keep your mouth shut."

Victor did his usual number, tossing Garth over his shoulder like he wasn't a person. Out of the corner of his eye, Garth could see Captain Donny lying in a pool of blood on the dock in front of his boat. Unbidden tears flowed from his eyes. He knew Donny had died trying to protect him and Li Li and didn't want anybody else to die protecting him. Especially his father.

# CHAPTER FIFTY-TWO

JAKE AND ALEKS traveled with Tony on an off-the-books Army AS365 chopper. One of Tony's buddies from Lewis McChord JBLM, the base just south of Tacoma, had "borrowed" it. Tony had the foresight to have it waiting nearby, as he told Jake, 'in case'. He said he figured he might need his friend Phil another time, and he wanted to spread the favors around. The pilot, Kevin Gage, said he'd explain it to his CO... later. Or never. No one said a word, and not only because it was too loud to talk. Jake looked ahead, intense. They were almost to Bellingham.

The pilot pointed down at a marina about a mile away. He indicated he'd land the bird in a parking lot on the far north of the docks, and shouted to them that the cops could take them the rest of the way. Jake nodded his thanks. He checked his gun, again, to be sure. Aleks and Tony were armed, but their weapons weren't visible.

As soon as they touched down, Jake's blood pressure rose when he received a text from Pelham that the local PD hadn't found anyone in the Harbor Master's shack and they were methodically checking on all the docks.

*Damn it, Garth. I knew you weren't going to listen to me. Damn it.* They were too late. Jake knew in his gut as soon as they headed down the pier to the Master's Shack that Garth was still nowhere to be found. He could read the body language of the local cops halfway down the dock.

When they entered the shack, there was no sign anyone had been there, except for the phone that Garth had left on the floor. Mark Feldmann, the Sergeant in charge, approached Jake. "We have four guys checking each of the docks, then we'll move to the boats. There are more than usual moored tonight because of the weather. But if he's here, we'll find him."

He was interrupted by shouting several docks over. They hurried outside to see one of the deputies waving his flashlight about 500 yards away. Jake ran, heart pounding, as the others followed. When they got to the *Belle Marie*, the deputy pointed to Captain Donny's lifeless body. "Still really warm. I don't think he's been dead more than a few minutes."

Sergeant Feldmann spoke into his walkie-talkie. "We may have an armed and dangerous suspect on the premises. Stay alert, people, and check every damn boat if you have to."

Jake leaned over Donny's body. "Single gunshot right through his heart. No screwing around." He boarded the boat without asking, Aleks right behind him.

"Hey!"

Jake looked at Feldmann. "I know how to do it. I won't screw up your evidence. It's all out here, anyway."

Jake and Aleks searched below carefully as if they were a team who'd done this a hundred times. They found nothing. When they came back out onto the dock, Jake reported to the Sergeant. "There are no trip logs of any kind. We don't know if he was covering his tracks or if the shooter was buying time. I'm guessing this is the guy who transported Garth."

Jake held it together, even though he knew that meant his son had been taken from him again, right when he thought he had him back.

They heard another shout from down one of the docks. A couple of the deputies, along with Tony, were leading Li Li towards them. Tony looked at Jake. "We found her hiding on one of the boats, under a canvas."

Li Li looked down at Captain Donny's body and sighed, a flicker of sadness across her face. Then she looked around at all the cops, settling on Jake. Fear was etched on his face. "Are you Garth's father?"

Jake nodded.

"I'm Li Li. You look like him. A little."

"Is he okay?"

"I don't know. He left me and told me to hide on a boat away from the shack where Captain Donny left us, and wait until you got here. I heard the sirens but I still wasn't sure it was safe."

"Is this Captain Donny?" Li Li nodded. "I'm sorry."

"Me, too. He helped us escape."

"Where did Garth go?"

"He asked me to tell you that he had a vision, and it was too dangerous for you to look for him. He wanted you to go home."

Jake looked down at this self-possessed child, and gently asked her again. "Where has he gone?"

"Back to my father's island. He was going to ask Captain Donny to take him back, but... Feng Wah must've gotten him instead."

Aleks and Jake looked at each other, then Aleks moved off quietly, calling his team at home with the information.

Jake knelt down next to Li Li. "So Feng Wah is your father?"

She looks ashamed. "Yes. For that I am sorry. My mother insists I must be grateful he gave me life."

Jake smiled, and gently probed. "Garth must've trusted you."

Li Li smiled and nodded.

"What exactly did he say?"

"He said that when we were on Captain Donny's boat he had the worst vision ever. He saw that he was the cause of many people dying. And my mother! And all the people my father sells. He was talking about a ferry boat!"

"Li Li, does your father keep all these people on the island?"

Li Li started to tremble. "Yes. For a while."

Jake put his arm around her and brought her close. "It's okay. I know you're doing the best you can."

Li Li's lip trembled. "It's been so... difficult."

"I can't even imagine. But you have people who will protect you now. I promise you that. And I still need your help."

Li Li was slightly comforted. "Okay."

"Where is your father's island?"

Li Li looked stunned. She had no idea. "I... I don't know. He never said." She tried to figure it out, then reasoned. "I know that it only takes him a little while to fly to the mainland."

"That helps."Aleks joined them again, and Li Li looked at the two of them, serious.

"My father is an evil man. He kills people for no reason. He has many people working for him and they all have guns. Big ones."

"Do you know how many?"

Li Li reported like a pro. "There are three shifts of guards. Three men watch the poor people, five patrol the island. And his head of security, Victor." She said the last with disgust.

"Twenty-four soldiers. And Victor." Now they understood what they were up against.

"We have to do this right." Tony was adamant.

"Garth takes top priority."

"Of course. But that doesn't mean we can't do it right."

Li Li interrupted them, excited. "I forgot the nuns! How could I forget them? I don't know how many there are, but they don't work for him. They're the ones who helped me and Garth get away."

Jake was shaken. The bells. Not the Church bells he dreamed or the ones reported by Lan, but convent bells. He filed away his acknowledgement of his abilities for a calmer time. "That's very helpful, Li Li. That should make it easier to find exactly which island Garth and your mom are on."

He looked at Aleks. "I'm going to give this information to Boris, and to my Captain. As soon as we know the exact coordinates, we can finalize the plans. We should be able to get this done by dawn."

Aleks put his hand gently on Li Li's shoulder. "I'm Aleks. You look cold, young lady. Let's get you back to Seattle, and I'll make sure you get a nice cup of Russian tea. With lots of strawberry jam."

Li Li looked up at the kind stranger, exhausted. Aleks picked her up like he used to with his own daughter, and she let him. When he carried her back to the chopper, Li Li finally relaxed and let him take care of her.

Jake and Tony followed, anxious to get started. They knew they had very little time to prepare for the war that was about to come.

# CHAPTER FIFTY-THREE

Feng Wah's plane descended quietly onto the island's landing strip and pulled to a gentle stop. Feng Wah turned to his pilot, calm and cool. "Refuel and wait here for instructions."

The pilot, Mel Moore, nodded. His eye twitched as he kept the rest of his face noncommittal. Feng Wah stepped out of the plane, and turned back to Garth, who was completely submissive.

"If you wonder how I found you, look under the sole of your right shoe. That's how I tracked you. That was clever of you to lie and ensure I was gone before making your way off the island. But you will never be as smart as I am, and if you attempt anything like that again, I will cut my losses and you will die."

Victor smiled and roughly pulled Garth along to keep up with their fast pace.

"Put him somewhere, then talk to the security team. Get the ferry ready to load and embark."

"The team is set. How long?"

"When I tell you I'm ready. I will rouse my daughter and my wife and gather my things. I don't want to be kept waiting."

Garth covered a gasp. Maybe Feng Wah had known where he was

all the time, but not Li Li. He let himself smile a little, certain that she was now with his dad. Safe.

As soon as Feng Wah entered the house, he discovered that Li Li was gone. The Butler ratted her out, trying to save his own skin. Feng Wah smashed him with a chop to the head. He hated sycophants.

He roughly dragged Garth to his study and had Pearl brought to him. He was livid. "You have nothing to do but provide for my child, and make sure she is obedient." He slapped her, hard, and she teetered backwards. She wouldn't give him the satisfaction of holding her face where it stung. "So I must assume you were responsible. You're no longer of use to me."

He turned to Garth, still undecided. He looked at Victor. "Take her to the huts. She will be part of the group we are ferrying. Keep the boy with you for now."

Victor grabbed Pearl and took pleasure in squeezing her arm tight. She did not flinch until he grabbed Garth's shoulder and pulled him along. "Will do."

Feng Wah was prepared for the worst. He opened his large standing safe, hidden behind one of the wood panels, and pulled out a fitted vest, filled with necessary documents and cash, as well as his weapon of choice, a Sig Sauer P226 Elite. The gun was comfortable, high-end, and deadly.

He didn't waste time looking around. There was no point. He had plans in place, always, to begin again, and in truth he had been getting bored. He would make the most of this situation, as always. His daughter's defection stung deeply, but he would think about that when he was settled elsewhere. He didn't know precisely where she was, but assumed she was with the police. She deliberately broke their bond, and would not escape his anger. But for now it was time to go.

The sun was still a couple of hours away from coming over the horizon as Feng Wah watched Victor and several security guards direct traffic. He showed no emotion when Pearl was herded onto a small private ferry with about 130 illegals. This was the largest group he had ever imported, and the knowledge of Pearl's deception infuriated him. As far as he was concerned, she deserved no more than to be treated as a slave.

The ferry had been rented from an event company, ostensibly for a destination wedding that was supposed to take place at sea, and then dock in Seattle at night. Feng Wah had contracted with the company with the proviso he would provide his own Captain and staff. He paid an exorbitant price for the boat and damage insurance so the company didn't care.

Victor came up to him, dragging Garth next to him. "What do you want to do with the kid?"

Feng Wah looked down at Garth. "I offered you a special place. You lied to me and betrayed me, as did my daughter. I will deal with her separately. You will go onto the ferry with everyone else, and you will join the rest of my merchandise below deck."

Garth's face was calm, but his lip quivered.

"And I promise you this: you will never again see your father or family. I thought that was a better punishment for you than an easy death."

Garth couldn't help himself, he bit back a sob but tears streamed down his face as Victor pushed him on board the ferry, in line with the others. Feng Wah turned away, not seeing that Pearl had been waiting for Garth. She slipped her hand into his, holding it tightly as she led him below deck.

The crowd was quiet as they were ushered into a holding room. There were four guards watching them carefully, all armed with M60s. Because it was a rental party boat, the accommodations were far superior to what the captives had been used to for the last weeks, including their journey from China and their brief time in the shacks. They were docile, grateful for the available bathrooms and running water. When a nursing mother asked for permission to use the washroom, and one of the guards indicated it was okay, a collective sigh of relief was felt throughout the room.

Pearl guided Garth to a corner under the watchful eye of two of the security guards who knew who she was. They hadn't been instructed how to treat her, so for now they were paying close attention to her movements. Pearl saw that Garth was in a state of shock, the events of the past few days finally sinking in. He turned to her, shaking. "I messed everything up."

Pearl shushed him. "You are only nine years old. It is right that you are scared. I promise I will do my best to take care of you, like you did for my Li Li."

"Everyone's gonna die because of me. I saw it."

"Child, we are not giving up. Never." She put her arms around Garth, and pulled him close to comfort him, as he wept the tears of a little boy.

# CHAPTER FIFTY-FOUR

## Fourth Day After

THEY'D FOUND FENG Wah's island. It was closing in on dawn and the Pashkovs' living room was buzzing with activity. Jake and Aleks had decided on the trip back from the Marina that they'd give information to Seattle PD – but not all of it. Thackery knew about Li Li, but Jake refused to take her to headquarters. She didn't know anything, she was safe, and he didn't want the system involved. She was with a friend and that's where she was going to stay.

Thackery didn't have the energy to argue with him. Even though it was out of their jurisdiction, they had another murder to add to this guy's list of crimes, and what they needed to do was find him. Jake's plan was he'd let them know about the coordinates for the small private island, but not until it was too late to catch up with them. He wasn't going to let anyone else try to save Garth. Aleks and Tony had gathered more information in two days than the Seattle PD, or, as far as he knew, the Feds had in four. Let his colleagues deal with the murders. His agenda was more important to him.

Tony came into the living room from the kitchen. "I have Phil's seaplane and Kevin Gage appropriated three Little Birds they'll 'lose' for the next twelve hours. There'll be Phil and five of us on the plane. We'll have two pilots apiece on the helos, and I've called in some favors for crew. Four on each bird. They'll be ready in thirty minutes, and it's about a forty-five-minute trip for the plane, with the birds tagging along. We're meeting them at a private airfield ten minutes from here. They'll all fly under the radar."

Aleks nodded. "Amazing work, Tony."

Jake thought so, too, but he wasn't surprised. His dad had been a badass soldier, and if the circumstances had been different Jake would have been able to take pleasure in his logistical abilities. But now they were simply necessary. "Do they know what they're walking into?"

"Yes."

"Okay." Jake followed Tony outside, Aleks right behind them with Boris and Peter.

Jake turned to Aleks. "Are you sure you want…"

Aleks cut him off. "…They won't stay here. The boys know how to use a gun, and they know how to take care of themselves. Don't worry about them."

"I won't, then." Nothing else needed to be said as they all headed to the cars.

When they got to the airfield, a Dornier Seastar was ready and waiting. It took off during another pelting sideways rainstorm. The plane's interior was climate-controlled and perfectly appointed. Tony was almost amused – this was way more comfortable than the Little Birds. He sat in the co-pilot seat next to his friend, Phil, who'd transported Jake to Vancouver. "Thanks for yesterday."

"No problem. It was good to do something real. Tourists can be a pain in the ass." This luxurious seaplane was only one of his fleet that did tours like his helos. Phil was also in the delivery business, but Tony never asked what he was delivering, nor did he care. Phil and Tony had served together and Phil would – and did – do anything for his buddy, and vice versa.

Jake sat quietly behind them, in one of the leather-bound passenger chairs, staring at the water below. His mind was on the task ahead. Aleks and his sons were two rows back, playing gin. Nobody could ever beat Boris, and there was nothing different about this time.

The three Little Birds were keeping pace behind them, each with its two pilots and four soldiers on board, ready to engage. Phil announced: "Five minutes to the coordinates! I've alerted the choppers and they're ready."

Jake turned to Tony, worried that they'd missed something vital. "I hope your friend in the Church…"

"…knows what he's talking about? He does. We were altar boys together and I trust him completely. No worries. Aside from the fact there's only one convent in the whole of the San Juans, the Order he described exactly fit what Li Li told us. Relax. We're headed to the right place."

"I get it, dad. And don't bother telling me that's not what I'm really worried about."

"Now that you bring it up… you need to let us military types take the lead when we land."

"You forget I was a military type, too. Is it that you don't think I can handle rescuing my son?"

Tony reacted with impatience and affection. "Of course you can handle it, asshole. But I want you to be careful. It's not that I don't think you're at the top of your game. But you know what Garth said. And damn, if I didn't believe that kid before, I sure do now."

Jake was frustrated beyond belief. "What nine-year-old kid deliberately walks back into the fire?"

"Your son. My grandson. He believes all that Kung Fu hero shit. I'm never gonna let him watch that goddamn show again. We're gonna have to train him better when he gets home."

"That's all I care about. Him home. Safe."

"You still have to understand he went back because he believed you'd be hurt if he didn't."

"I know he believes what he saw. That doesn't make it true. He's under enormous stress."

Tony sighed. "Right or wrong, be on your guard, okay?"

"Always."

The pilot announced they were three minutes from the target. Tony was all business. "Confirm to the choppers the approach is still from the north. The topography gives us more cover if we head in over the convent side of the island."

"They're confirmed."

Aleks and his sons put away their cards and checked their weapons. Aleks had his favorite old Sig Sauer. The boys went to Glock 26s. Tony had his old service revolver, a Beretta M9, and an M11 SigSauer as back-up. Jake stuck with his backup and the same SigSauer that Tony carried. And Tony had appropriated a few M67 frag hand grenades from the commando team, just in case.

They swooped in low over the convent, and Jake imagined he could hear the bells chiming. The island foliage was verdant and overgrown, a perfect hiding spot for illegal activities.

As they came across the hills, the plane let the choppers take the lead, and the commandos positioned themselves to jump to the target as soon as they were at the right altitude.

Jake spotted Feng Wah's compound and house first and pointed it out to Tony and Aleks. Closer to the beach he could see corrugated huts covered with camouflage. No wonder they weren't spotted by any satellite. In the distance they could see a short landing strip on the far side of the compound, near the water. A Seawind 300C, a luxurious seaplane, was parked at the beginning of the strip. From this height they saw no life. Tony signaled for the commandos to land near the compound and shacks. Phil was going to land in the water, below the landing strip.

The noise was deafening as all the air support came together, so there was no chance of surprise. They didn't know what resistance they'd face, but they were ready.

Colonel Jeremy Smith, another of Tony's long-time buddies, was piloting the first of the choppers, and running the mission. He signaled for his men to deploy. Their movements would have looked balletic if they hadn't been carrying heavy weaponry.

Jake motioned to Phil to land the seaplane on the strip instead of the ocean. "Can you land there and block the plane from taking off?"

"With pleasure." Phil maneuvered the Seastar to the short runway, changed to land mode with ease, and took the Seastar down gently. It stopped nose to nose with the plane on the runway.

Jake could see there was a Pilot in the Seawind, looking terrified. He immediately put his hands up. He knew he had no chance.

The twelve commandos under Colonel Smith began to search the compound and surrounding areas, expecting to encounter heavy fire. But aside from the pilot, the outside compound appeared to be empty. That left the big house, which is exactly where they headed.

Jake leapt off the Seastar, the others right behind him. He ran up to Feng's plane and roughly pulled the pilot, Mel Moore, out. "Don't shoot! I'm not armed."

"I don't give a shit if you're armed. Where is everyone?!"

Moore hesitated. "Gone."

"Everyone is gone? Then why are you parked here like a sitting duck?"

"I'm waiting for Victor."

Aleks pushed towards the pilot, speaking very quietly. "And where might Victor be?"

"He's late. He went back to the house for something. I heard you guys and he must have, too. He'd kill me if I left him here."

Tony spoke into his satellite radio to Colonel Smith. "At least one enemy in the house. Heavily armed. Proceed with caution."

Smith and several of his unit moved towards the mansion, fast and carefully, while one of his men tied up the pilot.

Jake began to interrogate him as a cop, annoying Tony and Aleks. "Who do you work for?"

"Man, I'll tell you everything I know, and it's not much. I work for

Feng Wah. Victor works for him. They both scare the shit out of me."

Jake was impatient. "Then why?"

"I have a family. They know it. Enough said."

"Does he own this plane?"

"Yes."

"Does he transport illegal immigrants on it?"

"No."

"Give me a little more here. Or I'll turn you over to the people who haven't taken an oath."

"I've never transported an immigrant, but I know they're kept here. He moves them by boat. I rarely fly Victor. Only the boss, and then to Vancouver and Seattle. Mostly Vancouver. I don't know what he does there or where he goes. He's not a sharing kind of guy."

They could hear shouts and gunshots coming from the estate. Alert, two of Colonel Smith's men circled protectively around Jake, Tony, Aleks, the boys and the pilot. The gunfire ended abruptly.

Jake was ready to move. "I'm going up there."

Tony put his hand on Jake's arm. "No, Jake. Let them handle it."

Tony was proven right when they saw the troops come down the hill from the mansion, dragging Victor with them. The hairs went up on the back of Jake's neck.

"That's him?" Aleks was calm.

"Yes."

"Good." Aleks indicated the boys should stand back. "Wait until we get every bit of information we can from him. That's Jake's province. But pay attention. You could learn something." Peter and Boris grumbled but acquiesced.

The commando team was not gentle. They had Victor's hands secured behind his back with ASP tacticals. He had a new welt on his face, his nose was still swollen and crooked, but there were no other overt injuries. Jake and Aleks watched Victor as he moved closer. His face had cuts and bruises from Anya's defense, but he had no expression, no fear, nothing in his eyes that resembled humanity.

Without communicating with each other, Aleks and Tony stepped forward and did a combination of body punches that left Victor coughing. They then backed off. Aleks turned to Jake: "He's yours. For now."

"Good. As much as I'd like to see him suffer a slow death, I need some information."

He hadn't even glanced at Victor yet. "If he doesn't give me what I want, it looks like there are lot of places to put him around here where no one will find him." He then turned to Victor. He didn't use his cop stare. He used his calm I'm going to fucking kill you if you don't tell me where my kid is stare.

Victor stared back, then smiled as best he could. "So you think you're a tough guy."

Jake's answer was a palm strike to his mouth. It hurt, he loosened some teeth, and blood dripped from Victor's mouth. "Yes. Any more questions?"

Victor's ears were ringing and it hurt when he shook his head no. "I want a deal."

"Multiple murders, kidnapping, assault on a cop with a deadly weapon, resisting arrest, smuggling across the border... I'm pretty sure you can make a deal with the Feds, they'll deal with anyone for information. My deal is: you'll live if you give me answers. You'll die if you don't. Slowly. Take it or leave it. You have thirty seconds." Jake looked at his watch, carefully.

"Deal."

Jake barely reacted. "Where is your boss?"

"He rented a party ferry from Executive Excursions for a fake wedding. He loaded the chinks on it."

"How many?"

Victor shrugged, then winced from the movement. "130, give or take. I don't know if he left any behind."

"None that we can find."

"Then 130."

"Who else is on board?"

Victor half-smiled, as best he could. "Yeah. That. His wife. Your kid. Feng Wah."

Jake stayed stoic. "Security."

"Twelve guys."

"What happened to the rest of his guards?"

Victor shrugged. "I guess he didn't need 'em anymore. They left."

"Don't make me drag this out of you. Where the fuck is the boat now, and where is it headed?"

"It's headed for Seattle. Berth 1, Pier 51 dock at the end of Columbia. 'Spost to dock late tonight. Had to fill the time so he could unload the merchandise when no one was around. The cover is it's 'spost to be a big wedding reception out at sea, so it's circling somewhere in the Strait until then. I don't know where."

Jake looked at him carefully. "What's his backup plan?"

"You're smart for a cop. He has one, but I don't know what it is. He only told me what he wanted me to know. Maybe the plane was 'spost to drop me off and then circle back for him. Ask the asshole pilot."

Jake knew Victor was holding back. "What aren't you telling me?"

Victor thought a minute, then shrugged. "Nothing."

"Bullshit. Deal's off. We're done here."

As Jake turned away, Victor told him. "The boat's booby-trapped with C-4."

Tony gasped, as Aleks stayed quiet. Jake couldn't breathe as he felt the air deflate from his lungs.

Jake had to hold Tony back. "All those people. You motherfucker."

"I do what I'm paid to do."

Jake maintained his calm. "Where are the explosives planted?"

Victor shrugged. "He didn't tell me. But I heard him talking to the bomb guy about putting them in the bulkhead and the engine room, and I'm pretty sure he has another place. For sure he has another backup plan to get off the boat early if there's trouble, but he wasn't interested in sharing that either."

Jake turned to Aleks. "Make sure he doesn't go anywhere. I'll be right back."

He moved off with Tony, out of range for Victor to overhear. "We have to get to that boat while it's in the Sound. Defuse the bombs, or evacuate the boat and explode them, before the ferry gets near the waterfront. That sonovabitch was counting on that to be able to get away."

"Yes. But we have enough people here to do that. At least two of them are bomb experts. Including me."

"I know that, dad. But we have no location on the ferry. If it's zigzagging through the Strait, there's no way to find it without satellite help. And that means the Coast Guard."

"Aleks' people can locate the ferry."

"It's time for experts to take over. I'm not saying don't use your guys. We will. But if we don't get the Coast Guard in, the people who know how to do this, and we lose everyone on the ferry, we're fucked and they're fucked."

"This isn't about ego, Jake."

"I know."

"They'll get in the way with all their rules."

"I won't let them. Let's see if they can locate it. I'm betting we're closer than they are anyway. We need to get out of here now."

Tony agreed. "My guys will get us there. We have the manpower, the firepower, and the know-how. The Coast Guard can clean up."

"And they can evacuate the boat. We don't have the men or materials to do that."

Tony nodded, but he was itching to get moving. "I'll fill Jeremy in. What do you want to do with the Pilot?"

"Disable his plane and leave him here, locked up. The County Sheriff can pick him up later. And tell Phil we'll need him to take Aleks and the boys home."

Jake called Tony back as he moved to join Aleks and the boys. "Dad." Tony turned. "Let Aleks have him. You have better things to do."

Tony hesitated, then agreed. "Okay, son. Your call."

Tony moved off to fill in the commandos as Jake walked back to Victor. "We're taking off. Phil will give you and the boys a ride back to the mainland." Aleks smiled and Jake started to walk away.

"Hey!" Jake turned back to see Victor, struggling.

"Oh. He's all yours."

Boris and Peter moved forward. Boris smiled. "Finally."

Victor looked at the two boys and freaked out for the first time. "What about my deal?!"

Jake looked at him for a long time, as if memorizing his face. "Victor Kasun. Somewhere from the Kosovo area, I'm guessing. You still have a slight accent."

Victor glared at Jake. "So."

"So, I imagine there's a lot of payback coming for whatever you did there. That's not my problem. My problem is what you did here. To my son. To my father. To my partner. No way on God's earth I'll let you get away with that. I couldn't live with myself if I did. I can live with myself for lying to you."

Jake ignored Victor's screams as Aleks, Peter and Boris dragged him off. And then he was gone.

# CHAPTER FIFTY-FIVE

GARTH AND PEARL were still huddled in the corner of the large area below deck. Garth couldn't believe he'd fallen asleep in the comfort of her arms. He was a little embarrassed and she knew it.

He looked around the room, and it was the same as before. Feng Wah was nowhere in sight. People drawn closely together whispering, under the watchful eye of the armed guards. Garth shuddered. The windows were open on both ends and it was really cold.

Pearl whispered to him. "Do you know where we are?"

Garth closed his eyes and let his senses receive information. He looked at her. "I'm pretty sure we're past the Strait of Juan de Fuca because it's calmer now. But I don't think we've moved much. Does it feel like we're going around in big circles?"

Pearl laughed softly. "That's what I thought, too."

Garth was puzzled. "Do you think they're doing it so no one can find us?"

Pearl sighed. "I stopped trying to understand the reasoning of my husband a very long time ago. But I am guessing he has a plan and the time isn't right. And no one in this little village of ours has any idea what's waiting for them."

Pearls words triggered something in Garth. "Why do you call this a 'little village of ours'?

Pearl shrugged. "Because in this moment, we are a small community facing the same challenges."

Garth understood. "I wish we could do what they did in Bossy's village."

Pearl was confused. "Bossy?"

"My godmother's great-grandmother. She always tells me the story before bed. All the people in her village got together and killed the serpent that ate Bossy. They saved her life."

Pearl looked at Garth thoughtfully. "Let me get you some water. We do not know how long we will be here and you must remain hydrated." She patted Garth's shoulder. "I will be right back."

Garth watched her move across the huge space for cars, now filled with people, and stare down a guard. He could see her pointing to a small area that looked like a mini-kitchen to Garth. The guard relented and let her through.

He sighed and closed his eyes. He knew what was coming, and at this point was too emotionally exhausted to resist. It was similar to the last vision, but more detailed.

*Jake is running through flames along the open deck. So much fire, that's all Garth can see. Hot and everywhere, surrounding his father, engulfing him. A shot is fired but the shooter is not visible. Jake is hit in the chest and the blood spurts like a geyser from his heart, and he falls backwards, overboard into the dark, churning waters. Garth's beloved San Juans turn into the fires of hell. Garth screams and screams as he watches his father disappear into the blackness.*

When he came out of his vision he realized he'd been screaming aloud. All of the illegals were watching him, terrified, and some began to shout at him. Garth was mortified and scared and did the only thing he could think of – he turned and faced the wall as if he were being punished for speaking out in class.

Pearl hurried over to Garth with water and made him sip it. She held him to stop his shivering and whirled back towards the crowd, addressing them in several Chinese dialects, sternly reprimanding them for yelling at a little boy. They grumbled and turned away, having let out their own frustration and fear. Pearl turned back to Garth, to comfort him again as best she could.

Garth was still trembling, but kept his voice low. "He's going to die! Everyone here is screaming. I can't stop it! I thought I could by coming back to the island, but I can't!"

Pearl remained calm. "Your father is a very enterprising man, Garth. You must have faith in him. Trust that he will be all right. That we all will."

Garth's eyes met hers. Without ego, he admitted to her. "I've never been wrong. Well, almost never."

Pearl actually smiled. "Never is a long time."

Garth sighed, still shaken. "Grandpa always says… 'never say never'.

"He sounds like a wise man."

"He's almost as smart as my dad."

"Then trust him. I like that. 'Never say never.' Because you may have a gift, Garth, but I have age and experience. And I know that my husband has won too many times. No one always wins. It's his turn to fail. And that's what we will pray for. Now drink this water, and then we will talk. I think because of you we have a plan."

# CHAPTER FIFTY-SIX

JAKE AND TONY huddled with Colonel Smith and his co-pilot, Brian. Jake explained about the explosives on the ferry, which was circling somewhere in the Straits, making its way towards the Seattle Harbor.

"We have people working on the exact location, but for now it's a cipher. As soon as we find it, I'll need to be dropped close enough to the boat so I can get there in a short time, but far enough away so they won't spot me. Is that doable?"

Tony objected. "Not I, Jake. We."

"You've all done enough. This is crossing into very dangerous territory."

Colonel Smith was matter-of-fact. "We're trained for this. It's why we do what we do."

"Is it possible?"

"Yes. The radar we have onboard should be able to locate the boat, regardless of what your people find. We know it's on a path to the Harbor, we know when they left, and so we need to look for an image that is moving more slowly than other boat traffic. That will narrow it down. I suggest we move now, and pardon the pun, do it on the fly."

"Okay. But we'll need to notify the Coast Guard."

The Colonel smiled. "We'll notify them. My plan is to be your primary back-up. I'll let the CG and Homeland know what we've 'discovered' on our routine mission. *After* you're in the water and close to boarding."

Tony couldn't help but mutter: "Told ya."

Jake was worried he was leading them into real trouble. "What happens if this goes south? And you lose a chopper. Or worse, one of your men."

"We're not going to lose anything or anyone. Including you. I have discretion on our maneuvers. It's the law of the sea that you rescue people from ships in distress. Don't worry about us."

Tony pushed. "Let them do what they do best, Jake."

"If it makes you more comfortable, as soon as we spot the ferry, I'll let the CG know we're on maneuvers in the area and spotted something suspicious. And offer to provide backup for them. That'll give you and my men time to board."

Jake hesitated and the Colonel became slightly impatient. "Look, Jake, none of my guys could live with themselves if they let a hundred people die when they could have been saved. Let us do our job and you focus on what you have to do. Besides, it's time Tony got off his duff and practiced his real craft."

Jake put his hands up. "I know when I'm outnumbered."

Aleks had come up behind him, Boris and Peter following. Jake asked no questions as he saw they were calm. They'd purged their anger, and there was no sign of remorse on their faces. "Outnumbered for what?"

"They've convinced me to utilize their expertise."

"Always a wise choice. So we'll take the plane back and work with our people. They should zero in on the ferry's location soon, although I imagine the Colonel's equipment can do it as well on the spot." Smith nodded his appreciation of Aleks' professionalism.

"And you know how to reach us if you need anything."

Boris and Peter started to object but Aleks put up his hand. "We've done what we needed to do. Now we'll do what we're best at doing. Let the professionals work."

He reached out and shook Jake's hand, then covered it with his other hand. "Go get your son."

"Thank you. Again."

Aleks gave him a big hug, then he and Anya's two brothers moved towards the seaplane.

Jake watched them go, feeling a sense of comfort he hadn't felt in a very long time. Then he turned and followed Colonel Smith and his father onto the lead chopper. They had work to do.

# CHAPTER FIFTY-SEVEN

PEARL KNEW SHE was taking a big chance. For once, though, luck was on her side. The security guard she thought she had the best connection with was standing closest to her and Garth. His name was Robin, and his eyes never stopped roaming over the crowd of people. Yet in the past she had seen an occasional glimpse of humanity in him, like when he nursed a wounded seabird back to health on the island. If she didn't make the effort, she'd never forgive herself for failing Garth and her daughter. She'd promised Li Li that she would do her best to get away, and so far her best wasn't good enough.

She whispered to Garth that he was to stay here and try to remain invisible. That meant no movements that could catch the attention of the guards. Or of the other prisoners. He said okay but sighed and closed his eyes and she saw he was afraid. She squeezed his shoulder and told him to keep having faith.

Pearl kept her cool and moved slowly towards Robin, approaching him quietly. His eyes followed her as she made her way towards him, and she knew he was hoping she wouldn't approach him. Robin looked pissed-off as he growled at Pearl. "Go back and sit down, Mrs."

Pearl smiled at him. "It's important I speak with you, Robin. And it's important for you that you listen. Why don't you walk me towards the bathroom as if you're watching my every move?" Robin stood there, frozen. She touched his arm. "I watched you feed those abandoned birds last year. I know you're not like the rest of them."

He hesitated, then barely whispered. "Okay." He followed alongside her slowly as she assumed he would. She made herself very small and submissive, which would look better to anyone who was watching. She was good at that.

Pearl kept her voice low. "I need your help to get me and the boy off the boat." She felt him slow down but put her arm on his and kept them moving. "I will pay you well. I have the resources, resources my husband is not aware of. If you don't do this, the boy and I will die."

He whispered. "I should turn you in."

She knew that if he hadn't given her away then, she had a chance to convince him. "If you do, I will die sooner, but I will die anyway. What you don't know is that you will be dead as well. My husband has explosives planted on this ferry. He's not aware that I know, of course. But the only people who will escape will be Feng Wah and the crew of the launch he has arranged to pick him up."

Robin and Pearl had almost reached the bathrooms. Her hand was still on his arm, and she felt his pulse begin to race. He paled. "I don't believe you."

She looked him in the eye and let him read her expression. "Tell me that you trust my husband more than you trust me. I know you're too smart for that."

Robin looked at her and blanched. He was barely breathing. "What do you want me to do?"

She told him only the part he needed to know. "Garth will become sick. I will accompany him. You'll take us to the back bathroom. From there they won't see us. You can convince Mr. Scott that we need air or Garth will throw up and that will make everyone down here throw up and he'll be stuck in the misery of 130 people vomiting at once. He won't like that and he'll let you escort us upstairs. You'll put us on one of the life rafts. And if you're smart, you will join us."

She saw he was torn, and trying to control his panic. She prodded him: "Think of it this way: possible death if you help us; certain death if you don't.

A moment later, self-preservation won. "Okay. Go on back with water for the kid. I'll let Scotty know he isn't feeling good now and you're going to try to settle his stomach. Once we get out of here, you'll have to do exactly as I say. And when we're back, you'll pay me $500,000.00."

Pearl smiled. "Done."

Robin half-smiled. "Too easy, Mrs. Make it a million." Pearl nodded. "Yes." She walked away, almost hopeful for the first time since she was forced to marry Feng Wah fifteen years before. She held on to that thought and knew it would have to get her through whatever was coming.

She reached Garth, who sat against the wall, leaning his back and his head against the wood slats, his eyes closed. Pearl gently touched his arm, and his eyes flew open, anxious. "Are you all right, Garth? Did you have another vision?"

"No." He hesitated, then: "But my father is close. I can feel it."

She worried this little boy wasn't going to be able to hold it together much longer. "I know it's hard, but you will see him soon."

Garth nodded, and held his stomach. "I want to see him so bad my tummy hurts."

Pearl put her arm around him, whispered into his ear. "Then get ready to follow me."

"What are you going to do?"

"Remember the story you told me about your Godmother and her great-grandmother's village?"

Garth's eyes widened, and he whispered. "Yes."

"It was very smart and we are going to follow her lead, and the people here will rebel and distract while we go with Robin."

Garth couldn't believe she had really listened to him. But he wasn't sure anymore that he'd been right. "But what about all the others?"

"They will save themselves. Which is what we will be doing. You must trust me, Garth. Feng Wah cares nothing about these people. He cares about me and you. And not in a way that is good for either of us." She took his hand. "I know it's frightening, but we need to go now." She felt his terror, but he allowed her to take him by the hand.

Pearl began moving towards Robin, who had positioned himself close to them. He had done what she asked, and the other guards ignored them. She leaned into Garth. "I have already spoken with the others. Soon they will begin to agitate. Keep moving towards Robin, no matter what happens. He has a lifeboat waiting for us."

She guided Garth along the edge of the room, nodding at the men and women she had alerted. Pearl and Garth had barely reached Robin when a murmur moved through the cabin. The group began to shout questions of the guards in multiple Chinese dialects. One of the guards started hitting the people closest to him with the butt of his automatic. He was soon surrounded and disarmed. A young, strong man smacked him in the face with the butt of his own gun, then spat on him, as the rest of the group surrounded the two other guards. Pearl had assumed and was correct they'd be hesitant to shoot, both because they knew they were outnumbered, and because Feng Wah would destroy them. The only way they had kept these people in check was by fear. Now they were the ones who would be afraid as they were overwhelmed and beaten unconscious by the captive immigrants.

Robin was in a hurry to usher them out. Two of the illegals, father and son, began to attack him and fight for his gun. Pearl stopped them, rebuking them in Cantonese and Mandarin. She quickly shooed them back. "Follow the plan! Take care of the other guards!"

She and Garth disappeared down the corridor after Robin. They hurried towards the middle deck, Pearl alert and praying no one else would see them.

# CHAPTER FIFTY-EIGHT

THE SEATTLE WEATHER didn't disappoint. As usual, the sky was dark and overcast, which the Colonel had assured Jake would work to their advantage. Jake could hear the noise of the chopper's blades even through the headset, but it didn't bother him. It focused him as his eyes scanned the hazy waters below. He knew the Colonel would spot the target on radar first, but searching gave him something to do.

He could see Tony doing the same thing on the opposite side of the helo. The Colonel's guys hanging off the side were as relaxed and alert as if they were riding a carousel at the amusement park. Jake knew they were watching the Sound as well.

Jake listened closely as the Colonel reported he thought they were nearing the ferry. He told them not to be concerned, as maneuvers by the military in this area were typical, and any ferry Captain would know that. His radar showed a slow-moving vessel, doing ten knots, about five nautical miles away. It could be doing wide circles, and if so, that would be their target.

He assured Jake that he had alerted the Coast Guard to their maneuvers and suspicions, and as soon as they confirmed the ferry, they'd coordinate with them and all the other involved agencies. The Coast

Guard needed time to secure vessels that could carry 130 plus to move into the Straits, and that's what they were doing while waiting for the signal to deploy.

Jake was grateful. He was calmer than he'd expected, mostly because the logistics were out of his hands. He knew he'd be on high alert as soon as he and Tony were lowered into the Sound onto the motorized military dinghy. The Colonel was going to send two of the four guys on this chopper with them. He'd deploy the other two in the next dinghy, and the rest of the troops when he deemed necessary. This was his operation, he was the expert, and he'd let Jake and Tony go first, but not without back-up. His craft, his decision.

Jake agreed, knowing argument would fail anyway. He was also grateful to have professionals right behind him. He had no idea what kind of opposition they'd be facing once they found the boat. Victor could have been lying about it all, and he was never going to be around to ask.

The Colonel pointed to the radar, circling his finger in the air, indicating there was a boat below that was circling. There was some static and talk between the Pilots, then the Colonel turned to Tony and Jake.

"We've identified the boat. It's definitely doing large loops. The ID matches the intel Aleks' people gave us. We're going to drop you and my men in a blind spot, and the other dinghies a few yards away. You'll follow in the ferry's wake and then you should board undetected from the middle of the vessel, where they store the lifeboats. Engines and propellers both fore and aft. Avoid them."

The chopper swooped down low enough to let the commandos drop a dinghy into the water. They climbed down the ropes as the wind whipped them around. Jake didn't remember ever being this cold and didn't want to know what the wind chill factor was. He had to ignore it. He was grateful that at least the chopper held steady as he and Tony slipped into the dinghy churning in the rough waters.

As soon as they were installed into the small craft, the lead commando, Dickie, waved the helo to lift off. The other choppers followed, to allow all the men to deploy. Dickie put his thumbs up: they were ready. Jake responded, thumbs up, and turned to Tony. Tony smiled and shouted above the noise of the waves and motors. "This will work. I know it."

Jake grabbed his dad's arm in a vise and looked at him. "One way or another, we'll get him back."

Tony nodded, trying not to shiver, and failing.

"And you be careful, dad. No hero shit."

The visibility was worse as the rain poured down, which was better for them. Jake thought it might snow, but he didn't care as long as their cover held. The wind howled as he and Tony and the team caught sight of the ferry ahead of them. They maneuvered behind its wake so they would be harder to spot, and the other chopper trailed behind.

The Colonel had strong-armed his buddy back on base to use their satellites to give them a visual of the boat. He was radioed the positions of the guards on the deck, and an ID of the weapons they carried. Three men were staged forward, and four in the Captain's cabin. They knew there should be guards below, but the heat images couldn't distinguish the guards and detainees on the lower deck, where most of the images were, so they planned to exercise extreme caution taking the lower deck. They also figured that the guards there were more concerned with controlling the crowd of detainees than about anyone boarding them from the water. The last thing they expected was an all-out assault from the Sound.

The ferry's engines, forward and aft, were loud enough to mask anything that might approach from below, but the guards weren't concerned with that. They scanned the skies regularly to make sure they weren't being followed. A chopper or a plane now and then was to be expected. But luckily for the rescue team, technology was way ahead of the mercenaries.

The commandos with Jake and Tony, Dickie and Roger, slipped over the edge of the dinghy as they had done so many times before in other parts of the world. They went quietly into the water, near the middle of the ferry. Jake and Tony watched them, knew they would do their jobs, and Tony and Jake would follow when they got the signal to move. The boat edged closer to the ferry.

"Stay out of their sight line."

"I know what I'm supposed to do, Tony." This was not Jake's milieu, but nothing was going to stop him from reaching Garth. Not the guns, not the sociopath holding his child, not the freezing spray from the chop in the Sound.

"Wasn't criticizing, son."

"Okay."

Dickie and Roger moved as a team, throwing their hooks on the starboard side of the ferry, then climbed as if they were walking up a staircase. They had the updated information on the guards' positions downloaded to them before they hit the deck. They knew where each guard was in real time, and moved onboard accordingly.

Once on deck they padded quietly behind the three mercenaries mid-boat and dispatched them quickly, silently and effectively. They weren't interested in taking prisoners and didn't. The last guard felt something going on, but turned too late. Taking care of him was a little messier, but done quickly.

Dickie signaled Jake and Tony to move to the makeshift ladders to be hoisted on board, as the two other commando teams, a total of ten men, had approached the boat on the port side and were scattering to the other decks to search out the rest of the guards. As Jake and Tony came on board, two shots rang out. Dickie spoke into his radio: "Report."

"Team okay. Seven hostiles down. One wounded. Three still missing. Send Dad below to deck four. Watch your six."

"Out." Dickie signaled to Roger to move to the top deck. "They've disappeared off radar. They're hiding up there."

Tony shrugged. "Bow engine room for me. Likeliest place for the big explosives."

"Glen will accompany you." A commando appeared in the mist, as if out of nowhere. "Go." He turned to Jake. "Go below deck."

They split up and Jake was cautious heading down, but moved quickly. He wasn't surprised when he found the original guards tied up, banged up and knocked out, and all the illegals milling around, ready to break for it.

Abe, one of the two commandos below deck, stopped him. "No sign of your son. One of these guys said he and Feng Wah's wife slipped out earlier with another guard. And there are still several guards on the upper deck near the forward Captain's cabin."

Jake was frustrated. So close. Abe touched his ear bud. "10-4." He turned to Jake. "Coast Guard is enroute to get these folks off. They're close. Tony's below in the forward engine room. He reported too many explosives for him to do alone."

Jake was torn. He wanted to help Tony but his primary mission was to find Garth. "Let Tony know I'll be down as soon as I recover Garth."

"No need. We sent two guys down to help him, and two more to recon the aft engines."

Jake took the stairs two at a time, quick but cautious. He'd been on ferries his whole life, and their configuration was not a mystery to him. This one was no different. If Garth was still on the boat, it would be in the top deck's Captain's quarters, with Feng Wah, and that's where he was headed, no matter what was waiting there.

# CHAPTER FIFTY-NINE

Garth and Pearl almost made it. They didn't screw up their escape — Feng Wah had expected her to try.

Right as they reached the life raft, one of Feng Wah's main mercs, Arnie, came out of the shadows and took out Robin. The gun was silenced so all Pearl and Garth saw was a hole appear in Robin's chest as the blood and life spilled out of him, exactly as Garth had seen happening to his father. Pearl covered Garth's eyes, but nothing would ever wipe out what he'd just witnessed.

Arnie pushed the two of them up a staircase, a hidden one that led directly into the forward Captain's quarters. Feng Wah was waiting for them in the spartan anteroom, dressed for the weather. The Captain was in the room beyond, behind a locked door and wide windows. He stared ahead, his co-pilot at the helm. They wanted to see nothing of what they suspected was happening.

Feng Wah looked at Pearl and Garth. He didn't indicate they should sit, and they didn't. Pearl fold her arms across her chest. He smiled. "You came very close. I am impressed. And surprised. I underestimated you. And Li Li."

She didn't respond as Feng Wah, unaware that the ferry was being taken over at that moment, looked down at Garth. "I believe we've reached the end of the road. You aligned yourself with the wrong side, foolish boy. I was willing to allow you your mistakes. You could have lived and eventually I would have let you become rich. That won't happen now. I made my way without you and I shall do so again."

He turned to Arnie. "Deal with them. I don't want them found."

Garth, still in shock from seeing Robin's death, shivered. Pearl stood her ground and faced her husband. "I don't think that would be a good business decision, son of a turtle."

She just called him a bastard, and Feng Wah's voice rose, betraying his fury. "You know nothing of business. Or anything else."

"Perhaps not. But I managed to keep Li Li safe." She smiled, which pushed Feng Wah to slap her across the face with no mercy. She fell backwards. Garth cried out and reached for her, but couldn't stop her from hitting the deck, hard. As she struggled to get up, she glared at Feng Wah. "Foolish man. You hurt me or the boy, you will never retrieve your money." She lifted herself off the ground and looked at him, calm and defiant.

That got his attention. "You babble."

"I've done many things in my life, some decent, some foolish. But babbling is not one of my dominant characteristics, as you should know by now."

He raised his hand again, as if to strike her down, but she didn't flinch. The look on her face told him he'd better listen. He stopped Arnie as he moved towards her. "Speak your piece or get out of my sight."

"I've transferred all of the money from your numbered accounts into different numbered accounts. In my name. And Li Li's. If you harm me or Garth, you will never find them. Ever."

For the first time in his life, Pearl had truly shocked Feng Wah. "I was a bookkeeper once, remember? And a very good one. If you think I'm being untruthful, check your accounts. Any one of them."

He turned away, disbelieving. Yet his heart pounded, knowing she wouldn't make the claim unless she could back it up. He pulled his

Galaxy from his parka, typed in some numbers, and checked his first account. Ten dollars left. His second. A few Euros. He knew better than to bother looking at any of the others. He whirled on her, livid. His face was red and he was bursting to kill her with his bare hands. But he knew she was right. If she died, his money, the fortune he spent the last twenty years building, was gone. "I'll make more."

"Perhaps. But it will take you much longer. And I'm sure the authorities know who you are now. But if that's your choice, I will accept it."

Her eyes never left his face. This was not the woman he thought he knew. He had a glimmer of respect for her but pushed it down. "What are your terms?"

"Safe passage for me and the boy. As soon as we are on the mainland, secure, I will transfer your money back to you. And you will never look for me or Li Li or try to contact us. Never."

He stared at her for what felt like an eternity. Garth was holding his breath. Garth sighed when Feng Wah turned to Arnie. "Give them a boat."

"I will need no help. It will be only the two of us."

It took all of his restraint for Feng Wah not to crush her on the spot. But if anything had gotten him to where he was, it was his self-control. He would not ruin himself by killing her now. She would die at a time of his choosing. "Go."

Pearl gave him a small, triumphant smile as she turned around and took Garth's hand. She didn't look back as she followed Feng Wah's thug out of the cabin. Feng Wah watched them leave, knowing he would find the right time to destroy them.

# CHAPTER SIXTY

JAKE RUSHED THROUGH the narrow corridors, up the steps two and three at a time, heading for the forward Captain's cabin. He slowed down and inched towards cover when he spotted a big man slamming out of the anteroom, indicating that someone should follow. Jake's heart leapt when he saw it was Garth, with a small, elegant Asian woman behind him.

He heard the footsteps moving his way, towards the aft. The armed man was focused on his goal, never expecting trouble on this deck. Jake clicked twice on his radio, the signal he and Abe had arranged, as he waited in the cubby for the guard to hurry past him. He quickly inserted himself between Garth and the guard, taking the man down from the back without a whimper.

"Dad!"

Jake made sure the guard was out, then turned back to his son. Tears were streaming down Garth's cheeks. Jake took him into his arms and held him tight. "I thought you were dead. My vision... "

"...Ssh, Garth, I'm fine. You're fine."

He looked at the woman behind Garth, who had a slight smile on her face, masking endless pain. "You must hurry. Feng Wah will come after us. He is not true to his word."

"You're Li Li's mother."

"Yes. Pearl."

"She's fine."

"Thank you. Now we must go."

Jake agreed, as Abe hurried down the corridor. "Abe. Get them off this boat."

"You?"

"I'm not finished yet."

"Done."

Garth protested. "Daddy, please please come with me. I saw a fire and people dying... and you didn't escape. Please."

Jake looked at Garth, shocked he had seen a fire on the boat. And surprised that he was still surprised. He kneeled down next to him, urgent. "I swear I will be fine. You have to go with Abe and Pearl so I can help these other people. To do that, I need to know you're safe, Garth."

Garth sighed. He never won arguments with Jake. He gave him one last hug. "Please come home, daddy. Please."

Jake kissed Garth's head and signaled to Abe. Abe rushed them down the corridor, towards safety. Garth turned around quickly, once, and waved. Jake smiled at him, thumbs up. Now that he knew his son was protected, Jake went after the sonovabitch who caused all of this. Jake allowed his fury to rise as he ran towards the Captain's cabin.

He encountered no opposition as he slammed open the door. The anteroom was empty, no Feng Wah in sight. He burst into the Captain's cabin and saw the Captain and First Mate on the floor, barely conscious. The boat was running on autopilot and Jake knew that wasn't good. That meant Feng Wah was making his escape and was going to trigger the explosives as soon as he was off. He moved to the Captain. "Where did he go?"

"I'm hurt. Help me."

"Help is on the way. Where is Feng Wah?"

"I heard him say he has a boat ready to pick him up on the bow. Please."

"Someone's coming…" Jake moved quickly, towards the bow. He radioed: "Colonel. Abort the mission. Get everyone off the boat ASAP. Big Dog is missing. If I find him near the bow, I'll take care of him."

"10–4. CG is evacuating now."

Jake knew he had very little time. He broke into a run, heading towards his fate. And Feng Wah's.

# CHAPTER SIXTY-ONE

It was cold, rainy and windy, almost snowing, exactly how Garth usually loved the Puget Sound. Not now. He and Pearl shivered as Abe lowered them over the side in the Captain's lifeboat. There was a steering mechanism and paddle, but nothing motorized. Abe maneuvered the craft into the water expertly and as gently as possible.

"Can you row away from the boat or do you need my help?"

Pearl motioned him to leave. "I can do it. Go help the others."

"There's a waterproof beacon under the flap in front. Flip it on so you can be seen."

Pearl nodded as Abe saluted and hurried to help offload the rest of the passengers. Garth looked at Pearl, worried. She tightened his adult-sized jacket as best she could. Then she did hers. "Good we have these. My parents never thought it was necessary for me to learn how to swim." She looked determined. "Li Li will learn."

Garth shivered, miserable. "I can swim. Grandpa Tony taught me." He looked around. "But not in this."

Pearl put her arms around him, sheltering him from the weather, their jackets glowing in the mist. He let her, but he was terrified. "Please God, please please please help my dad off the boat. Please. I'll never tell anyone about what I see again."

Pearl shushed him, firm, as she began to row away from the ferry. The wind swirled the water around them, gaining in velocity. She raised her voice to be heard. "Nonsense, Garth. You have a gift and a purpose. That's why we are here on this earth, to share our gifts with the world. Pretending they don't exist will solve nothing and help no one. The worst thing you can do is not honor what you have been given."

Garth shouted above the noise. "But I saw him die!"

"That doesn't mean you *made* him die. I promise you that your visions are possibilities of what might happen. We all can change our destiny some, our Ming, by the way we walk our path. By our Virtuous Actions. You'll know that as you get older. Besides, I have a great deal of faith in your father. He is a resourceful man. Who do you think you got that from?" She smiled at him and he trembled a smile back. "Look at what he's accomplished already. If anyone can defeat Feng Wah, it is he."

Garth wanted desperately to believe her. He shouted back to be heard. "Okay, Pearl. But do you think it's all right if I say a prayer that Anya taught me?"

"Always, little one. Always."

And he did, his little voice calming himself. "*Sh'ma Yisraeil, Adonai Eloheinu, Adonai Echad.* Please, God, keep my daddy safe."

Pearl added: "And keep us all safe. Amen." She continued rowing, determined to get as far away from the ferry as fast as possible.

# CHAPTER SIXTY-TWO

T**ONY AND TWO** of the commandos had finished dismantling the bomb in the forward engine room, but Tony had found two more in strategic spots. He knew in his gut that there was at least one more, but had no idea where. He realized the most important thing now was to get everyone off the boat. He had faith Jake would find Feng Wah, and do his best to take him down. But maybe not in time. One of the commandos signaled him across the room. "Tony. Time to go."

"Okay." The three of them moved quickly back to the deck to help offload the passengers. The sense of urgency was intense. No one knew if or when a bomb would go off, where it was, or who would be affected.

The rescuers were professionals, but that didn't mean they weren't aware of the danger. They moved as efficiently as possible, but it was still a fucking zoo. The fear was contagious among the passengers. Tony looked around, frustrated. He knew he was in the wrong place, and he knew he had to do something about that. Now.

# CHAPTER SIXTY-THREE

FENG WAH MOVED quickly, ignoring the chaos and shouting that surrounded him on the ferry. He knew he had very little time, and he knew his only escape was to remain calm, as he had done his entire life, to make safe passage. He almost laughed at himself – he sounded like an advertisement for one of those anonymous organizations for the weak and poor. Except they didn't preach his philosophy, which was to wreak havoc on those who interfered with him.

He had dispatched his guard to watch his back as he made sure the boat he had hidden off the bow was secure in the water. He had enough supplies to get him to his rendezvous, and he would be traveling alone. The security guard didn't know that yet, but he would find out. The fewer people who knew where he was, the better.

He had adjusted the lines on the boat when he heard the silence behind him. He turned. Nothing there. He finished lowering the small craft.

• • • •

JAKE SLIPPED OUT of the shadows to find Feng Wah readying his escape. He watched the man who had caused him so much pain. Feng Wah whirled around again, sensing the imminent threat.

Neither of them blinked. Jake hated the person in front of him with every ounce of his being, but he knew better than to give in to his emotion. He and Feng Wah were cut from similar molds, on opposite sides of the moral compass.

Jake calmly held his gun on Feng Wah. "Do you think anyone would know or care if I simply shot you?"

"Likely not. But you won't do that, Detective. I've met your child and he was not brought up by a vengeful man."

Jake seethed at the mention of Garth. "Put your hands behind your head. Slowly."

"As you wish." Feng Wah began to raise his hands, but when he did he had a ninchuk in his palm, and threw it towards Jake as he dove sideways.

Jake moved out of the way, but the weapon hit his upper shoulder, deep. He hung onto the gun but Feng Wah surprised him by not going overboard, but by jumping him.

They were evenly matched as Jake rolled over, out of reach and jumped to his feet. The blood on his shoulder was minimal, but Feng Wah went directly for it with a punch that spun Jake around. Jake landed in balance, turned quickly, with an uppercut to the solar plexus that knocked Feng Wah halfway over, then polished him with a right hook to the jaw.

Feng Wah landed on his back, but as Jake rushed him, Feng Wah used his feet and his momentum to toss him over his head, onto the deck. They both scrambled up, moving like it was a dance, but far more deadly. Feng Wah aimed a chop to Jake's neck, as Jake slid to the side and the punch didn't land. Then Feng Wah's surprise kick took him behind the knee and down.

They were both bloodied and beaten but wouldn't quit. They pummeled and pounded each other, never giving up. Jake was on his back, and avoided a damaging kick to his chest, but while he rolled away from it, Feng Wah limped to the side of the ferry, where he had dropped his motor launch into the water.

As Jake staggered up, Feng Wah smiled, gun in hand. "I wanted to wait, but you interfered with my plans. Again. Now I will do the same for yours."

Feng Wah pulled a remote from his pocket and Jake grabbed his backup gun and took aim. They both managed to get off a shot, Feng Wah hit Jake in his chest, the bullet's impact strong even with a vest, as Jake hit Feng Wah in his throat. But while Feng Wah was falling overboard, he pushed the button. As he slipped over the railing into the darkness, there was a horrendous explosion near the forward engine room. It rocked the boat, the concussion knocking Jake down on his back again, his head hitting the deck. He could hear screaming and terror from the other decks but couldn't move to do anything about it.

. . . .

FROM THE LIFEBOAT in the Sound, Garth, with the wind howling and the waves crashing against the small vessel, gasped as he watched fireballs light up the sky. It looked as chaotic and ugly as Garth had seen in his vision. He wept, terrified that his worst fear was coming true.

That's when the biggest wave Garth had ever seen slammed their lifeboat, turning it over and throwing Pearl and Garth into the churning waters of the Sound.

# CHAPTER SIXTY-FOUR

Jake was semi-conscious when he realized he was in a chopper, hovering near the burning ferry, circling to find survivors. He saw an anxious Tony hovering over him. "What happened?"

"You hit your head. And apparently you were shot in the center of your vest."

"I know that part... Garth."

"Abe put him on one of the small lifeboats with Li Li's mother. They were far enough away from the blast to be okay. They're looking now."

Jake's heart was pounding so loud he thought it would burst out of his chest. "They haven't spotted Garth?"

"Not yet. They will."

"And the others?"

"About fifteen injured, a few badly. Some missing. Four of Feng Wah's people dead."

"And?"

"Feng Wah bled out in his boat. Your shot went right through the larynx."

Jake nodded. "I figured he'd be wearing body armor so I aimed for his head. Guess I was a little off. Then the explosion and I hit my head as he went overboard... Who got me out?"

"I figured you'd be close to the action. Dickie helped me."

Jake looked at his father. "Thank you."

"You're welcome. Anytime. Well, not anytime. Don't do it again." Tony grabbed Jake's hand and held it as if he'd never let him go. "Promise."

The radio crackled with a message for the Colonel. Jake could barely hear it, but saw Tony go pale. Jake sat up quickly. "What?"

Tony didn't mince words. "All the boats are accounted for except Garth's. They can't find it."

Jake got the Colonel's attention. "You have a spotlight?"

Smith nodded, and turned it on. "Abe put them over the aft, not far from the Captain's cabin. I have two choppers looking. We'll find them."

They were being buffeted by strong winds. "Not if they capsized."

"They both have lifejackets on." He started to do a loop to the aft side of the burning vessel, shining the strong light on the water below. It was almost impossible to see.

Tony asked quietly: "What's the Beaufort?"

"About a 10."

"Gale force."

"Close to it. We can manage. So can they."

Jake ignored the pain in his head and chest, and the talk around him, as his eyes scanned the water and waves. The co-pilot handed him night binoculars to give him a better chance of seeing something in the water, anything in the water.

. . . .

GARTH WENT UNDER for the second time. Garth still had his jacket on, but it was so big and he was so little, it didn't give him the same flotation as an adult. He went under a wave and swallowed water as he frantically clawed his way towards what he thought was the surface. His eyes were stinging and when he finally came up for air, he was coughing and choking. Another wave hit and he fought not to go down again, when he felt two arms around him. It was Pearl. She was treading water and trying to hold him up.

"Don't fight me! We can float." She held onto him as tight as she could as the two of them hoped for mercy from the storm.

. . . .

JAKE WAS DESPERATELY looking for the lifeboat – for anything. He couldn't believe after all they'd been through it would come down to this. He refused to believe it.

Tony scanned the water as well, and Colonel Smith was using radar. "If the locating beam is on, we'll find it."

Jake ignored him. Talk was irrelevant. He wiped tears from his eyes that he didn't even realize he'd been shedding.

"What's that!?" The co-pilot was looking at a blip on the radar screen.

"Could be the craft. Take her down closer."

Jake tried to see, but the water was too choppy and the ride too bumpy for him to get a bead on what they were looking at. Tony pointed: "There!"

Jake saw what he was looking at, the worst thing he could imagine. All they could see through the rain and waves was the overturned life-boat, adrift. Jake's gut twisted as he screamed into the night. "Garth!"

# CHAPTER SIXTY-FIVE

GARTH AND PEARL were barely holding onto each other. It was freezing, they were exhausted, and they couldn't feel their legs. Garth whispered. "He'll find us. I know he will."

"Garth, don't let go of me. I think I saw the lifeboat. We have to try to get to it so we can hang on."

Garth was getting very sleepy. He didn't know it was called hypothermia, but he knew what it felt like. "I don't… I can't."

Garth could taste the salt water in his mouth, but was too tired to cough.

"Yes! You have to help us, Garth. You know I can't swim. It's over there!" She shouted in his ear.

Garth's forced himself to try to see where she was pointing through the sting in his eyes. "Kick your legs!" He showed her how and they tried to maneuver towards the boat.

Pearl looked up when she heard something above them. "Garth, look! Look!" She began to wave at the chopper as it was doing circles around the capsized boat. The waves were pummeling them, but they didn't stop yelling.

"Over here! Over here!" They knew there was no way they could be heard over the winds and the helicopter blades, but they screamed anyway. Pearl held onto Garth's jacket with the tightest grip she could keep, but waved with her other hand. Garth did the same.

And then a miracle happened. The chopper seemed to hover right above where they were treading water, and a very bright light illuminated them.

. . . .

ON THE CHOPPER, Jake and Tony cheered. They yelled down to Garth, knowing he couldn't hear them.

"Hang on, Garth. I'm coming!"

Tony and Jake lowered a rope ladder over the side. Tony was adamant. "I'm going."

"Bullshit. I'm fine. Get out of my way, dad." Jake already had a life jacket on.

Tony backed off, terror on his face. "Better do it right, then, or I'll have to come after you."

Colonel Smith held the chopper in position despite the winds. "Not much time and not much fuel, Jake."

Jake nodded. He slipped over the side, down the ladder, carefully moving from one swaying rung to the next, ignoring the stabbing in his head and chest. His foot slipped and he dangled there, being whipped by the terrible winds threatening to dump him into the waves. One more gust and he'd be in the water. His hands slipped and burned as he grabbed the rope tighter and pulled himself into a secure position through sheer will.

Jake kept going, until he reached the swirling waves. Tony lowered a harness down next to the ladder. Jake reached out and grabbed Garth and Pearl, who clung together. They could barely hear each other.

"Daddy! I knew you'd come!"

Jake yelled as loud as he could to be heard. "Garth, stay with me! I'm putting this around you and Grandpa will pull you up."

"Pearl!"

"She's next!" He fastened the harness around his son, not letting himself dwell on how small he really was as he signaled to Tony. "Go, Tony!"

Tony pulled Garth up into the chopper carefully. As soon as he got him safely aboard, he lowered the harness again. Garth was shivering uncontrollably, and Tony wrapped a hypothermia blanket around him.

Jake had secured Pearl, who was barely conscious, and the co-pilot pulled her up. When it was his turn to climb up the ladder, his hands and legs felt so heavy he wasn't sure he was going to make it.

Tony pulled Jake up the last few steps, and gave a thumbs up to Colonel Smith.

"Garth!?"

"Wrapped up warm! He'll be fine!"

As the chopper headed back towards land, and safety, Jake's eyes finally closed as he slipped into unconsciousness.

# CHAPTER SIXTY-SIX

## Fifth Day After

When Jake finally awoke, he came out of a restless dream without knowing where he was. He had no idea how long he'd been out. He gasped in panic until he realized that the babble in the background and the smell of disinfectant meant he was in the hospital. He opened his eyes slowly, wanting to adjust to the glare, and he saw Garth sitting two feet away, staring at him intently. When Garth saw him awake, he hustled to the side of the bed, his face anxious. "Dad? You slept a long time."

Jake tried to nod, but his head hurt too much. His voice was raspy. "You okay, Garth?"

"Uh huh. Now I am."

"All warmed up?"

"Yeah. They put me in this neat warming blanket. Pearl too."

Garth brought him a plastic glass with water, ice, and a straw without asking. Jake took it from him, his hand shaking, not realizing how dry he was. When he finished sipping the water, Garth put it back on the tray.

"You'd make a good doctor, son."

"That's what Mrs. D. said. And Grandpa."

Jake reached out his hand and Garth took it. "But I don't want you to ever have to take care of anyone again, not until you're a grown-up and become a real one, or a healer. You've got an amazing gift, Garth."

Garth was surprised hearing his father's words. "Okay, dad. Maybe."

"Can you at least promise me you'll try to only be a little boy for now? And I promise you I'll try to remember that, too. Plenty of time to grow up."

"Okay, dad." He hesitated.

"What?"

"Will it hurt if I hug you?"

Jake melted. "Even if it did, I wouldn't care."

Garth climbed on the bed and carefully hugged Jake. Jake kissed the top of his head.

"I want you to know how proud of you I am. You were braver than I have ever been. You're a good and really smart young man, Garth. And I love you more than anyone in the whole world."

Garth snuggled into Jake, a small smile on his face, a tear running down his cheek, but he couldn't help himself. Garth teased: "As much as you love Anya?!"

Jake was shocked, then started laughing. "You know too much."

"You said I was smart, dad."

He and Jake held tight, and the two stayed entwined that way until they fell asleep. When Tony came into the room to check on Jake, he came to a skidding stop, and then gratefully absorbed the image that would stay with him the rest of his life.

# CHAPTER SIXTY-SEVEN

Kate Dooley was leading Tony at a fast clip down the corridor in the CCU, where she'd spent the last week. You'd never know by watching her that she'd been released only an hour earlier."Why are we doing this, Kate?"

"Because I didn't trust you to get the right kind of chocolates."

"But you just left here."

"No buts. They wouldn't let me walk out, you have to be pushed in that bloody wheelchair. I want to show them what a masterful job they did making me good as new."

"I don't think they expected you to do a forced march today."

"Ha! Go see your kids, Tony, and I'll meet you there when I'm done giving these girls my thanks. Shoo now."

"I'm not leaving you to wander these halls alone. And my kids don't need me right now."

"Are you certain about that?"

"Positive."

"And I do need you?"

"I hope so."

Kate smiled and put her arm through Tony's. "All right, then. We'll do this together."

· · · ·

TONY WAS RIGHT — his kids didn't need him right now. They were in another wing of the hospital, in Anya's room.

She was resting in a chair, one IV line next to her. Or, to be more accurate, she was napping. She woke up with a start to see Jake and Garth sitting there quietly, staring at her. Jake was in a wheelchair, beaten up and bandaged. Garth looked fine.

"You okay?" she murmured.

Jake smiled. "Great shape. Better than you."

She tried to smile, but it hurt. Her face was still bruised and battered, her lower arm in a cast, bandages everywhere. "I'm okay. That's what they tell me."

He watched her lovingly. "Damn, you look like crap. And you're still beautiful."

"Ha! You must want something."

"Nope."

She took his hand, and they watched each other with the deep recognition that everything had changed between them, and they were fine with it.

Anya moved herself to be more comfortable. Garth rushed to her side to help.

"It's okay, baby. I have to learn to move on my own. It takes me a little longer than usual, that's all. But thank you."

Garth adjusted the blanket on her lap anyway. Anya reached over with her good arm and hugged him tight. "It's okay. I won't break. I promise." Garth hugged her back, eyes closed, so he could really feel her presence.

Anya pulled back and looked at him. "I understand you had quite an adventure."

"Grandpa said it's a story to tell at share day. Mrs. D. told him he was an idiot."

Jake and Anya laughed. "I love that woman. She's an angel and has been here every day. You'd never know she was recuperating from a heart attack the way she took care of me and mom. I think my mother and Mrs. D. are going to be BFFs from now on."

Garth looked at her carefully, and seriously. "You're really okay."

Jake laughed. "She's tough and strong, Garth. And very stubborn."

Anya glared at him. "Pot meet pan."

Jake laughed. "Guilty. And it's kettle." He wheeled his chair even closer to her. "They said if I try to get out of this thing they'll send me to hospital jail. But screw 'em."

He got up and put his arm around Anya and held her. They held each other. Grateful. And connected. Anya pulled away first and pointed. "Get back in that chair. I heard the words 'severe concussion' spoken."

"We match."

"Always did. Always will."

Garth looked back and forth between them, beaming. Anya turned to him. "So, young man. You're bursting to tell me something. I can feel it."

"It was Bossy."

Jake was puzzled. "Bossy?"

Anya smiled. "My great-great-great grandmother. What was Bossy?"

"Her story. That's what we did. I remembered what she did in the village, and I told Li Li's mom, and we did the same thing on the boat, and the villagers took over and that's how we saved each other."

Anya looked at him, blown away. "You amaze me, Garth Fortune. You are so brave. You took that story I've been telling you and turned it into a plan of action? I'm in awe, Garth. In awe. Under that pressure, I don't know if I'd have come up with that, and I'm a professional." She hugged him tight, tears in her eyes.

"It was really Pearl. But she listened to me. People don't usually."

Jake winced, furious with himself. "I swear I will always listen to you, Garth. I may not agree, but I'll hear you."

Garth laughed. "I know you will. Especially since you have dreams like mine!" Anya looked puzzled.

Jake shrugged. "For another time, Annie."

"Okay, but I'll hold you to that." Anya turned back to Garth.

"Honey, there's something I need you to know. When I was... gone, I felt so very far away. I could hear my mom, and other people, but they were way in the distance. I know they wanted me to come back, but I couldn't reach them. Then I felt you next to me, and I thought about my great-great-great grandmother and how hard she fought, and it gave me strength. You gave me strength, Garth."

Garth beamed. "I really tried hard to talk to you!"

"You succeeded."

"But I don't get it. I'm usually right. I talked to you and you heard me. But I was so worried about dad, and saw him dying, and I was wrong. I'm glad I was wrong but I've never been wrong before. Almost never..."

Anya took her time. "Well, while I had nothing to do here except get better and worry about you, I did a lot of reading. Or, really, my mother and Mrs. D. read a lot to me. I learned that even with what you see, sometimes it's hard to understand exactly what it means. You could be seeing something that's telling you one thing, but you hear another. There are so many possibilities, and maybe your actions changed the outcome of what you saw. I don't know. What is for sure is that you have a great gift, and if you want we – your dad and I – can find people, good people, who will help you figure it out. If you want..."

Jake agreed. "I've already talked to Aleks about this, Garth. He said he knows people who can help you control and understand what you see, and we can trust them."

Anya laughed. "That's my dad."

Garth sighed. "Okay. But I think I'm not gonna think about it anymore."

"Good idea, son. And FYI, whatever you see or don't see in the future, even if I'm not here, know that I'm never going to leave you. Not ever."

Garth put his arm around Jake's shoulder, and his other arm around Anya's, and sighed. "I'm so happy."

Jake and Anya looked over Garth's head. Jake mouthed to her. "I love you."

Garth interjected, without looking at either of them: "She loves you too, dad."

Jake and Anya's laughter filled the room, as their hands intertwined.

# CHAPTER SIXTY-EIGHT

## *Two Weeks Later*

THE WEATHER WAS cool, clear and crisp, with patches of blue sky and white clouds. The view was magnificent from the top of the hill in Kerry Park, with gorgeous scarlet fall foliage overlooking the water.

Flowers surrounded Chu Wen's exquisite pen-and-ink drawing of a smiling toddler, on an easel next to a beautiful urn resting on an elegant altar. Ling was surrounded by people praying and sending light towards the little life that was cut short.

Jake held on to Anya, who was leaning on a walker, next to Garth. Behind them, Max Woo was with Captain Thackery, next to Mrs. Dooley, who was arm in arm with Tony. Garth glanced at them, beaming. Several of the detectives from Jake's office were also there to pay tribute. They all stood in silence as the Old Woman and Ling moved forward, and the small casket was gently lowered into the ground. Pearl and Li Li stood off to the side, wanting to honor the baby but unsure of their reception. Ling graciously gestured for them to join the group. Li Li moved next to Garth, and put her arm around his shoulder. They were connected for life.

Jake had promised a proper burial for Ling's child, and he came through. Ling nodded in gratitude at all the people who came out to honor Xian. She told the attendees that her little boy had been a blessing, and she believed in karma and reincarnation and was ready to move forward with her life. She said she was certain that her child would come back another time to something better. Then she and Chu Wen sprinkled roses on the open grave, as the others covered it with dirt, one shovel at a time.

As the prayers ended, the day became warmer and lighter. Ling looked up and gasped. The others followed her gaze. Mt. Rainer appeared in all its glory.

Anya smiled. "The mountain is out. A good omen. A very good omen."

*THE END*

# ACKNOWLEDGEMENTS

So grateful: For Ma, Rose Shearer, endless champion, brilliant diagnostician of life. For Daddy, Jake Shearer, who's on every page of this book.

For my brothers and sister, Bernard, Beverly and Joel, and for every moment as family.

For my early readers, I treasure you, your fortitude and astute observations: Catherine Kurland (since the first day of the third grade), Howard Sunkin, Kelly Harrington, Julia Walker, and Sheila Gross.

For your lifelong support and insight, and to the decades ahead: Deborah Dean Davis, Beth Milstein, Jean Hester, Hannah Branstetter, Diane Levine, Paula Silver and Stuart Silverman, Beverly Magid, Laura Richter, Jennifer and Emilio Castellanos, Carolyn Kheel, Mike Cohen, Frank Kurland, Randy Mantooth, Kathryn Kuykendall, and Debbie Levy.

For my godchildren, Alexandra Marie O'Dowd, Char Branstetter, Stephen and Alex Lesefko, who bless my life. Keep slaying dragons.

For Barbara Tada, for your professionalism and patience; Linda Schwartz, for your extraordinary talent and extraordinary kindness; Amy Shaughnessy, for your calm, practical magic.

For Lorraine Wong, kind, brave and so missed; Dorothy (DC) Fontana, who supported me and all women writers in every genre.

And definitely not last or least: for Lillian Pearl Bridges. Your extraordinary legacy will never be forgotten.

Hannah Louise Shearer's passion for writing action, heroics and right vs. wrong began when she was a production assistant on the police drama *Adam-12*. This drive grew when she became the first woman line producer at Universal Television, on *Emergency!*, the iconic television show about firefighter paramedics.

As Executive Story Editor for *Star Trek: The Next Generation*, her writing was known for the ability to evoke emotion and humanize outer space. TV Guide said Shearer wrote one of the top ten quotes for the series: "Things are only impossible until they are not." She believes that with her whole being.

Shearer was recognized by the Writers' Guild of America for her work on *Star Trek: TNG*, one of the "101 Best Written TV Series ever."

When she's not writing, Shearer is following the Los Angeles Dodgers on the way to their next World Series championship.